Cruel as the Grave

Dean James

Hardcover ISBN 1-57072-111-4
Trade Paper ISBN 1-57072-127-0
Copyright © 2000 by Dean James
Printed in the United States of America
All Rights Reserved

1 2 3 4 5 6 7 8 9 0

For two extraordinary women:
Patricia Ruth McClain Orr
and
Megan Bladen-Blinkoff

When you have friends like these,
anything else is secondary.

Thanks for the many years of friendship.
Without your never-failing love,
encouragement, and support,
this never would have happened.

ACKNOWLEDGMENTS

It's time to express thanks to several people who have helped bring this book to the publication stage:

Julie Herman, who has taught me so much and with whom I've shared the birthing process of several manuscripts; here we are! Can you believe it?

Deborah Adams, who has offered much encouragement over the years, and who said, "Can you write me a book?"

Kaye Davis, who gave me the benefit of her considerable scientific expertise and helped me with some forensic information;

All the fine folk at The Overmountain Press who have worked so hard to give Silver Dagger Mysteries a good home;

Martha Farrington, owner of Murder by the Book, who has always encouraged and supported my writing; can you believe it's been nearly twenty years?

Ruth Williams James, who knows better than most what hard work and dedication really mean. Mom, I literally could never have done it without you.

> *. . . love is strong as death;*
> *jealousy is cruel as the grave:*
> *the coals thereof are coals of fire,*
> *which hath a most vehement flame.*
> —Song of Solomon 8:6

Chapter One

HER EYELIDS DROOPED farther and farther as her mind slowly ceased the struggle for comprehension. The book began sliding from suddenly powerless fingers. When the heavy tome landed on her bare toes, Maggie McLendon snapped awake.

After rubbing the aching toes, she retrieved the book, inserted a marker to keep her place, and then laid the book aside, yawning as she did so. She had known ahead of time that preparing for her qualifying exams would be less than fascinating, but she hadn't anticipated such frequent bouts of the "absolute yawners," as one of her friends referred to these periodic feelings.

Maggie was struggling through a detailed study of the development of medieval English law, written by someone who came to a point only after having buried it in a wealth of unnecessary detail. Once more eyeing the book with distaste, she sighed. At this rate she would never make it all the way through. But she had to finish it because, turgid though it was, it was an important new work on medieval English law. She had to be able to discuss the author's interpretations during her exams. Maggie, when she could stay awake long enough to ferret out the slim thread of the author's argument, admitted that the man did make some interesting points. How unfortunate, though, that the interesting and provocative points were buried in paragraph after paragraph of irritatingly inept prose.

The July skies still streamed with rain, having soaked Houston ceaselessly for two days now, making her unable to concentrate on her studies. Such weather cried out for reading, of course, but not for the reading of scholarly monographs. Maggie looked wistfully at her shelves of mysteries. She had several new books by favorite authors she was itching to read, but they would have to wait until she passed her qualifying exams in mid-August. Passing these oral examinations would make her officially a Ph.D. candidate. Then she would be free to concentrate on her dissertation.

But as she moved to look out her bedroom window, she could muster little interest in the task at hand. *Time for a break*, she thought as she made herself comfortable in the window seat. *Or else put myself to sleep with that dratted book!*

Gazing out at the relentless rain, Maggie again thought longingly of what she'd rather be reading. Maybe it wouldn't hurt to read a chapter or two in one of the new mysteries. Or she could pull an old favorite off the shelf. Perfect weather for that—certainly better for that than for assizes of novel disseisin and writs of right.

But, no, she thought as her eye caught the bright digits of her bedside clock across the room, *you'd better go get lunch ready instead*. The clock winked 11:53 at Maggie as she headed out of her room and padded barefoot down the stairs of the comfortable house she shared with her father.

Her father, Gerard McLendon, professor of medieval literature in one of Houston's fine institutions of higher learning, disliked having to prepare meals as much as his only child did. One important part of their amicable living arrangement was the agreement that they would take turns making meals, and they did their best to stick to the schedules. But neither one ever minded going out to eat if the other didn't want to cook.

From the foot of the stairs she glanced toward the front door to see whether the mail had been delivered. A pile of letters and circulars lay on the small rug in front of the door. Maggie retrieved the items, damp around the edges, then scanned briefly through the mail. Delighted to find the latest newsletter from the mystery bookstore in Houston, she tucked it under her arm as she quickly sorted through the rest of the mail. Nothing for her except the newsletter. The rest belonged either to her father or to the trash can. The circulars were jettisoned without a second glance, but she looked through her father's letters idly as she moved toward his study at the back of the house.

The small return-address label on one letter caught Maggie's eye: "Helena McLendon, The Magnolias, 1443 Oakhurst Drive, Jackson, Mississippi."

Smiling, she paused in the doorway to her father's study. Helena McLendon was Gerard's aunt, a delightful lady now in her early sixties. Maggie and her father received annual Christmas and birthday cards from her, as well as the occasional letter. She had come to Houston twice for brief visits when Maggie was younger, but they hadn't seen her for almost ten years now. *Has it really been that long?* she asked herself.

As Maggie entered his study with the mail, Gerard McLendon looked up from his book. A smile flitted across his face as he looked at his daughter, but she could see the strain in his eyes. He laid his pipe aside and absentmindedly fanned away some of the smoke swirling about his head.

She grimaced in sympathy. "Sinuses still bothering you?"

Gerard nodded. "Once this rain lets up, maybe the demons in my head will take a few days off."

"It can't rain like this much longer, I hope," she responded. "Then you'll start feeling better. Well, here's your mail." She placed the stack on the desk in front of him. She had purposefully left the letter from Helena McLendon on top of the pile, and she lingered in the doorway, hoping he would offer her the letter once he had finished it.

He picked up the stack incuriously, muttering his thanks. His hand stilled as he looked intently at the return address on the first letter. Oblivious now to Maggie's presence in the doorway, he put the other mail back down on the desk as he continued to hold the letter from his aunt in his right hand.

After a minute of silence, Gerard broke his gaze away from the letter in his hand and observed Maggie still standing in the doorway. "Was there something else?" he inquired with chilling politeness, speaking as he might to one of his students. A student, that is, with whom he was annoyed.

Okay, Maggie thought, chagrined. *I guess you don't want to open the letter right now.* "How about some lunch? Will sandwiches do?" she asked, masking her disappointment with a cheery tone.

"Sure," he responded, the fragment of an apologetic smile playing with the corners of his mouth. "I'll be along in a few minutes."

As Maggie left him, Gerard returned his attention once more to the letter. Making her way to the kitchen, she puzzled over her father's behavior. She shook her head as she opened the refrigerator door. "I guess he'll read the letter and tell me what she has to say eventually," she confided to the refrigerator. "Maybe it's just his sinuses."

While she prepared their lunch of sliced turkey sandwiches, leftover potato salad, and iced tea, she switched her thoughts to her father's family, most of whom she had never met. Helena, the only one she had ever seen, lived in Jackson with her elder brothers and sister in the family home. Henry, the eldest of the four McLendon siblings, was Maggie's grandfather. She had never met him, since he and Gerard had been estranged for as long as she could remember. Her grandmother had died when Maggie was only a year old, and she had no recollection whatsoever of the woman for whom she had been named Magnolia.

Also living in the family home were Henry's twin sister, Henrietta, and another brother, Harold. This much Gerard had told his daughter, but little else. Obviously whatever had happened to cause the rift between father and son had been bitter enough to extend to the rest of the family—except for Helena.

Maggie had naturally been curious about her father's family when she was growing up. Her mother, Alexandra, had died when Maggie was ten, and her maternal grandparents, the Hollingsworths, had died several years before that. The McLendons were the only family Maggie had, since Alexandra and Gerard had both been only children.

Curious though Maggie had always been about her

father's relatives, she learned early on that this was a subject he refused to discuss. On the two occasions when his aunt Helena had visited them, they had all enjoyed themselves mightily. Gerard clearly adored his aunt, and she, him. But Maggie could not recall that, during any moment of the time she had spent with her great-aunt, Helena had ever mentioned any other member of the family. Perhaps someday her father would confide in her the reason for his bitterness toward the rest of his family.

Maggie had placed everything on the kitchen table and was about to summon her father, when he saved her the trouble by stalking into the kitchen. He had his pipe going again and was puffing away furiously. She started to make a laughing reference to it, but the sight of his face stopped her. Whatever was in the letter had not been good news, judging from the scowl marring the features so similar to her own.

"What's wrong?" she asked, alarmed.

Gerard removed the pipe from his mouth and frowned into its bowl before replying. "Bad news, I'm afraid," he said, drawing out the words.

Maggie dropped into her chair as her father sat down at his accustomed place at the table. Laying his pipe aside on the table, he focused his attention on his daughter and, for the first time, seemed to realize that she was quite naturally perturbed by his behavior.

Flashing a brief, nervous smile, he began to talk. "You probably noticed that there was a letter from Helena in the mail. According to her, my father is gravely ill and hasn't much longer to live. He has a very bad heart and could go at any moment. She wants me to come home."

Quiet for a moment, allowing the odd feeling of shock to pass over her, Maggie regarded her father. His reaction—or seeming lack of one—to the situation puzzled her. He was usually laid back about almost everything, but surely he ought to be more upset about his father, even if they hadn't spoken in twenty-five years.

Maggie stood up, lunch forgotten. "Shall I start calling the airlines?" She moved toward the kitchen phone.

"No!" The word came with the force of a quiet explosion from Gerard, and she whirled in astonishment.

"I mean," he continued in a more level tone, "there's no need. I'll take care of it. And there's really no need for you to go. You'll be better off staying home and getting ready for your exams."

Maggie felt her mouth beginning to slide open in amazement. "What do you mean? Of course I'll go."

Gerard's jaw took on the same stubborn line which she had seen many times before. "There's really no need," he repeated firmly. "I'd rather you stayed home."

Suddenly irritated and not sure why, she snapped back, "And I'd rather go!"

He stood up, grasping his pipe. "There's no point in your going. I can deal with this on my own."

"Has it ever occurred to you," Maggie said, struggling to keep her temper in check, "that I just might want to have a chance to meet my grandfather at least once before he dies?"

Gerard's hand clenched around his pipe. "Even if I tell you I'd rather go by myself?"

"Dad," she said, trying hard to keep from clenching her teeth in response, "I'm going with you. Or I'll go by myself. Either way, I'm going to Jackson to see my grandfather."

"Start packing, then," he responded crisply, "and I'll take care of the reservations." He turned and disappeared through the kitchen door, his lunch forgotten.

Miserably, Maggie stared down at her own lunch. Her burst of anger at her father spent, she now regretted the sudden tension between them. He became grumpy only when he didn't feel good, and she knew he was suffering now with his sinuses. Perhaps he was so insistent that she stay home simply because he didn't feel good.

But, no, she thought. *He never speaks that way to me, even when he doesn't feel good. There's something he doesn't want to tell me. What could it be?*

Stirring from uncomfortable thoughts—not wanting to probe further at the time, and her appetite gone—Maggie wrapped the sandwiches in plastic and stuck them in the refrigerator, along with the potato salad. She slowly walked back upstairs to her room to pack.

Before she retrieved a suitcase from the closet and faced the difficult decision of what to pack to meet her family for the first time, Maggie went to her bookshelves and pulled out an old photo album. She sat on the bed and leafed through its pages. The earliest pictures in the album were of her maternal grandparents, who had died when she was too young to remember them. Her fingers traced lightly the contours of their faces, seeing in them little of her own facial features. She examined a portrait of her mother, again seeing little of herself there, except perhaps the determined set of her chin.

Maggie closed the album with a familiar sense of frustration. So much of her personal history was missing. Now, at last, she had a chance to fill in some of the gaps, but the circumstances were far from ideal. With a shrug, she put the album back in its place on the shelf, then went to her closet.

While she looked through her wardrobe for her best clothes, she pondered Helena's letter. Though she hadn't read it, she thought there was something peculiar about that letter.

Why had Helena written to inform them of her grandfather's condition? Surely, if he was so near death, Helena should have called.

But more puzzling than that, Maggie decided, was her father's reaction. Why didn't he want her to go to Jackson? At this point in time, there should be no reason for her not to meet the rest of her family. Unless, she considered uneasily, there was something—or someone—in Jackson her father feared for her to know.

Chapter Two

SEATED NEXT TO HER FATHER on the plane the next morning, Maggie waited with mounting impatience for takeoff. This was the only portion of the flight she detested, other than having to wait to board. Sitting there was uncomfortable, especially when it was so humid outside. They hadn't yet turned the air-conditioning on, and those little air vents really didn't do much good, she reflected. So she sweated in silence, using the airline's magazine as a fan to offset some of the stuffiness.

Gerard sat beside her, withdrawn into his own thoughts, as he had been all the previous evening and thus far this morning.

Maggie felt like she was almost dealing with a complete stranger. She and her father had always been close, and his shutting her out now disturbed her. She knew he was under considerable stress, and several times she was on the point of asking him to confide in her. But the cold, distant look on his face frightened her. She simply didn't know what to say to him. If only he would open up to her a little, she thought. But whatever was bothering him, he refused to confide anything in her. She'd have to be patient until he was ready to talk. She had many questions about his family, since Helena was the only one she had met, but her father was obviously in no mood to talk. She'd have to take everything as it came.

The aircraft jerked into motion, and Maggie came out of her reverie. She had ignored the repeated warnings of the flight attendants to buckle her seat belt, and now she hastily did so.

Once they had changed planes in Dallas and were again in the air, she decided to venture a question, which she thought might be a neutral topic. "Who's going to meet us there?"

For a moment Maggie thought her father hadn't heard her, so intently was his gaze focused out the window. Then he turned toward her, a slight frown on his face. "I don't know. Helena's a little too scatty to be a good driver, but my father probably has someone who drives for him. He's always hated doing it for himself." He turned back to the window.

Maggie shrugged—another attempt at communication turned aside. Muttering under her breath, she reached for her book bag and pulled out one of the books she had to read for her exams.

About an hour later, she wrenched herself back into the present when the irrepressibly perky flight attendant reminded her to put her bag of books underneath the seat once more. They were approaching Jackson, and as she put her books away, Maggie could feel her heart begin to beat faster.

Making sure that her seat belt was secure, she then thrust her head next to her father's as she strained to look out the window and get her first glimpse of his birthplace. The skyline didn't quite compare with Houston, Maggie saw, but she was pleased to view an abundance of trees amidst all the buildings. Jackson might be the biggest city in the state of Mississippi, but it didn't seem like it was too far from the country, no matter which way you looked.

Jackson's airport was tiny, compared to the sprawling expanse of the terminals at Houston's Intercontinental. *Is that the only terminal?* Maggie wondered.

The flight from Dallas to Jackson had been considerably less crowded than the flight from Houston to Dallas, so the McLendons had little trouble making their way out of the plane. Once they had gained the relative quiet of the waiting area, both Maggie and Gerard looked around for anyone remotely resembling a welcoming committee. There seemed to be no one waiting for anyone from their flight except a tall, blond man, dressed casually in khakis, polo shirt, and sneakers.

As Maggie looked curiously at the man, she noticed that

he gave a start upon looking directly at her, then moved quickly toward them.

Surely I don't look that bad, she told herself. *Now I'm scaring total strangers in airports.* She looked down surreptitiously at her dress, a dark green cotton sheath she had always thought flattered her figure and her complexion. Reassured that she still looked presentable, Maggie stared back at the man. *This stranger is not anything to scare little old ladies,* she thought. *In fact, he probably charms them right out of their rockers and savings accounts.*

He had to be one of the best-looking men she had seen in the flesh. His blond hair was thick and curly. His eyes, as she noticed when he stopped his progress diffidently in front of Gerard, were a dark green. His shirt, a shade reminiscent of his probing eyes, clung snugly in all the right places to a physically fit body.

"You must be Gerard McLendon," the stranger said, proffering a hand. His voice was low and musical, not gruff and unmannered, as she had perhaps subconsciously expected. "I'm Adrian Worthington. Miss Helena McLendon sent me to bring you and Miss McLendon back to the house."

As she heard herself called *Miss McLendon* in that cultured and velvety-smooth Southern voice, Maggie began to blush. She wasn't quite sure why, but it might have had something to do with the look of cool appraisal that Adrian Worthington had given her.

As she felt the blush receding, she tried—just as coolly, she hoped—to return the man's glance. She couldn't help liking what she saw, because physically he had most of the characteristics she found attractive in a man. Rugged good looks, a body that obviously benefitted from regular exercise, and—most important of all—he was at least three inches taller than her own often-troublesome six feet.

"How do you do?" she said, almost blushing again when she heard how stiff and unfriendly her voice sounded.

One of Adrian's eyebrows arched slightly. "Welcome to Jackson, Miss McLendon." His voice chilled her.

Now, Maggie chastised herself, *he probably thinks I'm a*

snob. But there seemed little else she could do at the moment.

"If you'll follow me," Adrian said, as he abruptly turned on his heel, "we'll collect your baggage and be on our way."

Father and daughter followed, Gerard somewhat huffily, Maggie easily matching her strides to those of the two men.

They waited in silence several minutes for the baggage to be unloaded. Adrian made no attempts at conversation. Maggie stood quietly between the two men. Gerard's mood was even more tense than before, and his edginess seemed to have increased tenfold once they were on the ground in Jackson.

"There they are," she said suddenly, pointing to the two large suitcases belonging to her and her father. She reached out for them, but Adrian was there before her, swinging the luggage off the belt as if the suitcases were empty.

"Shall we go?" he inquired politely—and rhetorically, since he was already heading toward the exit when he asked.

The car toward which Adrian headed, once they had reached the parking lot, was—surely Maggie was mistaken—a Rolls Royce!

After taking care of the two large suitcases and the three smaller bags which Maggie and Gerard had carried on the plane, Adrian opened the door to the backseat and courteously ushered them inside. Maggie's eyes were wide as she looked at her father in mute inquiry. As her gaze traveled around the interior of the car, she noticed the glass partition which separated her and her father from Adrian.

"I have a feeling there's something you haven't been telling me," Maggie commented wryly once her perusal of the car's interior was finished.

"What do you mean?" Gerard's brows were knitted together in concentration. He had not been paying any attention to their mode of transport.

"This!" she replied, motioning vaguely around with her right hand. "It's a vintage Rolls Royce, in case you hadn't noticed!"

"Oh," he muttered blankly. "I thought it looked familiar."

Her nerves tightened a little further. Noticing the expression on his daughter's face, Gerard hastily continued. "I never told you, because I didn't see any point in it, but my father is a wealthy man."

Maggie leaned weakly back against the seat and contemplated her father in silence. *I can't wait to find out what else you haven't told me!* she thought. But there was no point in a confrontation right then. She concentrated instead on seeing what she could of Jackson out of the frosted windows of the Rolls.

Presently they left the busy thoroughfare for a quiet and noticeably prosperous residential area. She noted with interest that the farther they went in this particular area, the more opulent—and widely spaced—the houses were. Eventually they came to a block which seemed to be nothing but trees, but then she spotted a driveway, into which the Rolls sedately turned.

As Maggie looked through the glass which separated her and her father from Adrian Worthington, she could see through the windshield ahead very large and sturdy iron gates barring their progress. But as she watched, the gates slowly began to part, and the Rolls entered the grounds of a large estate.

The driveway wound through the trees ahead of them, but once they had rounded a small curve, she could see quite clearly the large house which lay before them. There was a niggling air of familiarity about the mansion, although Maggie couldn't recall ever having been in Jackson before.

Suddenly she began to laugh as she realized how she knew the house! Any moment now, Scarlett O'Hara could waltz out the front door, crinolines billowing, because it looked like an overgrown replica of Tara from the movie version of *Gone with the Wind*.

Maggie chuckled as she climbed out of the car. She tried to nod her thanks gracefully as Adrian opened the door of the Rolls, but he remained impassive as he stood aside for her to climb out. Then she couldn't stop the laughter from bubbling up. She didn't know whether she was to be awed or amused by the sight before her.

The resemblance of her grandfather's mansion to Tara was more than casual, but this building looked much larger than the cinematic one. For once Maggie felt dwarfed as she gazed up the broad front steps and on up to the roof far above. The wings of the mansion stretched many yards on either side of her. The gleaming white of the walls was brilliant in the morning sunshine. A broad veranda ran the length of the front of the house, and soaring columns emphasized the massiveness of the whole structure. The solidity of it intimidated her, because she had never imagined her roots traceable to such a setting.

Maggie laughed again, more uneasily this time, and started when Gerard asked her gruffly what was so funny. Adrian and the car had disappeared while she stood there gaping and giggling.

"This!" she indicated with a broad sweep of her hands. "You didn't tell me I should pack my hoopskirt!"

That came out more sharply than she intended, and Gerard flushed at the note of criticism in her voice. He shrugged his shoulders, struggling for a reply, then was saved when the front door opened and someone burst forth.

Helena McLendon, dressed in a violently red warm-up suit, hopped down the stairs, two at a time, until she reached a bemused Maggie and Gerard at the bottom of the flight. Once her feet, clad in well-worn sneakers, had steadied her in front of her nephew and his daughter, Helena paused to catch her breath before she flung her arms around Gerard's neck. He was not expecting the onslaught of so enthusiastic an embrace and almost keeled over backwards from the force of it. He managed to steady himself and cautiously wrapped his arms around his aunt and squeezed her back.

After a few seconds Helena and Gerard released each other, and Helena turned a tear-streaked face toward Maggie, who held out her arms for another enthusiastic embrace. Helena gave her a quick, wordless hug, then stepped back to look up into her grandniece's face.

Helena, youngest of the four McLendon siblings, was sixty-three. She was also, at five-ten, the shortest. Iron-gray hair, attractively cut in a short style, framed a mobile, intelligent face. Sky blue eyes darted back and forth between Maggie and Gerard while a radiant smile lent a shine to her whole face. Maggie didn't think the woman had aged much in the ten years since they'd seen each other. The hair was perhaps a bit grayer, but she looked otherwise the same.

When her great-aunt at last spoke, Maggie felt the memories come flooding back. The voice had always seemed impossibly youthful to her, on those rare occasions when Helena had visited them. Bursting with energy, it held a current of enthusiasm matching the vigor with which Helena attacked life. Maggie, at the moment, felt old and tired beside her; Helena's warm-up suit covered a fit and well-exercised body.

"My, you two are a rare sight for these tired old eyes!" Helena nearly shouted at them. She grabbed them each by an arm and almost dragged them up the steps. Gerard stumbled and started going down, but she held on tight, and he managed to right himself.

On Helena's other side, Maggie had to stifle a giggle. Helena had pulled Gerard up like a yo-yo. *Lord*, Maggie thought, *she's got more energy than a hyperactive gerbil!*

Maggie caught her breath at the top of the steps, but when Helena had swung open the massive front door, Maggie lost it again as she contemplated the entranceway.

Helena stepped ahead of them and turned to face Gerard and Maggie. "Welcome to 'The Magnolias,' Maggie. I'm so glad you're finally here!"

Maggie gaped at the grandly sweeping staircase ahead of her. The entrance to the house looked large enough to accommodate several overweight elephants, but the stairs lent the impression that the area was almost crowded. Any moment now she expected to see Vivien Leigh come rushing down in a vain attempt to keep Clark Gable from uttering that fabled line.

Helena smiled benignly at Maggie's obvious amazement, but her smile faded when she looked at her nephew. Seeing the alarm in Helena's face, Maggie turned to her father and was astonished to find him sweating profusely, his face pale and his eyes blinking rapidly.

"Dad, what's wrong?" The sharpness in Maggie's voice as she moved to his side and grabbed his arm roused Gerard from his curious state. "What's wrong?" she repeated urgently.

Wiping a shaky hand across his forehead, he brusquely assured the two women that he felt a little queasy. "Probably that wretched tomato juice I had on the plane," he muttered. "It didn't taste right."

Maggie didn't believe him and was about to say so, when a strident voice assailed them: "Helena! Don't stand there like a fool, girl—bring them on into the drawing room!"

Maggie turned her head in the direction of the voice but caught only a quick glimpse of a rigid back and a mass of stiffly-sprayed gray hair as the owner of the voice moved out of sight into a room to their left.

Helena blushed and motioned for Gerard and Maggie to follow her as she moved immediately to do the voice's bidding.

Through the open door of the drawing room, Maggie saw several heads turned expectantly toward them. The voice belonged to a tall, elderly woman who stood in the center of the room. Dressed in immaculate lilac silk, her resemblance to Helena was striking, but she had to be at least fifteen years older. Her hair was cut in a style similar to Helena's, but the effect was rather ruined by the fact that every hair had been threatened into place by excessive application of hair spray. Fascinated, Maggie watched for the hair to move, but every time the woman tossed her head—which she did at irregular intervals—not a hair stirred.

Neither of the other two people in the room, an elderly man and a woman only a few years older than Maggie, had said anything, waiting, it seemed, for the holder of center stage to make the first move. Helena waited nervously beside Gerard and Maggie. Gerard, apparently calm once more, waited also.

Maggie was tempted to say something, anything, just to break the silence, but as she opened her mouth to speak, the woman—who Maggie had decided by now must be Helena's older sister, Henrietta—laughed harshly. "I hope you weren't expecting the fatted calf, Gerard," she said, the venom in her voice making Maggie flinch.

"No," he responded, eyeing her insultingly. "One raddled old cow is quite sufficient, thank you."

There was no mistaking whom he meant, and for a moment Maggie held her breath, expecting the worst. Instead, Henrietta laughed. "At least you didn't go soft, teaching poetry all these years. I'm glad to see you haven't lost your waspish tongue."

"I certainly had a good role model." Gerard smiled as he moved forward to hug her.

Helena giggled nervously, then urged a speechless Maggie forward. "Maggie, my dear, this is my elder sister, Henrietta McLendon Butler." Helena made the introduction tartly, getting a little of her own back with emphasis on the word *elder*, Maggie was amused to note.

"But everyone just calls me Retty," responded the elder sister with a flash of the eyes at Helena. She put her head to one side and subjected Maggie to a searching gaze. "No need to tell me who you are! Magnolia to the life!" She swept Maggie into a fierce embrace, surprisingly strong from someone nearly eighty.

Once Retty had released her, Maggie stepped back and began to mutter some incoherent words of greeting, but Retty had already turned to motion her two companions forward.

"This is Harold," Retty said, "my brother."

Harold, though he obviously found it difficult to take his eyes from Maggie's face, gave Gerard a big hug, then moved to Maggie, tears forming in his eyes. "You are so like her," he whispered as he bent to give her a chaste kiss on the cheek.

"Like my grandmother, you mean?" Maggie said, her tone more waspish than she intended. "I wouldn't know."

Harold drew back in surprise, his face clouded by dismay. Gerard, engaging in more verbal fencing with his aunt Retty, hadn't heard. Maggie wanted to poke her father in the ribs to get his attention. She felt overwhelmed by all this.

Then she took another look at Harold's hurt face, and she felt ashamed of herself. *This wasn't his fault,* she reminded herself sharply, and she smiled a rueful apology. His face clearing rapidly, he smiled back.

She studied him and her two great-aunts covertly. The resemblance ran strong among these three McLendon siblings. Retty and Harold were about the same height, a flat six feet like Maggie, and Harold had the same thick gray hair which graced his sisters' heads. They were decidedly a handsome family. Not to mention a bit on the intimidating side, all together like this.

The final occupant of the room had moved forward to offer her greetings. "I'm Sylvia Butler," she said shyly to Gerard, who clasped her proffered hand and gave her a quick peck on the cheek.

"Sylvia, I'd never have recognized you," he said.

"Of course not," Retty complained. "You haven't been here in twenty-five years. No way you could recognize the girl. She was only a child the last time you were here."

"At least," Gerard said, his eyes sparkling with mischief, "she doesn't take after her grandmother, thank the Lord. She's quite lovely."

"My granddaughter," Retty said, ignoring Gerard, as Maggie held out a hand to her cousin. Sylvia shook her hand, smiling.

Sylvia's face seemed vaguely familiar to Maggie, who struggled to place it in her recollections. Shining dark hair framed a lovely oval face. Maggie envied her cousin her luminescent skin and the expression of calm which had now replaced her momentary nervousness as she resumed her seat.

That's it! Maggie thought. *Sylvia looks like a Renaissance Madonna.* Her face had that same quality of ethereal repose which had made Maggie so fond of Renaissance pietistic art.

No one would accuse Sylvia's grandmother of looking either pious or calm. Retty's sharp tongue had already put Maggie a bit on edge.

"Well, why don't we all sit down," Helena chirped into the uneasy silence which had suddenly befallen the group.

She suited action to words by plumping herself down on one of the three sofas which stood at the center of the large room. The sofas formed a cozy C-shaped area around a small table holding an extravagant arrangement of magnolia blossoms made of porcelain. There were chairs and small tables scattered throughout the rest of the room, affording small pockets of isolated intimacy should anyone choose to move from the forced conviviality of the room's center.

They all quickly followed Helena's example. Maggie sat beside Helena on one sofa, while Harold and Sylvia sat down across from them. Retty motioned for Gerard to sit beside her on the sofa which served as the crosspiece of the grouping. Maggie privately dubbed it the Queen Bee's Throne, smiling inwardly.

"We're only going to sit for a few minutes," Retty announced, "because lunch will be ready any moment. It's a little later than we're accustomed to, but just this once we thought we'd deviate from the routine, since you decided to grace us with your presence today."

"Thank you," Gerard responded drily. "We all know how you adore your routine." He threw up his hands in mock dismay. "I did my best with the airline schedules, but apparently they weren't aware of your schedule, Retty. Perhaps you should let them know, for future reference."

Maggie again gaped at her father. *Did he and his aunt carry on all their conversations like this?* she wondered. There was a vein of humor in his riposte, but there was no mistaking the hostility.

"I daresay I'm predictable," Retty acknowledged, "but who else is going to keep this madhouse running the way it should?" She glared pointedly at Helena. "No one else in this room, I can tell you that! And certainly not those who've abandoned their responsibilities to the family."

Everyone else laughed politely at this little exchange, but Maggie felt increasingly uneasy. There were dynamics at work here which she had no preparation to understand. Once again she felt like poking her father with something sharp.

Helena sensed some of her nervousness, because she turned to pat Maggie's arm soothingly, saying, "Don't mind those two, my dear—they have twenty-five years of unused insults to trade." She smiled wickedly, and Maggie could see the impishness in her eyes. "Retty and Gerard always got along famously, because he's the only one who ever gives her back as good as she hands out."

"Well, my goodness," a voice exclaimed loudly from behind them, "the prodigal son is finally home."

Maggie turned to see who the speaker was and almost fainted from the shock.

For a long moment everything wavered, and Maggie thought the room was going to spin around her. Then she took a deep breath as the woman moved closer. The silence held.

The woman returned Maggie's gaze steadily, the faint hint of a frown stirring around her lips as she stared at the younger woman. She cocked her head to one side and said, "Goodness me, you're like a ghost from the past."

Retty broke the uneasy silence. "Maggie, this is your grandmother's sister, Lavinia Culpeper. Lavinia, your great-niece, Gerard's daughter, Maggie."

Maggie stood as the woman came closer. Lavinia Culpeper was perhaps two inches shorter than Maggie, but the square-ness of her shoulders and the spareness of her lean frame lent her the impression of height. Maggie felt as if she were staring into a mirror, but one which distorted the view some-what, showing her what she could look like after forty years of dissatisfaction with life. Lavinia had an abundance of dark auburn hair, dramatically streaked with white over the tem-ples, and she was dressed in a dark green linen dress, much like Maggie's own, which highlighted the green of her probing eyes. She had an angularity of feature which marked her face with a vague air of horsiness enhanced by the thick, long hair. The aura of discontent came powerfully to Maggie. *Why, she wondered, is this woman so bitter?*

"I'm not in the least surprised you knew nothing about me," Lavinia said, her voice dripping with venom. "After all,

I'm just an in-law here in the McLendon stronghold. Welcome home." She turned to Gerard. "You had the sense, once, to get away from here. Why did you come back?"

"Hello, Lavinia, it's wonderful to see you, too," Gerard said in a neutral tone. Neither he nor his aunt made any effort to embrace. "I thought it was time I came back and introduced my daughter to her family."

Lavinia regarded him in silence. "Lunch is ready." She turned and walked away.

"Come along, everyone," Retty said, standing up.

Still a bit stunned by what had just transpired, Maggie followed the rest of the family out into the hall and into the dining room next door.

The table could comfortably accommodate fifty guests, Maggie decided as she focused on the room in order to regain her equilibrium. One end of the long table was elegantly set with expensive-looking china, polished silver, and sparkling crystal. Maggie slid into the seat Retty indicated she should occupy, then bowed her head as Harold commenced to say grace.

Harold spoke with fervent thanks for the fact that two members of the family had returned home after a long absence. Something suspiciously like a snort came from the head of the table where Retty sat, but Maggie couldn't be quite sure. It might have come from her father, seated on Retty's left.

Once Harold's prayer ended, Retty rang a small silver bell, and Adrian Worthington appeared through a doorway bearing a platter of fried chicken. As Maggie observed more of her surroundings, she noticed that the elegantly furnished table already held a number of vegetable dishes—corn on the cob, mashed potatoes, two varieties of peas, and lima beans, or "butter beans" as Helena called them when she passed them to Maggie. There were also plates of corn bread, homemade rolls, biscuits, and a boat of thick and creamy white gravy. Maggie, who disliked cooking almost as much as she disliked exercise, felt her taste buds stir in anticipation. She refused to think of the effect on her waistline of a steady diet of such fare. No wonder Helena jogged.

After taking the platter of fried chicken around to everyone and seeing that they all had what they wanted to drink, Adrian seated himself in the vacant chair to Maggie's left.

Startled by his unexpected movement, Maggie, in the act of reaching for a fluffy, steaming biscuit, upset her water glass and sent liquid cascading all over Adrian's plate. Mortified, she mopped ineffectually at the mess with her linen napkin, apologizing all the while, as her victim tried to mask his mingled irritation and amusement.

"It's quite all right," he told her as he gently took the napkin from her hand. "They do allow me to eat with the family from time to time, and I did have my bath this morning." He got up and found her a fresh napkin on the sideboard.

Maggie blushed an even deeper red, by now beyond words, because the man had somehow picked up on a stray thought of hers. She risked a quick glance at his face as he took his seat once more and was reassured to see that he was looking friendlier than he sounded. Thankful that she didn't seem to have offended him, she smiled an apology, which he accepted by an answering smile.

The rest of the meal was agony for Maggie, made nervous by the presence of the very attractive man at her side. All she could think of was how clumsy she must have looked to him, pouring water all over him. She didn't pause to analyze why she should worry about his perceptions of her. She concentrated instead on eating, handling her cutlery and glasses with great care. There was desultory conversation around her, all on neutral subjects, but she did not take part.

From time to time as she ate, she looked over at Lavinia, who frowned back at her. Maggie felt too intimidated by the woman to attempt any conversation with her, even to demand an explanation for her rudeness. Lavinia did not seem in the least happy to have her and her father as guests.

But, then again, Maggie wondered, were any of them, except Helena, really happy to have her and Gerard at The Magnolias again?

"Well, Gerard," Retty said in her sharp voice, as if she'd

read Maggie's thoughts, "I suppose Henry will be up to seeing you this afternoon, if you care to look in on him." She patted her thin lips primly with her napkin, then took another sip of her tea as her mischievous eyes regarded her nephew.

"If he feels up to it," Gerard replied mildly, "I think both Maggie and I would like to see him. If a man on his deathbed is allowed two visitors at once." His eyes roved across the table, coming to rest on Helena's face, which had taken on a decidedly odd look.

"So you thought he was dying?" Lavinia finally spoke. "Is that why you rushed back so quickly, bringing your daughter? So you could still find time to make it into the will?"

Helena hissed in outrage, and even Retty seemed taken aback by such a frontal assault. Maggie wanted to throw something—preferably something hot—into Lavinia's face, because the venom in her aunt's voice was like acid thrown in her own.

Gerard laughed. "Lavinia, you always were a first-class bitch. Frankly, if you had mellowed any over the past twenty-five years, I'd have been greatly disappointed." He raised his glass to her. "Here's to the woman who has elevated nastiness into a true art form." He drank deeply from his iced tea.

Appalled by this little exchange, Maggie waited for a further eruption. Lavinia coolly raised her own glass, drank from it, then set it down. She stood and dropped her napkin on her plate, pushed her chair aside, then left the room without saying another word.

Maggie had no appetite left. Her hands trembled in her lap, and she wanted nothing more than to leave this house and go back to the quiet and safety of her home in Houston. No wonder her father had been reluctant to come back to Jackson.

"And she thinks the Culpepers were ever so much more refined than the McLendons," Retty snorted.

To Maggie's amazement, that was the only comment offered on Lavinia's behavior.

Retty continued, scarcely skipping a beat. "Where on earth did you get the fool idea that Henry is on his deathbed, Gerard? The old fart isn't running any marathons, I'll grant you, but he's not doing as bad as all that just yet."

Gerard smiled grimly. "Now why am I not surprised to hear that?"

Helena squirmed in her chair. Maggie in her turn wasn't all that surprised to hear that her grandfather's health wasn't as precarious as Helena had led them to believe. Helena's letter had been more than a bit odd, and now she was beginning to understand why.

"Perhaps I did exaggerate the situation just a little in my letter," Helena admitted.

"What letter?" Retty asked, her eyes narrowing in suspicion. "I thought you said Gerard called up out of the blue and announced he was coming home for a visit."

Helena squirmed again. Maggie caught her father's eye and tried not to laugh. He was enjoying this, to a certain extent. He had probably known all along that his aunt had engineered the whole thing to get him to come home, and now she would have to explain to everyone what she had done. But as Maggie watched him pick up his glass of tea, she saw his hand tremble slightly.

Helena smiled nervously as she cast her eyes around the table, seeking support from someone. All she found was amusement at her discomfiture, except from her sister, who was clearly annoyed.

"Well," Helena coughed in a deprecating manner. "Henry is certainly not getting any better, and he *is* almost eighty years old, after all. I just thought it would be nice to have Gerard and Maggie come home, so I . . . um . . . exaggerated the situation a bit. I'm sorry," she finished lamely. Lips pursed, she looked around the table again.

Gerard, along with Retty, looked sternly back at her, while everyone else tried hard not to laugh. Sylvia had to stifle a giggle, and Adrian kept his head turned away. Maggie could see his shoulders trembling from suppressed laughter. After the unpleasant scene with Lavinia, Maggie was glad that Helena managed to provide a bit of comic relief.

"You silly girl!" Retty said at last. "If you couldn't find

something to meddle in, I don't know what you'd do for entertainment!"

Helena's head snapped back, and her eyes flashed. "Well, I certainly learned how from the best meddler in the state of Mississippi!"

Adrian's shoulders were heaving convulsively now, and both Sylvia and Harold had their faces pressed into their napkins. Maggie was tempted to follow suit, the situation having developed so quickly into a farce, but she wanted to see what her father would do.

Gerard shook his head dolefully. "Helena, my dear, they really should lock you away in the closet, or at least give you a good spanking."

The picture of a physically chastised Helena was too much. They all—except Helena, who was now beet red— broke into unrestrained laughter at his pronouncement.

"A very good idea, Gerard!" Retty proclaimed. "Any volunteers?" She wiped her eyes one last time with her napkin, then stood up. "Whatever the method, it's still good to have you both home. I'll go up now and talk to Claudine—that's Claudine Sprayberry, Gerard—who's Henry's nurse, and see if you can visit with him this afternoon."

Retty marched at a brisk pace out of the dining room, and Maggie marveled once again that the woman could be almost eighty years old. Her face bore the weight of all her years, but her body was that of a woman years younger.

The rest of the company moved slowly out of the dining room and down the hall to the drawing room, except for Adrian Worthington, who remained behind to oversee the clearing of the table by two young black women dressed in dark green uniforms.

They were all still smiling as they seated themselves on the three sofas in the drawing room. Maggie was pleased to see her father amused by the revelation of Helena's duplicity, but as she watched him she was startled by a strained look in his eyes which his laughter failed to mask. Despite all the amusement engendered by Helena's forced confession, Gerard still looked worried about something.

.Helena chatted with a slightly subdued Gerard, while Harold questioned Maggie about her academic interests. Harold, Maggie was delighted to hear, had been a professor of literature at an eastern state university. Having never married, upon his retirement two years before, he had returned to Jackson to live with his brother and sisters.

While she chatted with Harold, Maggie heard snatches of the conversation between her father and Helena. Evidently, someone named Ernie was coming to visit in the next day or two. She didn't quite catch what connection Ernie had to the McLendon family, but her father seemed pleased that this Ernie, whoever he was, was coming.

Retty marched into the room with an announcement then, and both conversations ceased.

"Henry's finished his lunch now, and he said he'd like to see you both. Come along." She marched back out of the room without giving either Gerard or Maggie a chance to offer any response to the abrupt summons. Hastily they got to their feet to follow her, Gerard a few steps ahead of his daughter. His face had become suddenly and completely remote, and Maggie made no attempt to talk to him as they followed Retty.

Surely now she would learn something about why her father and her grandfather hadn't spoken to each other in twenty-five years.

Chapter Three

AT THE HEAD OF THE STAIRS, Retty turned to the right and strode at a brisk pace down the hall, stopping after she had passed three or four doors. Maggie had meant to try to keep count of them, but Retty's hectic pace and her own chaotic thoughts defeated her intention. What on earth was she supposed to say to the grandfather she'd never met?

Retty rapped smartly on the door before opening it. She motioned Maggie and Gerard in behind her. Just inside the door they were met by a slim, poised figure in a white uniform. The nurse moved forward to shake Gerard's hand, but at the same moment Maggie stepped from behind her father and startled the woman.

The nurse looked fully into Maggie's apologetic eyes. The woman blanched, and she took an involuntary step backwards. Color bled slowly back into her face as she made a visible effort to tear her eyes away from Maggie's face.

After having met her great-aunt Lavinia, Maggie was beginning to understand why people reacted so strongly at the sight of her. But that didn't make it any more pleasant, or make her feel any more welcome.

Gerard reached out a steadying hand. "Claudine," he said warmly, "I can't really believe it's you—grown up after all these years!"

Claudine Sprayberry, Retty had said her name was, Maggie remembered. Here was, yet again, another person from her father's past. What was her connection to the family, besides being Henry McLendon's nurse?

From what Maggie could see in the rather dim light of this part of the room, Claudine was hovering around forty, two or three years either way. Her body, shapely in the crisp nurse's uniform, looked younger, but there was a suggestion of hardness about the full lips and icy blue eyes that made Maggie settle on forty as highly probable. Thick, brownish-red hair coiled around her head. Slightly put off by the woman's reaction to her, Maggie scolded herself mentally for her bitchy assessment of the woman's looks. *Just try to relax a bit,* she thought. *They're all probably as much on edge as you are.*

Though the top of her head barely reached his shoulder blades, Claudine reached out and pulled Gerard down for a quick peck on the cheek. "It's good to see you again, too," she responded, her voice light. "But I do feel the tiniest bit old seeing this young lady here with you. I can still remember the time you came home to tell everyone about her!"

This made Retty and Gerard tense up, and Maggie could feel her father's unease almost palpably in the room with them. *What on earth happened in this house twenty-five years ago?* she wondered yet again.

Claudine gave a faint smile, then continued, "Well, time enough for chatting about old times later. Someone wants to see you." She turned toward the center of the room and nodded her head.

For the first time, Maggie was more aware of her surroundings. She and Retty stood in a corner of the room, just inside the door. The room seemed large, though perhaps the lack of furniture—save a king-sized bed, a bedside table, and a couple of chairs—lent the impression of space. The lighting was dim, the curtains pulled against the glare of the early afternoon sun, and the color scheme did nothing to lessen the gloomy feeling. Everything seemed to be some combination of gray and mauve—a tribute, Maggie learned later, to the school colors of her grandfather's college, Mississippi State University. At the moment she found the whole scene rather unsettling.

A thin, frail figure dominated the bed. His skin was deathly white against the mauve of the bedspread, but Henry McLendon lay there with fires banked, waiting impatiently for them to approach. Quietly, both Maggie and Gerard moved forward to stand by the side of the bed. With a shock, Maggie found the outlines of her father's face carved into the hideously old contours of her grandfather's visage, and the image frightened her. What had once been the fullness of flesh had shrunk away to reveal the uncompromising sharpness of the bones beneath, and Henry McLendon's face was now nothing but planes and angles. Yet from this physical wreck burned a fierce energy; she could see it in his eyes. Henry McLendon had not yet made up his mind to die, and that was enough for now.

Those brilliant eyes glanced at Gerard, then moved on to Maggie's face. In them she read an appeal she couldn't answer, for she knew that, if only for a moment, he was seeing someone else, probably her grandmother. *Please, God,* Maggie thought, *not Lavinia!* Then the eyes dimmed, and the old man blinked.

When he spoke, the voice came out strong, like a leather whip cracking in the air. "You're a little early, I haven't given up yet."

Maggie flinched as if he'd reached out to strike her. Gerard, surprisingly, laughed aloud. "You old bastard," he said with affection, though his voice was strained.

Maggie couldn't take her eyes off her grandfather's face. Though his expression changed very little, she would have sworn that her father's reply had pleased him. His words confirmed it. "I see you didn't go completely soft teaching poetry."

"It kept me from going insane writing wills and drawing up contracts, not to mention bilking widows and orphans of their property," Gerard conceded tartly.

Henry chuckled, a dry, raspy sound that Maggie mistook for a cough at first. "He always did have brass," he confided to her. "Even as a toddler. Your grandmother had quite a time trying to potty train him." He smiled. "He *had* to be tough, in this family. Else he'd've been eaten alive, and not just by his father. I'm glad to see he stayed that way. What about you?"

Still dazed by mental images of her father's toilet training, Maggie didn't know quite what to reply. "I've lived with him for nearly twenty-six years," she said. "Does that qualify me?" *Now I'm beginning to sound like the rest of them,* she thought.

Henry laughed again. "You'll do, my girl! You'll do." He extended a hand to her, urging her to sit on the bed beside him, while Gerard pulled up one of the chairs. Retty and Claudine, completely ignored, had faded into the background.

"Your grandmother," Henry began. The pain in his voice nearly made Maggie wince. "Your grandmother never got a chance to see you, thanks to a lot of foolishness and stubborn pride. Not on her part, of course. She was too intelligent for all that. I hope your intelligence comes from her, and not from either one of us feebleminded men." The tone was jocular, but the intent was serious.

He turned his head slightly toward Gerard. "We've wasted a lot of important time over pride. I was too stubborn to call you myself, so I asked Helena to write to you for me. God knows what she said, but I apologize now if the silly girl dramatized everything."

"Father, I—" Gerard began, but Henry motioned for him to be silent. Maggie was amused to see her father shushed in this way.

"Your father and I have quite a bit to talk about, my dear," Henry told her as he squeezed her hand. "I hope you won't mind if I ask you to leave us alone right now."

Maggie frowned. This wasn't what she had hoped to hear. "Frankly, Grandfather," she said, the name sounding strange even as it rolled off her tongue, "I was hoping someone would finally get around to telling me just why you and Dad have been estranged all these years. What on earth happened?"

Everyone froze around her. Henry McLendon frowned. "Your grandmother died the last time your father was in this house. Hasn't he ever told you that?" Suddenly he closed his eyes, and for a moment he looked so still and frail that she was afraid he'd died even as he spoke.

Her heart thudding, Maggie whispered, "No, Grandfather,

he never told me."

A faint spot of red colored Henry's cheeks. He opened his eyes, and she breathed more easily. She didn't dare look at her father. She had felt him draw away from her earlier when she spoke her mind, tired of the shilly-shallying.

"You're direct," her grandfather said, regarding her with a small smile of approval. "But for now you're just going to have to wait. Your father is the one who should tell you what happened, and I want you to promise you'll wait and let him tell you. Not anyone else. Do you hear me?"

"Yes, Grandfather," Maggie said, taken aback at his insistence.

"We'll have time to talk later. But I want you to know that having you here at last makes everything worthwhile." He smiled again.

Touched by this last remark, though still burning with curiosity, she leaned forward to kiss him lightly on the cheek, and he clutched her hand. Blinking back tears, Maggie stood up. Looking down at him, she wondered whether they really would have much time to talk. Seeing him like this, she thought perhaps that Helena hadn't exaggerated in her letter. Now that she and her father were here, would he cease fighting and die, once he and his son made their peace? Or would he fight to stay alive to spend more time with his only grandchild?

Overcome with sadness, Maggie moved slowly toward the door, where Claudine Sprayberry waited with Retty. When Maggie glanced back, Gerard had taken her place on the bed beside his father. His head bent low, he murmured something to Henry, who replied quietly.

Claudine in a low voice told Retty and Maggie that she would go to her room while the two men talked. "Mr. Henry looks fine for now, but Gerard really shouldn't stay too long. Sylvia will be up soon to take over. It's nearly two. They should be fine until then." She ushered the other two women out the door with her and followed them back down the hall to the next door.

This, it turned out, was Claudine's room, connected by

an inside door to her patient's bedroom. "It used to be a dressing room," she told Maggie with a frown. "But they've made it into a really comfortable room for me." Impulsively she touched Maggie on the shoulder. "I'm sorry I was so strange earlier, but when I first saw you, it was like a ghost coming out of the dark."

Maggie made a moue of resignation. "I'm afraid I'm rather used to that reaction by now."

Claudine smiled her thanks at Maggie's acceptance of her apology. "I hope we'll have time to talk later, but right now I've got to change so I can go shopping. This is my afternoon off." She opened her door briskly and closed it before Maggie had a chance to stammer out a reply.

Helena approached them, having just come upstairs, and Retty motioned to her. "Helena, take Maggie to her room. I think she probably needs some time alone right now."

Maggie nodded gratefully. Retty patted her on the shoulder and walked away, toward the stairs. Helena, reading the distress in her face, gave her a quick hug, and Maggie struggled with her emotions, feeling completely overwhelmed.

As she followed Helena down the hall, Maggie forced herself to breathe deeply and evenly. She tried to distract herself by thinking about The Magnolias and what she had seen of it thus far. The only thing in her experience to which she could liken this mansion was a large and very grand hotel, once a stately home, in which she and her father had stayed in England. The plush carpet on the floor, which deadened all but a faint whisper of their footsteps, and the very massiveness of the building around, over, and underneath her unnerved Maggie. Her own house back in Houston, once roomy and comfortable, now seemed oppressively small in comparison.

Helena made no effort to explain what lay behind the various doors they passed. By the infrequency of their appearance Maggie estimated that each of the rooms was much larger than any of the rooms in her own house.

Finally Helena paused before a door near the end of the long corridor. Diffidently she said, "I hope you won't mind,

Maggie, but Henry insisted that you have your grandmother's room."

Maggie's hand, which had been reaching for the doorknob, faltered. Her grandmother! The few times Gerard had ever discussed his estranged family with her, he had not mentioned his mother, other than to explain that she had died when Maggie was nearly a year old. Learning more about her was her innermost thought, especially after everything which had occurred this day.

When Maggie hesitated, Helena took action by opening the door and ushering the younger woman inside.

Sunshine cascaded into the room from two sets of French doors which led out onto a wide balcony. The light dazzled her eyes momentarily as it bounced off white walls and golden fixtures. The room appeared to Maggie at least twice the size of her own bedroom, which itself had been remodeled from two rooms. A beautifully carved antique bed dominated one side of the room. Another wall consisted of floor-to-ceiling bookshelves. There was space also for a small sofa, two chairs—each with its own reading lamp—and a desk whose woodwork matched that of the bed.

Maggie swallowed a lump which had come unbidden into her throat. The room had a cozy, welcoming feeling for her, and for the first time she had a burgeoning sense of home-coming.

As she turned toward Helena to express something of her emotions, Maggie noticed for the first time a portrait on the wall to her left. The wall was bare except for the portrait and a door.

Near life-size, the portrait drew Maggie toward it irresistibly. For a moment she thought she was staring at herself, but as she came closer she could see that the woman in the portrait was older, perhaps thirty-five or forty. Dressed in a ball gown of emerald satin, the woman had the same deep, rich auburn hair and green eyes that Maggie had. The face, intelligent, humorous, and loving, gazed searchingly back at her, the hint of a smile upon the full red lips. One hand casually smoothed back the abundant hair; the other clasped a book. In the background of the portrait Maggie could see a small replica of the mansion. This, then, was her grandmother, Magnolia Amelia Culpeper McLendon.

Helena had drawn close to her grandniece, placing a comforting arm around trembling shoulders. "We all loved her so very much," Helena whispered, her voice husky with emotion. "She was so excited when you were born, and she fussed so when she heard that Gerard had named you for her. 'Why on earth does he want to name that poor child "Magnolia"?' she asked. 'That's no name for a modern girl!' But she was so proud anyway!"

The image of her grandmother blurred slowly, and Maggie reached with an unsteady hand to wipe some of the tears away. "She's so lovely," she said unselfconsciously, then realized what she had said.

Helena smiled as Maggie turned to her and asked, "Do I really look that much like her?"

Helena nodded. Maggie blushed.

"And Lavinia, too, more's the pity," Helena said.

Maggie widened her eyes. "Not too much, I hope," she said dryly.

"Honey, that's such a long story, Lavinia and her nastiness, it would take years to tell you," Helena said, sighing. "And right now I expect you want to be by yourself for a little while. Am I right?"

"Not just yet," Maggie said, now feeling a need for company, for someone at least a little familiar. "Stay with me a little longer."

Helena drew Maggie away from the portrait and back toward the center of the room. She explained that the door near the portrait led into the bathroom.

"After Magnolia died," she said sadly, "Henry just couldn't bear to change this room, so he left it pretty much the way it was. We've kept it up well, though."

"She died not long after I was born, didn't she?" Maggie asked hesitantly, mindful of her promise to her grandfather.

Helena nodded. "You were just about a year old, bless your heart—you never even got a chance to know her. But she had all sorts of pictures of you." She smiled. "They're still here in this room, I think. None of her things have been disturbed in all this time—almost twenty-five years." She walked over toward the wall of books. "Henry used to come in here sometimes—after she passed away, that is—and sit and talk to her." She glanced sheepishly back at Maggie. "I did, too. We all missed her a lot."

"You called this my grandmother's room. Didn't she and my grandfather share a bedroom?" Maggie realized the question might be considered a bit indelicate, but she wanted to know.

Helena laughed. "The room Henry's in now was their bedroom. This was just Magnolia's private sitting room. One of the good things about having a house this large."

Maggie joined her at the bookshelves and squeezed her great-aunt's arm gratefully. "Thank you for telling me these things. Since I have no memories of her of my very own, it's very nice to share yours."

Helena patted Maggie's arm in response. "I know, dear." She moved closer to the shelves. "These were Magnolia's books. She was quite a collector, and whenever she disappeared for a while, you knew you'd find her reading somewhere." She ran a hand lightly along the spines of a row of books.

Maggie moved closer to read the titles and blinked when she realized what she was seeing. Her grandmother had obviously been a devoted mystery reader, because here were what looked to be complete sets of the works of Margery Allingham, Maggie's own favorite, as well as Agatha Christie, Ngaio Marsh, and Dorothy L. Sayers. Reverently she pulled from the shelf a copy of *The Nine Tailors* and glanced inside. A first edition. Her breath tightened in her chest.

She glanced quickly through more of the books while Helena watched. In addition to the large collection of mysteries there were classics of British and American fiction of the nineteenth and early twentieth centuries. Jane Austen, George Eliot, Edith Wharton, D. H. Lawrence, and Henry James, along with Josephine Tey, Henry Wade, John Rhode,

Elizabeth Daly, and Phoebe Atwood Taylor.

Then Maggie's eyes lighted upon one particular title, and she frowned. There on the shelf stood a copy of Agatha Christie's *Sleeping Murder*, which she knew had been published several years after her grandmother's death. She pointed this out to Helena.

"Henry kept up her collection after she passed away," Helena said. "She had loved her books so much, it just seemed one small way for him to remember her." She laughed lightly. "Several of the rest of us are mystery readers, too, and Magnolia was always generous about letting us borrow books, although she was mighty particular about the way you treated them!" She laughed again. "Anyway, I knew all her favorite authors, so it wasn't hard for me to keep track of them for Henry and make sure they got ordered. Of course, now they're nearly all passed away, too, so there haven't been many additions lately."

Maggie was touched by the story and pleased also to have found this link with her grandmother. As she rested one hand lovingly upon a row of books by Allingham, she felt even closer to her namesake. She turned shining eyes toward her aunt and said, "Thank you! You don't know how much this means to me. So many of these people are writers I love myself, and knowing that I share the same taste in literature with . . . my grandmother means so much."

Helena engulfed Maggie in a sudden, fierce hug which left the younger woman breathless. "You're just what we all need!" Helena declared when she had stepped back. "I haven't felt so good in years."

Maggie had to smile at her enthusiasm. Now, thanks to Helena and her memories of her grandmother, she felt she really had come home, despite her father's great reluctance to bring her here.

Helena said, "I'm sure you're ready now, my dear, for a little time to yourself to try to absorb everything." She gave Maggie another hug. "I'll see you later."

The door closed behind her, and the silence in her wake was almost deafening. Everything about Helena was so vital that the moment she left the room even the sunlight seemed to dim a little. Maggie smiled as she remembered her father's nickname for his favorite aunt. "Hurricane Helena" suited her very well.

Maggie decided that freshening up a bit wouldn't hurt, so she went into the bathroom. The opulence of it seemed almost indecent to Maggie, accustomed to the functional style of her own bathroom in Houston. The combination of marble and gold looked terribly expensive. She could probably live comfortably for a year in Europe on what it had cost to fit out this bathroom.

She peeped hesitantly into a walk-in closet. Her clothes looked like orphans in one corner. The closet was bare except for her own things. Her grandmother's clothes, if they had been kept at all, were not here, although the closet had enough space to house the wardrobes of several women, or so it seemed to Maggie.

She bathed her face in cool water and patted it dry with a thick, golden towel. Since someone had already thoughtfully laid out her toilet articles for her, she picked up her brush and tried to convince her hair to be a little less unruly.

Feeling somewhat calmer, she was still frustrated by not knowing the answers to several important questions. Her grandfather's revelation about the timing of her grandmother's death had stunned her. The last time her father had been in this house, his mother had died. Was she supposed to think that her father had played some role in his mother's death?

She shrugged that off as nonsense as she walked back into the bedroom. Surely she was letting the unpleasant undercurrents among the family members get to her. Lavinia was enough to rattle anyone, she thought sourly.

As she was sitting down on the bed, a knock sounded at her door. "Come in," she called out.

The door opened slowly in response, and her father stood framed in the opening. Tentatively he advanced into the room, shutting the door behind him. Gerard's eyes focused immediately upon the portrait of his mother, while Maggie watched for his reaction.

The silence lengthened as he stared at the portrait. The obvious tension in his body, betrayed by the set of his shoulders, gradually drained away. After several minutes he turned to face his daughter, who was not surprised to see tears glistening in his eyes.

Gerard walked over to the bookshelves. His right hand reached out to caress the spines of several books. "Even your taste in literature you inherited from her," he remarked, his voice devoid of emotion.

Maggie kept her voice low. "It seems so."

He came to sit beside her on the bed. "She would have been very proud of you. Even though she never went to college, she was the best-read person I've ever known. These books here"—he waved his hand at the nearby shelves—"were her favorites, but she read all the classics, not once but several times." He shook his head admiringly. "I don't quite know how she did it, because there were so many demands on her time, but she always managed to read at least a couple of hours a day. Even my father," he laughed, "knew better than to interfere when she settled down with a book."

This sharing of memories by her father was what Maggie had wanted. The fact that it should have taken place years before was ignored at the moment. She sensed that her father was finally ready to talk about his past, and she was too curious about what he would tell her to criticize the timing.

She did venture a comment. "I gather you had a good talk with your father."

Gerard smiled tiredly. "Yes. We talked about a lot of things—things we should have discussed years ago, of course, but we were both too stubborn to make the first move."

"Until Helena made it for you," Maggie said neutrally.

"More or less," he replied. "Father prompted Helena to do it. I suppose he thought I would ignore a direct appeal."

"Would you have?"

He frowned. "I don't know. He's always set my back up,

ever since I was an adolescent." Gerard laughed suddenly. "He probably still has a hard time seeing me as anything but that gawky teenager who defied him at every turn."

Maggie amused herself for a moment, imaging her father as a rebellious teenager. She grinned.

"Anyway," he said shrugging, "we finally cleared the air."

"If you don't mind my asking"—she couldn't quite keep a note of irony from her voice—"why were you estranged in the first place?"

"It was partly over my choice of careers," Gerard answered, then hesitated a moment. Taking a deep breath, he plunged ahead. "But the main reason was that I was responsible for my mother's death."

Chapter Four

STUNNED BY HER FATHER'S ANNOUNCEMENT, Maggie felt the silence in the room smothering her. She drew a ragged breath as she stared incredulously at Gerard, struggling with the implications of what he had said. Then her mind cleared, and she seized upon one word. "You said 'responsible.' What do you mean?"

Abruptly Gerard got up from the bed and walked to the French windows, standing with his back to her. "As far back as I can remember, my father and I never agreed on anything. There was always antagonism between us. I don't know why it should have been that way, except our personalities are so fundamentally different." He took a long breath. "My father has always been aggressive, going for what he wanted, no matter what obstacles stood in his way." He turned back to Maggie and gestured with his hands. "That's how he amassed the wealth to build a house like this. He built up a network of influence, took on high-profile cases with big payoffs, you name it. And he made a fortune."

"So the family wasn't wealthy to begin with?" Maggie asked. She was desperately curious to get her father to the point on his responsibility for his mother's death, but she could see that, for now, he needed to tell the story his way.

Gerard laughed, a little bitterly. "No, the McLendons were just ordinary, middle-class stock until my father came along. He seemed to have the Midas touch when it came to anything to do with money. It was Mother's family, the Culpepers, who had the breeding. They were once immensely wealthy, before the Civil War, but time and change eroded all that. Father rescued Mother and her family from 'genteel poverty' when he married her." He snorted in derision. "My grandparents could hardly stand to look at my father, but they were sure enough glad to get their hands on some of his money!"

Maggie smiled, briefly, at her father's defensive tone. He might argue with his father, but he wouldn't let others denigrate him needlessly.

Gerard turned back to look out the window. "Father ended up supporting pretty much the whole damn family! Retty married a man who went through money like it was water. Helena has never made much of an effort to try to support herself. Harold did, but apparently he lost all his savings a couple of years ago in some kind of financial disaster, and he's had to come crawling back home, begging." He snorted in derision again. "Lavinia, of course, has been a parasite all along."

He turned back to Maggie, his eyes blazing. "Can you see now why I was so determined to get away from him? I wanted to make my own way, call the shots for myself."

"And you did," she said quietly. "You've made a very good life for yourself, and I've never wanted for anything." She grinned. "Except for that pony I wanted when I was ten. And the Jaguar when I was sixteen."

Her father laughed, some of the strain leaving his face.

Maggie patted the bed, and Gerard came to sit beside her. "What happened when you left home?" she asked.

He shrugged. "All through graduate school, I never heard from my father, but Mother, Helena, and Harold wrote to me regularly. When your mother and I got married, my mother and Helena flew up to Boston for the wedding. Mother never said anything, but I know my father was furious with her. But she always went her own way.

"When you were born, I thought my father would finally soften up a bit. I kept waiting for some response to the telegram I sent as an announcement. Mother, of course, called immediately, but not a word from him." He stared down at his hands, clenched in his lap. "I waited nearly a year. Then Helena called to tell me that Mother had been very ill with pneumonia and wanted to see me. I left you and your mother in Boston and came down here right away. Mother was very weak, just beginning to recover. For her sake Father was trying hard not to argue with me. He thought there was no way I could be supporting his granddaughter in any suitable manner on what I was making at the time, and I could tell that he was furious with me for your sake, odd as that may sound."

Unaware that she had done so, Maggie made some small sound of denial, and Gerard squeezed her shoulder reassuringly. She leaned against him and wrapped an arm around him.

He took a deep breath. "I had been here just two days when we had the worst argument ever. Mother was upstairs in her room—she really wasn't strong enough to leave it—and Father and I had gone into the drawing room right after lunch. I don't remember now what set him off, but we were going at it hammer and tongs for at least half an hour. One or two people came into the room but left so quickly that, to this day, I don't know who they were." He fell silent for a long moment.

"Finally I could see I wasn't getting anywhere with him—as usual—so I stormed out into the hallway. He followed me and grabbed me by the collar when I ignored him. I swung around and had raised my hand to strike his arm away when I heard Mother cry out for me to stop."

Now Gerard's breathing was labored. Maggie pulled away from him in some alarm as he struggled with the memory of what had happened twenty-five years ago. She clasped one of his hands, and he held it like a lifeline.

"I looked up," he continued shakily, "and there she was at the head of the stairs. She was still very weak, much too weak to be out of bed. She was propped against the banister, because she didn't have the strength to come all the way down the stairs. Everything about that moment seems so vivid, even after all these years." He took a deep, steadying breath. "Both Father and I were speechless. I think the sight of her shocked us both back to reality. Then, before either of us could move, she jerked forward suddenly, fell, and started rolling down the steps. By the time I reached her she was dead. The blow on her head when she fell had killed her."

He was crying silently now, the tears slipping carelessly down his face. For a long moment Maggie was paralyzed by a vision of herself rolling down those cold marble steps. Shakily she reached out to encircle her father's shoulders with her arms, and the two clung to each other for several minutes until both felt somewhat steadier.

Maggie had no idea what to say. She had never imagined anything like this. But she had to say something to her father. "Did your father"—she couldn't call him "Grandfather" right now, she just couldn't—"actually hold you responsible for what happened?"

Gerard looked squarely at her. "For a long time, we *both* held me responsible. The last words I ever heard her say were 'Gerard, stop!'" His shoulders slumped in self-reproach. "How could I blame my father, when I considered myself just as guilty as he did?"

But Maggie could tell from the sound of his voice that Gerard had wanted all along for his father to absolve him of that guilt. Obviously, something had happened during their conversation this afternoon to lessen something of Gerard's sense of responsibility for his mother's accidental death, but he wasn't completely free of the old feeling yet.

"Dad, it was an accident. A very tragic one, but nevertheless it was an accident." Maggie stroked his arm. "You aren't to blame."

He shook his head. "Maybe not. But I didn't improve the situation any by the way I behaved. 'Pride goeth before destruction,' and all that. I was too proud to try to make peace with my father."

"And it sounds like he was just as bad, refusing to acknowledge your right to choose your own path in life," she said heatedly. "Why is he any less at fault than you?"

"I know that," Gerard said quietly. "The rational part of my mind has been telling me that for years, but the irrational part can never forget the way my mother looked just before she fell down those stairs." He looked away for a moment, toward the portrait of his mother. "But, thank God, this afternoon my father and I did what we should have done years ago. We talked it out, and I guess we more or less forgave each other for what happened." He laughed sadly. "Age finally accomplished what nothing else could. He's mellowed, at least a little bit."

"I'm happy you've been able to make your peace with him after all these years." She hugged him, and he squeezed her back.

"If we both hadn't been such stubborn jackasses we could have done this a long time ago and saved everybody in the family a lot of grief." The sudden pain in Gerard's face made Maggie hurt also. "All the years we lost simply because of pride, not to mention what it cost you—the opportunity to know your family." He laughed shortly in an attempt to lighten the mood a little. "At least I came by it honestly—my stiff neck, I mean."

She weakly smiled back, not knowing quite what to say. The reconciliation with his father meant so very much to him, but—and this was the most awful aspect of the situation— even knowing that it had been an accident did little to abate completely the feelings of responsibility.

But a healing process had begun, for which she was thankful. Their decision to come to Mississippi had been a good one. Her father could settle his debts with the past, and they could both look forward to a future which somehow included the rest of the family.

Gerard stirred restlessly from the bed. "Father wants to see you for a few minutes this afternoon. I think he has a surprise for you, and if it's what I suspect, I know you'll be delighted."

Maggie immediately felt uncomfortable. "But I don't want any gifts," she protested. "There's no need for him to give me anything, Dad."

Gently he reached down and tilted her face up toward his. "Just talk to him, and it will be all right, I promise you. He's trying the best way he knows how to make amends, of a sort. So do your best to let him, okay?"

She smiled her acquiescence. She stood up beside her father and said, "Let me have a few minutes to myself before I go to see him." She kissed him on the cheek, then pushed him gently toward the door. "I'll see you later. Why don't you go lie down for a while? I think you could use some rest, don't you?"

Gerard gave her a quick hug before leaving her.

Now that she was alone and could think about it, Maggie considered what her father had told her. The violence of her grandmother's death shocked her. Sensibly she didn't blame her father or her grandfather for the accident, but the tragedy of it saddened her. The longer she dwelled on it, though, the more likely she was to spend the afternoon crying in her room.

Resolutely closing the door behind her, she strode down the hall toward her grandfather's room. Her heart beating a little rapidly, Maggie knocked on his door.

Sylvia answered Maggie's knock, but this was a Sylvia Maggie hadn't expected to see. Sylvia, the nurse, was cool, professional, a brisk efficiency having replaced the aloof, Madonna-like woman from earlier in the day. *Maybe it's the uniform*, Maggie thought in amusement, as Sylvia ushered her into Henry McLendon's bedroom.

"Here's Maggie, Uncle Henry," Sylvia announced cheerfully, rousing her patient from a slight doze.

Henry McLendon blinked once, twice, then Maggie could glimpse the vitality she had seen earlier return to his fierce eyes. He was visibly more tired than he had been earlier in the day, yet he still contained the spark of energy that wouldn't let him give in completely to the restrictions of age and illness.

He stretched out a welcoming hand that wavered only slightly before Maggie grasped it in her own. Impulsively, she bent forward to kiss his cheek, and she could tell that her action pleased the old man. He patted the bed beside him and motioned for her to sit there, rather than in the chair drawn up for visitors.

For a long moment they gazed unblinkingly into each other's eyes. Apparently what Henry saw pleased him, for a satisfied smile creased his worn face. She couldn't help but smile back, although the unwelcome vision of her father in old age frightened her.

Her grandfather's expression turned serious. "I suppose by now Gerard has told you everything?"

Maggie nodded. For a few moments she had forgotten her feelings of resentment, still half-realized, toward this old man for his unreasoning stiffness toward her father, and the recollection of those feelings now disturbed her. Henry read something of this from the expression in her face, for he laughed softly.

"Don't fret, child, it's okay if you want to be aggravated with me just a while longer. The Lord only knows I deserve worse." He sobered abruptly. "Your father wasn't to blame for Magnolia's death, and I knew that all along, I suppose."

Watching him closely, Maggie nodded, "No, he wasn't, and neither were you."

He smiled again. "You're straightforward with your feelings—I like that. I'm not going to ask for your forgiveness—it's a little late for that, I'd say—because all of that's really between me and your father anyway, and we've made our peace. I reckon I lost more in the long run than you or your father, because I cost myself a son and a granddaughter, and there's not much I can do now to rectify that. Though I can't make up for all the mistakes I made in the past, I can set things to rights about your grandmother's death, however, after all these years," he added obscurely.

She opened her mouth to ask him what he meant, because the tone of the remark puzzled her as much as its content.

Watching her, Henry shook his head and said, "There's time enough for that later. Just something I should have taken care of long before now." He patted her hand affectionately. "In the meantime, there's something else I wanted to talk to you about."

Maggie inclined her head warily. "Yes, sir?"

"Your father tells me that you have the same taste in reading as your grandmother did," he said.

She smiled, and Henry's hand tightened upon hers as she replied. "Yes, sir, I could hardly believe it when I walked into her room and saw all those bookshelves just stuffed with books by most of my favorite writers. That, and seeing her portrait, really made me feel like I had come home, in a sense."

Her grandfather smiled sadly. "I'm delighted to hear that, because I want you, from now on, to consider all those books yours."

He smiled again, happily this time, at Maggie's gasp of surprise and incoherent words of denial. "Now, my dear, don't argue with me over this. It's not like I'm really giving them to you. I know your grandmother would love for you to have them all—it's more of a trust I'm passing on to you than an actual gift. What do you say to that?"

She thought back to what her father had said to her. Why deny her grandfather the obvious pleasure of this gift? Especially when it would mean so much to her in the years to come. "Thank you," she whispered, her voice husky with unshed tears. She leaned forward to kiss his cheek again and give him a hug, resting lightly against him. He returned the pressure briefly. Maggie drew back.

Seeing the tiredness in his eyes, she stood up slowly. "I think I'd better go so you can get some rest. This has certainly been a busy day for us all." Awkwardly, this was all she could think of to say.

Henry McLendon inclined his head on the pillow. "I think you're right," he replied. "I'm glad you and your father came home, child."

"So am I, Grandfather," she said, doing her best to hold back tears. He looked so frail and so old to her.

As Maggie moved back away from the bed, she stepped against the bedside chair, which in turn caused something propped against it to slide to the floor with a muffled thud. "What on earth?" she muttered as she bent over to retrieve a baseball bat. As she picked it up, she saw that the varnish that had once protected all the names hastily scrawled on the surface was flaking off here and there.

Henry laughed. "That's just an old souvenir your father got out of his room—at my request. I daresay he'd forgotten all about it, but that's the bat he was using when he hit a home run his senior year in high school. He won the state championship for his team with that bat—it was the only home run he ever hit."

Maggie knew that her father was a big baseball fan. Very little ever interfered with his watching games on the weekends, and he attended as many Astros home games as possible. He had never talked much about playing himself.

Smiling fondly, she propped the bat once more against the chair. "I guess he'll be back to get it later." Feeling something on her hand, Maggie inspected her palm and discovered a few small flakes of varnish from the bat. She brushed her hand absentmindedly against her skirt.

"I imagine so," Henry replied tiredly.

Sylvia stepped forward then. "You really need to get some rest now, Uncle Henry," she chided him fondly. "You've been talking to somebody or another all afternoon, and it's time you took a nap. You'll have plenty of time to visit with Maggie tomorrow."

"I'll take a nap if you'll hush fussing at me," Henry grumbled. "If you had your way I'd never talk to anybody. I'd just sleep all the time!"

Sylvia laughed as she guided Maggie toward the door. "Don't pay any attention to him—he'll talk the horns off a billy goat if you give him the chance." She lowered her voice as they reached the door. "But all this talking really does wear him out, and he's had practically the whole family up here this afternoon, along with you and Gerard. I'm afraid he's overdone it a little."

Maggie nodded. "You're right, I know, but this has been a pretty big day for us all."

Sylvia patted her on the shoulder. "I'm really glad you've come home, especially for his sake." She bobbed her head backwards in Henry's direction.

Squeezing Sylvia's hand briefly, Maggie slipped out the door with a smile. "See you later."

Maggie went once again to her bathroom to bathe her face in cold water. Staring in the mirror, she said, "This is ridiculous. No more crying today." Her head ached slightly, and she wished for some aspirin. She checked the medicine cabinet and, sure enough, there was a new bottle of aspirin, its seal still intact. She opened it and filled a glass with water, then downed two tablets.

Back in the bedroom, reclining on the bed, she contemplated what she should do next. Before she could give it much thought, a knock sounded at her door. Startled, she got off the bed and called out, "Come in."

Briskly the door swung open, and Adrian Worthington stepped into the room. He flashed a brief smile at Maggie. "Harold asked me to let you know he'd see you at dinner. Your father told him Mr. McLendon had asked to speak with you, so Harold thought you'd probably rather wait until later for a tour of the house."

An attractive butler in khakis and polo shirt was outside the realm of Maggie's experience, so she stood there not knowing quite what to say to the man, even how she should address him. "Thank you for letting me know," she finally stammered. "I was thinking about my uncle and how to find him when you knocked on my door."

He smiled again, which did nothing to ease the onslaught of her jitters. "That's pretty easy, actually, Miss McLendon." He moved to the telephone beside her bed.

"Please, call me Maggie," she said hurriedly, uncomfortable at being called "Miss" by someone only a few years older than she.

"Maggie," he repeated, and she swallowed convulsively as she stepped closer in answer to his motioning hand. She rather liked the way he said her name, the way he lingered slightly over the first syllable. *Better watch it*, she admonished herself silently. *Why?* herself asked back.

Quickly and concisely Adrian explained to Maggie the in-house phone system. Each phone had two lines, one an outside line and the other for in-house calls only. Under the phone lay a handy list of all the house extension numbers.

"And if you can't catch up with the person you want to talk to," he said, "you can always dial the extension in the butler's pantry. It rings in the kitchen also, so during the day, anyway, someone will always answer that line and get a message to me."

"Thank you," Maggie responded. "I think I can handle this. It certainly makes sense to have a system like this in a house this size." She shook her head wonderingly. "Otherwise I don't know how you'd ever find anybody."

He nodded. "Yes, it is handy. Now," he said as he turned toward the door, "is there anything else I can help you with?"

"Yes, there are two things, actually. The first is: When is dinner, and how should I dress?"

"Dinner's at six-thirty, and dress around here is always pretty casual. What you're wearing now is fine." His eyes moved appraisingly—and approvingly—over Maggie's figure.

Coloring slightly—whether from irritation or pleasure, she wouldn't stop to decide—Maggie posed her second question before she lost her nerve. "What should I call you? I've never known a butler before—if that's what you are, because I'm really not sure—and I have no idea what you prefer." *That sounded pretty ditsy*, she told herself. *Now he thinks you're a complete idiot!*

He pursed his lips to keep from laughing. "You can call me whatever you like. Worthington, or Adrian, if you prefer. The family isn't very big on formality, you may have noticed." He opened the door, and Maggie stared at the muscles in his shoulders. The polo shirt fit his body very nicely. "And butler will do just as well as anything for a job title."

"Um, thank you for all the information . . . Adrian." She collected her thoughts enough to say this before the door shut behind him. He gave her a wink in farewell.

Limply, Maggie sat down on her bed. Adrian, as she now forced herself to call him, definitely intrigued her. His manner of speaking marked him as well-educated, and he had an assurance of manner with nothing servile about it. Perhaps a little probing of Helena—discreet, of course—would yield some information about his background.

Yes, she was interested in him. And, for some reason, she thought he might be interested in her. Otherwise, why would he come up to her room to deliver Harold's message, when he could as easily have called her on the efficient house telephone system?

Shrugging aside her speculations, Maggie decided to explore her grandmother's—correction, *her*—collection of books before dinner. She was touched by her grandfather's gesture, and it was one she hadn't the heart to refuse. This link with the grandmother she had never known was a precious one, and these books were a gift she would always treasure simply because they had been loved by her grandmother.

In complete happiness Maggie lost track of time exploring the contents of her new collection, finding several wonderful surprises. With a start, she noticed the time around six-fifteen. Hurriedly she went into the bathroom to wash her hands and face and to brush her hair again, deciding as she did so that her traveling clothes would have to do for dinner, because she didn't want to spend time dithering over what was suitable to wear. Besides, Adrian had told her the family didn't really care about formalities such as dressing for dinner.

Downstairs, she found that Adrian had meant what he said. Helena had changed her red running suit for one in strident purple. Of them all, only Retty appeared to have "dressed" for dinner, this by having added a cashmere sweater to her outfit of the day.

The food was superb and plenteous. Afterward Maggie couldn't remember what they had actually had to eat, because the conversation was so lively she never had time to concentrate on what she was putting into her mouth. The fact that Adrian was sitting beside her again occupied her thoughts more than did the food.

Retty and Gerard kept them all laughing with a mock argument over the virtues of life in Houston. Helena couldn't resist baiting her elder sister, and Harold jumped in loyally to support Helena when Retty thundered a broadside in her direction. The mood of the dinner was rather frenetic, and

Maggie and Adrian sat quietly while the others kept the conversational ball zipping around the room.

Claudine Sprayberry joined them as they were all sitting down at the table. In contrast to the nurse's white uniform she had been wearing earlier, she now wore a bright yellow, sleeveless dress. Across her shoulders, Maggie noticed enviously, she wore a scarf interwoven with streaks of blue, red, and green. As cool air from the house's overly efficient air-conditioning system drifted across her shoulders, Maggie wished that she too was wearing a scarf. Then her attention turned to the food, and she forgot about being cold.

After dessert—homemade vanilla ice cream that was so wonderful Maggie had no trouble eating a second helping— Retty steered them all toward a room at the back of the first floor. This room was their entertainment center, Retty explained to a curious Maggie. There was a state-of-the-art sound system and a huge collection of music. Mounted against one wall was a huge television screen, which looked to Maggie more like a small movie screen. Otherwise the room was furnished with leather chairs and small leather sofas scattered casually about, and the dark richness of the leather Maggie found oddly reassuring. This room, at least, looked like a place where someone spent a lot of time.

Sylvia joined them as they were discussing what movie to watch. She had given Henry his dinner and left him to sleep, she reported as she patted a beeper in her pocket. "If he can't sleep or if anything bothers him, all he has to do is press a button, and I'll be right upstairs," she explained to Maggie and Gerard.

Helena suggested they should let Maggie or Gerard pick the movie for the night. Gerard waived his choice in favor of his daughter's, so Maggie contemplated the astounding video collection. There had to be several hundred tapes in the specially designed cabinets in one wall, but finally her eyes rested on one title, "The Lion in Winter." She hadn't seen that one in quite a while, and it was one of the Audrey Hepburn movies she hadn't bought for herself yet. "How about this one?" She handed it to Helena.

"Oh, we're all Hepburn fans here," Helena said, pleased with Maggie's choice. "You'll get no argument from me!"

Everyone else—including Adrian, Maggie noted with pleasure—seemed amenable. Adrian set everything up while the others arranged their seats. She found herself with Helena on a small couch directly in front of the screen, about eight feet back. The others settled themselves in chairs scattered in a loose semicircle behind the couch. Adrian turned off the lights, found his own seat, then clicked the remote control. Maggie snuggled down contentedly in the soft leather to watch one of her favorite movies.

For two-and-a-quarter hours she sat, barely moving, enthralled with a movie that she could quote in some scenes. Vaguely she was aware that, behind her, some of the others on occasion moved around, but her attention focused upon the screen. Helena beside her seemed just as absorbed in the movie as Maggie; she also never left her seat.

When the movie ended, Adrian flicked on the lights and set the tape rewinding. Retty had nodded off during the movie. The bright lights woke her up, and rather shamefacedly she rubbed her eyes as she smiled at Maggie.

Sylvia stretched before announcing that she was going to run upstairs to check on Henry. As she went out the door, Adrian asked them whether anybody would like something to drink. Before he had gone completely around the room, taking requests—Helena having dithered between a Shirley Temple and a Bloody Mary—Sylvia reappeared in the doorway, her face a grotesque caricature of horror.

She grasped the doorknob for support as her legs threatened to give way. "Somebody's killed Uncle Henry!"

Chapter Five

FOR A LONG MOMENT Sylvia's words hung in the air, while all activity in the room froze. Stunned and disbelieving, Maggie glanced quickly around at the rest of the family.

The faces of her relatives were curiously blank, she noted. Adrian and Claudine were the only two in the group, besides Gerard, who evinced any emotion. Adrian was swallowing convulsively, while Claudine hugged herself and shivered, running her hands up and down her arms, her hands coming to rest on her bare shoulders.

The expression on Gerard's face registered unbelieving horror, and Maggie could feel her own face slipping into a mirror image of her father's as she finally accepted what Sylvia had told them. Trying not to cry, Maggie clutched at her father's hand. He grasped it in his own. She noted dully that his hand felt as cold as hers.

Claudine moved first, her bright yellow dress a sudden blur of color and movement, pushing her way through the door, jostling Sylvia aside. Quickly Adrian followed her, and after a moment they could all hear the footsteps of the two rapidly ascending the marble steps. Gerard and Maggie began to follow, while Lavinia herded Sylvia toward a chair, clucking solicitously over the young woman. Retty, Harold, and Helena remained where they were, standing aimlessly near the doorway, still trying to absorb the impact of Sylvia's announcement.

When Maggie and Gerard reached Henry McLendon's bedroom, they found Claudine leaning against the closed door. "Don't go in there," she advised them bleakly. "Dear God above, it's awful. I'd better go call the police." She proceeded on shaky legs down the hall and disappeared inside her room next door.

The door opened, and Adrian stepped out. Pale of face, one hand rubbing his stomach, he glanced nervously between Maggie and her father. "There's nothing any of us can do now," he said blankly. "You'd better go back downstairs."

He tried to push them gently back toward the stairs, but Gerard stood firm. "What happened?" His tone of voice was stern, a tone which had forced many a cocky graduate student to quail. Adrian's normally assured manner was no proof against the older man's air of command.

"He's dead, and someone killed him," Adrian said, his breathing ragged. Let's just leave it at that. Please." He closed his eyes and covered them with one hand.

"Could someone have gotten into the house and done this?" Maggie asked, trying to control her trembling.

"No," Adrian said, his voice flat. "I switched on the security system before we started the movie. No one could have gotten in."

"Oh, my," Gerard said softly. He reached out blindly for Maggie, who herself felt as if the floor were about to disappear beneath her. They clung to each other for a moment, until Adrian, recovering slightly, urged them to go downstairs.

With Adrian on one side and Maggie on the other, Gerard moved down the stairs as if he had aged forty years. This frightened Maggie for several reasons, not the least of which was the fact that she had never seen her father in such a state. But at the back of her mind, she fretted over the fact that one member of the household was a murderer. Someone in the family had killed Henry McLendon.

By the time they reached the entertainment room again, Sylvia had evidently recovered enough to tell the others what she had found. Helena, pale but curiously dry-eyed, sat in the corner by herself, her fingers picking ceaselessly at something on the leg of her tracksuit. Retty sat with Sylvia, who cried quietly, while Retty patted her hands soothingly. Harold stood in a corner, his back to everyone else in the room. Lavinia sat curled up in a corner of one of the couches, nursing a glass of some dark-colored liquid.

Gerard's entrance roused Helena from her quiet perch. After one long look at his face, she moved quickly to a cabinet in the wall, fetched out a decanter and a glass, and poured a generous amount of what looked to be brandy into the glass.

"You look like you need this," she said gruffly to Gerard as she pushed the glass into his hands. "Drink up."

Maggie weakly smiled her thanks at her aunt, who promptly fetched another glass for Maggie, whose pallor she seemed to notice for the first time. Gratefully Maggie sipped at the liquid while she watched the color come back into her father's face. His breathing became gradually less labored, and Maggie's concern for him ebbed a fraction.

"The police are on their way," Claudine announced from the doorway. She headed for the brandy and poured herself a generous amount. Her hands were unsteady as she lifted the glass to her lips. She bolted back the shot of brandy like it was orange juice, then put her glass away. She plopped down on one of the sofas and leaned back, her eyes closed. Her arms crossed across her chest, Claudine massaged her shoulders through the thin material of her dress.

The silence grew uncomfortably longer as every person in the room glanced surreptitiously at the other occupants. The only exception was Gerard, whose eyes were fixed unwaveringly on the nearly empty glass in his hands. As she observed each of her relatives in turn, Maggie noted curiously that the blankness of expression had not cracked. *Why wasn't anyone saying anything?* she wondered. *Were they all still so stunned that they couldn't absorb what had happened?*

Or were they afraid to look one another in the eyes, knowing that one of them had murdered Henry McLendon?

All at once, Maggie wanted nothing more than to leave the house, to go outside and breathe deeply of the outside air. The tenseness of the atmosphere crowded in on her, making her claustrophobic. She forced herself to calm down.

They sat in that chilling silence for perhaps ten minutes, not a one of them ever speaking. When the doorbell rang, Adrian got up to answer it. The others waited patiently for his return. A few minutes later he ushered into the room ahead of him a distinguished-looking man Maggie guessed to be about her father's age.

He went immediately to Retty. "Mrs. Butler, I can't tell you how sorry I am to hear about this. I promise you we'll find out who's responsible as soon as we can."

Retty took his proffered hand listlessly. "Thank you, Arthur. I know you all will do your best."

Arthur nodded to the others, then his gaze rested on Gerard. "Good lord, nobody told me you had finally come home." He moved forward to extend a hand.

Gerard looked up at him for a moment, unable to focus upon the smiling man in front of him. After a few seconds his gaze cleared, and a slow, strained smile broke across his face as he stood up to shake hands. "Arthur Latham! I thought they would've run you out of town years ago. Don't tell me you're a cop."

Latham smiled back. "They couldn't run off their top man, now could they?" His gaze rested on Maggie, and she registered his slight intake of breath, though he tried to cover it with a courtly nod of the head. "This young lady must be your daughter."

Maggie stood up to offer him her hand while Gerard performed the introduction. "Arthur and I go way back," he told his daughter. "He got into so much mischief as a teenager, I figured he'd be a life-resident of Parchman by now."

Seeing the puzzled look on Maggie's face, Latham explained that Parchman was the state penitentiary. She smiled dutifully back, uncomfortable over the man's scrutiny of her. She matched him look for look, noting the streaks of gray in the dirty-blond hair and the many lines etched in a face burned red by the sun. His body, slightly overweight to judge by his incipient paunch, looked powerful. His shoulders strained at the seams of his fashionably cut—and expensive—suit.

Abruptly the lighter mood of reunion vanished as Latham switched his attention to the matter at hand. Nodding at Adrian, he announced, "I'll take a look around upstairs, then

I'll be back down to talk to each of you while my men go about their business." He strode quickly from the room, followed by Adrian.

Before the door closed behind them, a young man in uniform, his cap deferentially tucked under one arm, stepped inside. He smiled politely at them as he assumed a stance of seeming indifference near the door.

Latham's energy had managed to break through Gerard's state of inertia, Maggie was relieved to see. Despite a lingering air of incredulity, Gerard looked more like his normal self now as he sipped the remainder of his brandy.

Under the seemingly disinterested gaze of the policeman, they all sat quietly and waited. Occasionally someone moved an arm or a leg into a more comfortable position, but for the most part the room was still, except for the sound of breathing and an irregular, unconscious sigh.

Maggie sat, one shoulder touching her father's shoulder. She drew comfort from his presence while her mind busily tried to think of anything it could besides the awful implications of her grandfather's murder.

From her many years of reading mysteries and reading about real crimes in the Houston newspaper, she knew only too well that the murderer had to be a member of the family. Who else would have had the opportunity? She couldn't believe, as much as she would like to, that someone had wandered through the extensive grounds and into the house to murder her grandfather. The fact that Adrian had set the alarm before they sat down to watch the movie clinched it.

She glanced warily around the room, feeling bereft. She had come here this day and had found a family, only to have all that taken away from her by a brutal murder. Until the police could figure out who was responsible, Maggie wouldn't feel she could trust any member of her family except her father. And perhaps Helena.

Helena had never moved from her side while they watched the movie. And surely, Maggie thought, it must have been during the movie that the murder had taken place. The opportunity would have been too good to miss for someone bent on mischief. In the darkened room, and during a long movie, anyone could have slipped out for a few minutes without any of the others paying much attention.

If her idea about the timing of the murder was correct, Maggie decided, then both she and Helena would have an alibi. Each could attest that the other never left the room during the movie.

But what about her father? Maggie's stomach churned in fear. Would the police think he had no motive for murder? Or would they see Henry McLendon's murder as the result of an attempt at reconciliation gone violently wrong?

Don't do this to yourself! she admonished herself silently. *Don't manufacture problems before they arise on their own!* She tried to take comfort in the belief that the police wouldn't be that shallow.

Latham returned, his face set in grim lines. He no longer had about him any air of a friend of the family. His relaxed and friendly manner had retreated behind a cool mask of professional imperturbability.

He spoke first to Retty, requesting the use of Henry McLendon's downstairs study as a suitable place to interview them all. Woodenly Retty gave her consent, and Latham requested that Sylvia follow him, as he wished to interview her first. Everyone else he told to remain in the room until called for.

Sylvia stood on shaky legs to follow him. Retty's voice stopped him in the doorway. "Arthur, if you don't mind, I'd like to talk to you right after you finish chatting with Sylvia."

Latham nodded. "That's fine by me, Mrs. Butler. I'll send someone for you. It shouldn't be too long." He turned on his heel and was gone.

The silence settled around them once more, and Maggie drained the last of her brandy from her glass, wishing desperately for more but not having the energy to get it for herself. Adrian had come back into the room with Latham, and seeing Maggie gaze longingly at the brandy decanter, he hastened to refill her glass. After doing so, he sat down on the couch beside her, acknowledging her low-voiced "thank you" with a slight smile.

From that point onward, in intervals of fifteen or twenty minutes, Latham sent one of his men to call each of them to be interviewed, until finally only Gerard, Maggie, and Helena were left. When Gerard was called, Maggie and Helena sat quietly for a few minutes under the watchful eye of the young policeman.

Abruptly Helena got to her feet and went to the opposite corner of the room, away from the door where the policeman stood. She glanced significantly at Maggie, who was slow to realize that Helena wanted her over in the corner with her.

With a languid stretch of her arm Maggie placed her brandy glass on the table beside the couch and got to her feet. She walked over to Helena with an inquiring look.on her face. Casually the policeman took a couple of steps away from the door.

Helena flashed him a sweet smile before turning her back to him. "You and I are going to have to stick together, my dear," she told Maggie in a whisper.

"Why?" Maggie whispered back, puzzled.

"I've been thinking, and if Henry was murdered during the movie—which seems pretty likely—then only you and I have an alibi," Helena replied triumphantly, pleased with her reasoning—so pleased, in fact, that she had let her voice rise above a whisper. As soon as she realized this, she glanced guiltily over her shoulder at the young policeman, who smiled back.

Amused, in spite of the situation, Maggie nodded. "I think you may be right. About the timing, that is, and of course the other follows right along with that. We'll just have to wait and see, though, won't we?" This last came out a little plaintively. "Anyway, I know that you and I didn't do it, and of course Dad didn't either, but I can't imagine why any one of us would have. Why would anyone do this?"

Helena's face twisted into an oddly uncomfortable expression. "My dear, that's what's so awful about all of this! Every member of the family had a good motive for murdering Henry—including me!"

Chapter Six

AGHAST, MAGGIE STARED BACK at Helena. "You can't be serious!" Her stomach tightened into a cold little knot.

Helena nodded. "I'm afraid so. We've got so many skeletons in the family closet, you could have a Halloween parade. And Henry put most of them there." She glanced furtively at their silent companion, then dropped her voice to the merest whisper. "We obviously can't talk about it here and now, but later on I'll come to your room and we'll talk, okay? These are certainly things you should know about—now, anyway."

Reluctantly Maggie voiced her agreement. "Okay."

Helena moved back to the couch and sat down, her face once again blank. Listlessly, Maggie walked over to the cabinets housing the videotape collection and glanced through the contents. She was getting a headache, trying not to think about all the family secrets Helena intended to reveal.

About ten minutes later, another policeman came to the door to ask Helena to accompany him, leaving Maggie alone with the guard, as she now thought of him. Without the presence of one family member, she felt completely isolated from what was going on in the rest of the house. She shivered.

The police were probably still upstairs in her grandfather's bedroom, poking around all over the place, trying to find evidence. Resolutely Maggie blocked from her mind thoughts of her grandfather lying dead in his bed. Since the discovery of the murder, she had distanced herself as best she could from the grief she thought she should feel. But now, when she had opened her mind tentatively to emotion, she felt nothing. Perhaps this emptiness was a form of grief in itself. But she had known her grandfather only a few hours, had spoken to him twice, before his life had been ended violently.

More than grief, she felt a sense of irretrievable loss. Those precious few minutes they had spent together were all she would ever have. Even they might be lost in the aftermath of his murder. Unhappily she mulled over the possibilities in her mind while she waited for her turn to be interviewed. Could she really imagine Retty, or Harold, or Helena a murderer?

Mercifully for Maggie, her wait was brief. After about fifteen minutes, the officer serving as courier came back to escort her to her grandfather's study.

Arthur Latham stood up from behind a desk as Maggie entered the room. "Sorry to keep you waiting so long, Miss McLendon. Please have a seat." He indicated a chair beside the desk—Henry McLendon's desk, she realized dully.

As she sat, Maggie made a quick survey of the room. Dark, rich paneling, shelf upon shelf of leather-bound tomes of law, and heavy, ornate furniture gave the room a brooding, uncomfortable feel. That was somehow suitable to its present business—the conducting of a murder inquiry. She shivered again.

Maggie looked at Arthur Latham, forcing herself to focus on the policeman and what he wanted of her. What was he, she wondered, a lieutenant? Given her grandfather's wealth and prominence, Latham just might be the chief of police. After all, he had referred to himself as the "top man."

He smiled, but that gesture of friendliness did nothing to put Maggie at ease. He opened his mouth, but she anticipated him, none too politely. "Yes, I do look incredibly like her."

The lines around his mouth tightened a little, and for a moment Maggie feared she had insulted the man. She grimaced in self-deprecation. She had to get a grip on her emotions; antagonizing this man needlessly wouldn't serve any purpose. "Sorry, I didn't mean to be rude, but that's the first thing anybody has said to me all day long, and I couldn't resist beating you to the punch line, so to speak."

He accepted her apology with another smile. "You should take it as a compliment, young lady. Your grandmother was one of the most beautiful women that I ever had the privilege to know."

Disconcerted by the rebuke, despite its being politely uttered, Maggie murmured a thank-you. She was relieved when Latham asked her to recount the day's activities. Settling her mind to the task at hand, she began to organize her thoughts.

"We arrived this morning around eleven or eleven-thirty. As you may know, this is my first visit here." Latham inclined his head slightly. Relieved that she wouldn't have to go through the story of the family estrangement, Maggie continued. "I met several members of the family—Retty, Harold, Helena, and Sylvia, and of course, Adrian Worthington—before we had lunch. After lunch I met my . . . my grandfather"—she stumbled a little over the word—"for the first time, as well as his nurse, Claudine Sprayberry." She swallowed hard.

"I talked to my grandfather for several minutes before leaving my father alone with him. They had a lot to discuss, and I knew—at least, I thought—I'd have plenty of time to talk to him later." *Don't dwell on it, move on*, she told herself. "I went to my room—actually my grandmother's room—to try to rest. I could hardly sleep last night"—she smiled shyly at Latham—"I was so excited about meeting everyone today. Then my father came along and told me about his talk with my grandfather. They had reconciled after all these years, and my father was very happy about it." She couldn't—at least, not now—tell him about the real source of the estrangement. But perhaps he already knew, since he seemed well-acquainted with the family.

Latham nodded his encouragement for her to continue.

"Well, then my father told me that my grandfather wanted to talk to me, so I went along to his room. Sylvia was with him then. He seemed rather tired, but we talked for several minutes. He gave me—or rather he passed along to me—the most wonderful gift."

"What was that?" Latham asked, frowning.

"My grandmother's books," Maggie said. Then she wondered what he thought about that. Was he thinking her grandfather's gift to her might be a motive for murder?

Latham urged her on. "And then?"

"He really looked tired by then. Sylvia said he had had several others with him before me. So I told him I thought I should go, and he agreed. When I stepped back from the bed, I bumped into the chair and knocked over a baseball bat which had been propped against the chair. I couldn't imagine what it was doing there, and my grandfather explained that it had belonged to my father and that he had asked Dad to bring it to him."

"Did you touch the baseball bat?" Latham asked casually.

Maggie frowned, remembering. "Yes, I did. Why . . ." Her voice trailed off. With sickening certainty, she knew why Latham had asked. The murderer had used the baseball bat to kill Henry McLendon. Suddenly she felt like vomiting. "That was the murder weapon, wasn't it?" She gripped the sides of the chair.

Latham stared at her. "I'm afraid that's something I can't discuss just now. But of course we're going to need to get your fingerprints, since you were in your grandfather's room today."

Numbly, Maggie nodded her assent. Latham wouldn't confirm it, but she knew she was right.

Taking a deep, steadying breath, she said, "Okay, where was I?"

"You had just talked to your grandfather for the second time," Latham prompted.

"Oh. Well, after that, I guess it was about four-thirty by then, I went to my room." She paused for a moment. There was something about the conversation with her grandfather that teased her memory, but for the moment the memory refused to surface. She went on, "Just after I got there, Adrian Worthington knocked on the door. He passed along a message from Harold. We had been supposed to talk this afternoon, but Harold kindly offered to wait, since he knew I had been talking to my grandfather and probably wanted some time to rest before dinner." She paused for a much-needed breath. The memory surfaced, and Maggie stiffened. Should she tell Latham about Henry McLendon's odd remark about her grandmother's death? No, better talk to her father first and find out more about it.

Latham looked curiously at her but did not press her for an explanation. Quickly she continued before the pause became uncomfortably longer. She decided without really thinking about it not to mention her conversation with her father.

"Adrian told me when dinner would be, and then he left. I spent the rest of the time before dinner looking through my grandmother's books. I made it downstairs just in time for dinner. Everyone except Sylvia was there. After dinner we went into what they call the entertainment room, where Sylvia joined us, to watch a movie, "The Lion in Winter," which they let me pick out. It lasts a little over two hours, I think. Helena and I sat together on a small sofa nearest the screen, and neither one of us moved from it until the movie was over."

Maggie took another deep breath. "While Adrian was asking everybody what they wanted to drink, Sylvia went upstairs to check on my grandfather. She came immediately back to tell us that somebody had . . . somebody had killed him."

"Thank you, Miss McLendon," Latham said briskly. "You've given a concise and clear report." He stood up. "I think that's enough for now. We'll probably be talking again sometime tomorrow when we know more."

Maggie stood also. She longed to ask him whether he had any idea yet about the time of death, but she decided that they would know in due course and that he probably would misinterpret her reasons for asking.

She bade him good night and made her way wearily through the hallway to the stairs. Slowly she mounted them, dreading the thought of having to pass her grandfather's bedroom. Crossing her fingers, she hoped that the police had finished, at least for now, with the room. When she reached the top of the stairs, she looked apprehensively down the hallway but could see no one going in or out of the room, so she hurried down the hall toward the comparative safety of her room.

Maggie opened the door and flicked on the light switch. As she came face-to-face with her grandmother's portrait once again, she thought about the one thing she had decided not to tell Arthur Latham—at least not yet.

In their second—and last—conversation, Henry McLendon had told her that there was little he could do to repair the damage he had done to his relationship with her father, but that there was something he could do about her grandmother's death.

What bearing did that odd remark have on her grandfather's murder?

Before Maggie had time to speculate further, someone knocked on her door. She opened it just enough to peer through the crack and was relieved to see her father standing there. Stepping back, she swung the door open to allow him to enter.

Gerard's eyes as he looked at his daughter expressed a mixture of bewilderment and hurt, as if he still couldn't quite comprehend what had happened. Added lines of doubt and worry had been etched into his face over the last several hours, aging him ten years. He sighed.

"I just don't know what to think about all this. I can't believe that someone deliberately killed him." He shook his head. "I can't help feeling, in some strange way, that if we hadn't come here, he'd still be alive."

She took his hand in her own and squeezed it tightly. "Don't start thinking things like that," she protested, her voice sharp. "Don't load yourself down with guilt that doesn't belong to you." Even as she spoke, however, Maggie couldn't overcome the feeling that her father might be right. Somehow their visit might have served as a catalyst to Henry McLendon's murder. Did it have anything to do with Magnolia McLendon's death twenty-five years ago?

This was a question Maggie wanted to explore with her father, but he didn't need to discuss the deaths of his parents right now. Her immediate concern was to get him into bed, where a good night's sleep might do something to restore his shattered equilibrium.

"You need to try to get some sleep," she told him firmly. "Where's your room, by the way?"

Gerard took a moment to focus on what she was saying. "Oh, it's next door, sort of. My bathroom is next to yours, and on the other side of that is my bedroom."

"Well, come on, then," Maggie urged him gently. "You're going to bed." She led him to the door and then down the hall to his bedroom.

The room reminded Maggie of Gerard's bedroom in Houston. Obviously, in some matters of taste, he had changed little in the years since he had grown up in this house. She speculated now that his discomfort with—or more likely rejection of—his father's wealth explained his preference for spartan furnishings in this most personal of all rooms. While his study might be crammed with comfortable chairs, books overflowing from their shelves, and a rack of pipes and expensive tobaccos in their containers, Gerard's bedroom betrayed the ascetic side of his personality.

Sitting on the one straight-backed chair in the room, Maggie waited patiently while her father changed into his pajamas in the bathroom. He sat wearily on the edge of his bed. She bent over to brush his brow lightly with her lips in a good-night gesture.

"Be careful," he urged her, his voice tired. "Lock your door, and don't let anyone but me in."

"I'll be fine," Maggie promised. "You lock your door after I leave, and then get some rest." She kissed him once more and left the room, then waited a moment to hear the lock click into place.

Ministering to her father as if he were an overtired but docile child left Maggie feeling confused. This reversal of roles disturbed her, because she had never seen him in such an emotionally delicate state. Wearily, she made her own preparations for bed, after locking her bedroom door. Things would look better in the morning—that was her prayer, at least.

She was settling into the bed, about to switch off the bed-side lamp, when someone knocked quietly but insistently on her door.

"Damn!" she muttered, remembering that Helena had said something earlier about talking to her. Maggie had hoped that her aunt would have forgotten about it until the morning.

Cautiously she unlocked her door, opening it slightly, and peered out at Helena's worried face.

"Come on in," Maggie invited, none too graciously, but Helena paid no attention to the tone of her voice. She plumped down on the bed and motioned for Maggie to join her. After locking the door again, Maggie did so, wishing that instead she might burrow under the covers and ignore whatever frightful revelations Helena had come to bestow upon her.

"Now then," Helena said comfortably, once Maggie was settled beside her. "We have quite a lot to talk about if we're going to sort this out between us."

Maggie forced back a yawn and asked, "What do you mean?" But she had an uncomfortably certain feeling that she knew what her great-aunt was going to propose.

"Well," Helena said, "since you and I are the only ones who have an alibi for the apparent time of the murder, we really should stick together and try to figure this thing out."

Maggie shook her head. "You're getting a little ahead of yourself."

Helena cocked her head to one side interrogatively. Maggie explained patiently, "We don't know yet when . . . when it happened, so we can't know for certain that you and I do have an alibi."

Helena waved this objection aside. "A minor point, I promise you. I'm sure we'll find out tomorrow—or whenever—that it must have happened while we were watching the movie. The whole family—well, everybody except you and Gerard, that is—knew we usually watched a movie after dinner, so the murderer could count on carrying out his plan to murder Henry then. Don't you see?"

Exasperated, Maggie nodded. "You've made a good point, but you're still arguing from the wrong end of the stick, so to speak."

Helena laughed. "You just wait—you'll see that I'm right."

Maggie conceded for the moment. There was nothing to be gained right now from arguing with Helena over a mere point of logic. The issue of premeditation, which Helena seemed to endorse, bothered Maggie. She thought it more likely that the murderer had adapted his intent to the household routine, rather than mapped out a cold-blooded campaign to murder her grandfather. But, she thought dully, that still makes it premeditated to a certain degree.

But for the moment Maggie was more interested in the question of motive. Opportunity would have to wait until they learned more about the time of Henry McLendon's death. She watched Helena for a moment. For a woman whose elderly brother had just been murdered, Helena seemed remarkably untouched by grief. Maggie wondered why. Perhaps that was what Helena intended to tell her.

Hoping to nudge her great-aunt toward the point of this nocturnal visit, Maggie reminded Helena of her earlier remark about the skeletons in the family closet. "What were you talking about?"

Helena grimaced. "I don't want you to think of me as some acidulated old gossip-mongering tabby who has nothing better to do than talk about her relatives." Maggie had to smile at the idea of Helena as "acidulated," but Helena did momentarily have something of the smug feline about her.

Maggie nodded encouragement, and Helena continued. "I might have exaggerated slightly when I said that we all had reasons to murder Henry. But not by much!"

Holding on to the fraying edges of her patience, Maggie replied, "For example?"

"Before I launch into a catalog of the family secrets, I think I ought to explain to you a little about Henry." Helena glanced sideways at Maggie but could tell nothing from the stillness of her face. "When you saw Henry today, you saw someone who had mellowed considerably in the last few months. Serious illness affected Henry more than I would've ever thought possible. That, plus the fact that he was almost eighty."

She shook her head. "The tragic thing about it, of course, is that it came years too late. Henry was the most stubborn, infuriatingly self-righteous person I've ever known, and believe me, in this family that's quite an accomplishment. He was always stiff-necked about everything, and he never would admit he was wrong about anything. Gerard is just like him in some ways, but at least your father has the saving grace of a sense of humor so that he doesn't always take himself so seriously. Henry could never unbend that much.

"Gerard went his own way, and Henry thought it was foolish of him, but you couldn't talk either one of them into seeing the other's point of view. Magnolia tried. We all tried, at one point or another, but we finally gave up. Then, when Magnolia died, something in Henry just seemed to close itself off from everyone, and he was worse than before." She sighed. "He never relented all those years. We couldn't even mention Gerard's name in this house. I used to pretend I was going to Atlanta to visit an old friend those few times I came to Houston to see you."

Helena removed her shoes and tucked her legs underneath her on the bed. Maggie leaned back against the headboard, resigned to a long conversation. Interested as she was in what Helena was telling her, Maggie nevertheless was having to fight to keep from yawning into her aunt's earnest face. She was too tired to hold herself up any longer.

"Then," Helena went on, "like I said, when Henry had his first stroke about nine months ago—there were a couple of others after that—he changed. I think he was kind of superstitious about dying without talking to Gerard first, because he knew all along that he was wrong. But he was just too damn proud to admit it. He put it off for months after the first stroke, but he finally hinted to me that he wanted to see you and Gerard. And the rest I did myself."

Helena looked apologetically at Maggie, who suppressed a yawn in order to smile in a forgiving manner at her aunt. She truly harbored no resentment over Helena's ploy to bring

Gerard home to Mississippi.

"I talked to Henry this afternoon," Helena said softly, "and he was very happy that he and Gerard had patched things up. And he was delighted with you, too." She patted Maggie's nearby foot fondly.

Quickly Maggie blinked back the threat of tears. At the moment she was too tired to think about her grandfather and her all-too-brief memories of him in a detached fashion. She attempted to steer Helena toward the intended topic of their conversation, the possible motives for murder, acknowledging to herself as she did so the contradictory responses to her grandfather's death.

"What about the motives you mentioned earlier?" Maggie reminded her.

Helena looked studiously at her hands. "Guess I might as well start with myself first." She looked somewhat defiantly at Maggie. "We all blamed Henry for a lot of things, but if we hadn't been pretty weak-spirited creatures in the first place, I guess he'd never have walked all over us the way he did. He controlled the purse strings, and we all grew up having money. Our father wasn't as rich as Henry became, but we did okay. Usually all he had to do to keep us in line was threaten to cut off the money supply, and we jumped when he hollered 'Frog!'"

Seeing no condemnation in Maggie, only interested concern, Helena relaxed. "I went to college, but I didn't get any kind of useful degree, and there never was much question of my going to work. I was supposed to marry into one of the right families, produce a gaggle of the right children, and turn into a respectable old vegetable."

Tired as she was, Maggie couldn't keep from laughing at this. She had a brief vision of Helena as a gray-haired carrot toddling around an imposing house, and she had difficulty controlling her laughter.

"I'm sorry," Maggie gasped. "When I'm really tired, I get silly, and I couldn't help myself, thinking about you as a vegetable." She took a deep breath to steady herself.

"Well," Helena smiled in return, "that's okay, and thanks

for the compliment—I think.

"Anyway, I was a little like Gerard. I didn't want to do what everybody else thought I should, but I never really had his courage, or I would have gotten the hell out of Jackson a long time ago. Instead I managed to insult every man—and his family with him—that Henry trotted out for me to marry. All except one, that is." Her face reddened suddenly, and again she concentrated on her hands.

"One man they paraded in front of me I didn't find just awful. In fact, I fell in love with him, and he with me. We were getting ready to announce our engagement to the family when Henry found out that my . . . my intended was about to be arrested for embezzling from the company he worked for. Henry couldn't stand the thought of one of the McLendon sisters marrying a criminal—and frankly I wasn't too fond of the idea myself—so he simply faded from the scene while the rest of the family pretended he had never been admitted into this house. Henry was always very good at getting rid of anything—or anyone—that threatened the good family name," she added bitterly.

She looked squarely at Maggie, who was embarrassed by her intensity. "There was just one thing which Henry didn't know," Helena continued softly. "We had anticipated our wedding, if you know what I mean, and I found out right afterward that I was going to have a baby."

Horrified, for she could see what distress this revelation was causing Helena, Maggie could only sit there and gape. If she had been more alert, she might have guessed that something like this had happened, but her aunt's admission had taken her by surprise. The next thing Helena told her, however, jolted her wide-awake.

"When Henry found out, he was livid of course. And then he tricked me into giving the baby up for adoption. I never, ever forgave him for that!"

Chapter Seven

HER HANDS CLUTCHING HER STOMACH, Helena swayed slightly back and forth on the bed. Her eyes were shut as she made an effort to maintain control of her emotions. Maggie, left speechless by the blunt announcement, rested against the head of the bed, waiting for her to amplify the statement, unsure whether she should attempt to comfort her great-aunt.

After a few moments Helena felt able to continue. "I know that must sound to you like I was an idiot or something, but I was barely twenty-one at the time, and I hadn't really realized yet just how ruthless Henry could be. When he found out I was pregnant, he was so solicitous about my condition he really had me fooled. He insisted that I go to Boston to a specialist he had heard about. Our mother had had a difficult time with all four of us, and Retty had trouble with her one child, and I was awfully sick right away. Henry said he didn't want anything to happen to me, so I believed him when he said he wanted the best for me."

She wiped a stray tear from her cheek. "At the time I was so confused by everything. The man I had been prepared to spend the rest of my life with turned out to be a crook, and I just didn't know what to do, so I sort of let Henry take over my life. He sent me to Boston with Retty. We saw the doctor the day after I arrived, and after examining me, the doctor informed me that I was in such a delicate state that if I wasn't very careful, I might miscarry at any time."

Maggie frowned, and Helena laughed shakily. "Of course, what I didn't know at the time was that the doctor was acting on instructions from Henry. No doubt Henry had promised him double or triple his usual fees! And back then, a woman never dared question her doctor. I never thought twice about what the doctor told me."

"So what happened next?" Maggie asked.

"The doctor had me admitted to a private hospital there in the Boston area. Retty flew home, and there I was alone. I stayed at that place for nearly six months, until the baby came." Her breathing grew labored, and Maggie extended her hand. Helena clutched at it.

"They told me the baby had died during delivery," she said, her voice without inflection. "I was stunned at first, but I didn't believe them. I had memories of hearing the baby crying. They told me I was just imagining things, that I was just hysterical because I'd lost the baby. They kept me in the hospital another two months, and they drugged me most of the time. But I never really believed that the baby had died."

Maggie was struggling to hold back her tears. "What did you do?"

Helena grimaced. "I came back home. And I snooped and snooped. It took me nearly a year, but I found out what Henry had done. The baby hadn't died. Henry instructed them to tell me that, so the baby could be put up for adoption without my knowing about it. I've despised him ever since."

Helena then retreated abruptly somewhere that Maggie could not reach, exhausted by her revelation, and the two women sat in silence. Maggie was appalled beyond anything she could have imagined, and Helena was locked into a private pain that she could not share. For a few minutes Maggie watched her great-aunt nervously, made fearful by the woman's pallor. Finally Helena wrenched her mind away from its private torments and gazed at Maggie.

A ghastly smile twisted her face. "I'm sorry to subject you to this," she apologized, "especially after all that's happened today, but this might come out now, and I figure it's better that you hear it from me than from someone else." A shadow—whether of pain or fear, Maggie was not certain—passed briefly over her face before she continued. "Only the family knows about my . . . my 'skeleton in the closet,' and you can bet Lavinia, if she ever finds out, will be happy to tell anyone if she thinks there's anything to be gained by it."

What could Maggie possibly say to her that would make any difference? She held open her arms, and Helena leaned forward into the embrace.

"What happened to the baby?" Maggie asked softly when Helena sat back. "Did you ever find out who adopted her? Or him?"

"Him," Helena smiled sadly. "Yes, eventually I did. And by that time I figured he was better off with his adoptive parents. I've never made any attempt to get in touch with him, to tell him about me. I figure that if he ever wants to find out who his natural mother is, he'll come looking. I don't want to disturb him or his adoptive family, if he doesn't want to know, himself."

"That must have been so very hard for you," Maggie said.

Helena shrugged. "I never forgave Henry for what he did. That's something the Lord and I still have to work out, but I did manage to come to terms with it, or they would have hauled me off to Whitfield a long time ago." Seeing Maggie's raised eyebrow, Helena explained that Whitfield was the state mental hospital. "Anyway, I guess I figured that Henry could damn well support me the rest of my life after what he did, and he never begrudged me anything I wanted."

Helena smiled grimly. "That's how I came to have five master's degrees. I spent the next ten years or so after it happened in school, getting one degree after the other. I'm a born dilettante, so I took advantage of the situation and did just what I wanted to do." She looked sideways at Maggie. "I don't know if you can understand what I did, and why I did it, but that was the way I chose to cope, and it served well enough."

Maggie had little idea what to say. She merely nodded in response to the plea implicit in Helena's voice. It was too late, and she was too tired, to be able to cope with the things she was learning about her grandfather. The less thought she gave to anything right now, the better off she'd be.

"What about the others?" Maggie asked, curious what further horror stories Helena would tell her. She'd rather hear it all now, while the surreal nature of the situation shielded her somewhat from the awful truth.

Helena took a deep breath. "Retty was very happily married to a man named Lionel Butler. He died about twenty years after they were married. They had one son, Lionel, Junior, who grew up to be a lawyer just like his father and his uncle, and he married a lovely young girl named Louise. They had one daughter, Sylvia. They were such a beautiful little family," she sighed. "Everything seemed perfect for them, except that Louise couldn't have any more children. Lionel, Junior, was doing well in Henry's law firm, even though he was kind of spineless. Like the rest of us, he never could stand up to Henry over anything, and eventually it cost him his life."

Helena frowned down at her hands, remembering. "Lionel was terrified of flying, especially in small planes. Henry had to have a deposition for an important case, and he insisted that Lionel fly over to Starkville to take it late one afternoon, then fly back that evening so Henry could have it for court the next morning. Lionel didn't want to go because the weather didn't look very good—they were predicting thunderstorms—but he was more afraid of Henry than he was of flying, so he said he'd go. Louise offered to go with him, because flying didn't bother her, and she knew she'd be able to keep Lionel calm. Something went wrong on the way over to Starkville, and the plane crashed, killing Lionel, Louise, and the pilot.

"Retty just about went out of her mind, because Lionel was the most important thing in her life after her husband died. We were all horrified, of course, and Henry was very upset, but he insisted that it wasn't his fault. But we all knew that Lionel and Louise would never have gotten on that plane if it hadn't been for him, so Retty always held him responsible for their deaths. She called him a murderer to his face more than once."

Helena with a strained smile looked at Maggie. "Sylvia grew up very bitter at Henry. That's the way Retty taught her to be, because she raised the girl. In the last few years I think Sylvia got over some of it, especially since Henry paid all her fees for nursing school, but I guess she figured—just like the rest of us—that it was the least he could do. Blood money, if you will."

Helena slowly unlocked her legs from their tucked position and stretched them downward until her toes touched the floor. She stood up. "I need a sip or two of water, I think." Her body wilting with fatigue, she walked into Maggie's bathroom.

Maggie could hear the splash of water in the sink as she waited for Helena to return. *How much more could there be?* she wondered.

Helena came back to the bed and sprawled across it on her stomach. "Including Gerard, that's three down, two to go," she announced with a faint attempt at striking a lighter note. "Harold's next, I guess." She shifted onto one side, her face toward Maggie and her head propped on one hand. "Gerard in some ways is a lot more like Harold than he was like Henry," she said musingly. "They used to sit for hours on the odd occasion when Harold was home from the university where he taught, talking nothing but literature. Henry was always jealous, I think, because he had no patience for such things, and he resented the fact that Harold and Gerard had something like that in common. So, being Henry, he took it out on Harold. Every chance he could, he ridiculed Harold because he was a college professor and didn't have a real job making real money. And about the time your father left home for college, we found out that Harold . . . um . . . was having an affair with one of his colleagues. And the colleague turned out to be a man." She glanced sideways at Maggie to gauge her reaction.

"That doesn't make a bit of difference to me," Maggie replied gently to the question on Helena's face.

Relieved, Helena continued. "Naturally, that was something that Henry just couldn't understand, so Harold wasn't welcome in this house for a long time. He hardly ever came home as it was. I guess he just didn't feel comfortable around the rest of us. Anyway, he retired about two years ago from his teaching job, and we thought he'd be living comfortably on his Social Security and his retirement benefits, but Retty and I found out he had given all the money he had managed to save to a sort of protégé of his.

"This young man was going to turn it into a fortune for Harold, but of course he lost it all, and Harold was practically penniless. Well, it took Retty and me quite a while, but we finally got Harold and Henry to talk, and Henry asked Harold to move back home a little over a year ago." She took a deep breath. "For the first couple of months it was awful. Henry kept making these pointed remarks—even though he had told me and Retty he would let Harold alone—about the wisdom of letting 'perverts,' as he called them, handle large sums of money."

She looked apologetically at Maggie. "It was sort of a relief when Henry had that stroke, because he was driving Harold crazy with all the snide remarks. They almost got into a fight one day, and Adrian had to pull them apart. It was awful." Dolefully she shook her head.

"Is that everyone, then?" Maggie asked tiredly. She wanted sleep, anything to keep her from thinking for at least twelve hours.

Helena grimaced. "Well, there's Lavinia." There was so much venom invested in the way Helena said the name that Maggie blinked awake again.

Admiringly Helena continued, "Lavinia was the only one—before tonight, that is—who ever had the gumption to try to kill Henry."

Chapter Eight

HELENA GLANCED DEMURELY at Maggie to see how the younger woman reacted to her statement. Maggie was now wide-awake again, paying close attention to what the older woman had to say. Helena continued.

"Lavinia was fifteen years younger than Magnolia, and they looked a lot alike. Even their voices sounded alike. But your grandmother was a lady, and Lavinia's just a spiteful bitch who's never been satisfied with anything."

The venom in Helena's voice kept Maggie alert. There had been little hint of Helena's feelings toward Lavinia earlier, Maggie thought as she cast her mind hazily back over the events of the day. Now that she thought about it, she couldn't remember too many instances when anyone had had much to say to Lavinia. Did they all dislike her as much as Helena obviously did?

Spiteful herself, Helena went on, "Lavinia always wanted everything her big sister had, including her big sister's rich husband. Lavinia tried her best to get Henry into her bed, but that's one thing I'll say for him, he had better sense than to fall for a trollop like her. He was devoted to Magnolia—he could never see another woman as anything more than a walking dress, even when Magnolia was nowhere around. Even after Magnolia died, Lavinia wouldn't give up. She finagled Henry into inviting her to live here, but being under the same roof made him dislike her just that much more." Helena laughed maliciously. "In the end, Lavinia had as much reason to hate him as the rest of us. And, like I said, she's the only one of us who ever had the nerve to try to kill him."

"What happened?" Maggie asked.

Helena rolled her eyes. "I guess it's not so funny now, really, but this all happened about a couple of years after Magnolia died—before Lavinia realized that Henry'd rather bathe in acid than have anything to do with her. Anyway, Lavinia's got an awful temper, just like Henry, and one day they got into a real knock-down-drag-out. Lavinia had been messing about in here, going through Magnolia's things, and Henry cussed her out, but good. She followed him back down the hall—they were still screaming at each other—and when they got to the stairs, she pushed him. Luckily he didn't hurt himself, and of course she realized she really had gone too far, so she couldn't apologize enough. She was afraid he'd kick her out of the house, and by then she didn't have enough money to live like she wanted on her own. Henry accepted her apology and let her stay here, but after that he never had too much to say to her."

Helena stifled a sudden yawn as she looked at her watch. "Good gracious, it's almost two! I'd better go and let you get some sleep. Tomorrow's going to be a pretty rough day." Wearily she stood up.

Maggie was ready to get some sleep, but a little bump of curiosity remained unsatisfied. Stifling a yawn herself, she quickly asked, "What about Claudine and Adrian?"

Helena smiled indulgently. "Well, they really are like family, I guess—especially Claudine, since she pretty much grew up in this house. Her mother was our housekeeper for nearly thirty years. She died of cancer a few years ago." She smiled again. "I can still remember the day she and Claudine came here. Claudine could just barely toddle around, and she was the most beautiful baby. Her mother had worked for Magnolia's family at one time—there was some sort of trouble there, we never did find out exactly what—and when Magnolia found out that Lorraine needed a job, she hired her as the housekeeper. Claudine was so cute, and she just adored Henry. For a long time I believe she actually thought he was her father." She laughed, but then sobered quickly.

"When she was a teenager, though, Claudine went through one of those stages," Helena continued. "She was just hateful to everybody. I think it really bothered her, growing up in this house, seeing all the money all around her, and she couldn't have the kinds of things that Sylvia had. But later on she settled down—just grew out of the rebellious stage, I guess. She's a wonderful nurse."

That explained Claudine, Maggie thought, but what about Adrian? Startled, she realized that she had spoken her question aloud.

"I think I'll let you ask him that yourself," Helena announced pertly. She bent over to give Maggie a quick kiss on the cheek, admonished her to lock the door, then hurried out of the room before Maggie could question her further.

Blushing furiously, Maggie did as Helena had bidden, feeling suddenly vulnerable without the company of her exasperating great-aunt. Maggie climbed in between the covers of her bed, letting the firmness of the mattress soothe her tired back. She turned off the overhead light from a convenient switch on the bedside table. The sudden darkness of the room smothered her for a moment, and she forced herself to breathe slowly and steadily until her eyes adjusted to the darkness of the strange room.

Gradually her breathing became more regular, and she concentrated on slowing her chaotic thoughts so that she could sleep. She began conjugating verbs in Latin, a trick that rarely failed her, and soon had drifted into sleep.

Dimly Maggie was aware that someone was poking hundreds of little needles into her right hand. She shifted her head groggily from beneath the pillow, and the pale sunlight filtering into the room assaulted her eyes. She shook her hand to get the blood flowing back into it and turned over onto her back, wondering what time it was.

As she turned, Maggie, still half-asleep, noticed that someone had pulled a chair next to the bed. And that someone was smiling seraphically at her.

Maggie screamed, but the figure only frowned in dismay. It didn't leave. In fact, it moved solicitously closer, stretching out a hand.

"Who the hell are you?" Maggie, now wide-awake, asked as she inched as far away from the questing hand as she could.

While the unknown visitor struggled to frame a reply, someone knocked on Maggie's bedroom door. The visitor moved to unlock the door, and Gerard, dressed in chinos and button-down shirt, his hair still damp, burst into the room. He frowned in relief as he saw Maggie lying puzzled, but unhurt, in the bed. Then his gaze took in Maggie's companion. He grinned broadly as he said, "I might have known!" He engulfed her in a hug, held her tightly for a few moments, then stepped back. "Ernie! How the heck are you?"

"I'm doing well, Gerryboy." The woman grinned at Gerard, displaying a magnificent set of teeth for someone Maggie judged to be around sixty. She turned to Maggie apologetically. "I'm so sorry I scared you—I just came up to pay my respects to Magnolia, not having any idea that anyone would be sleeping in here. And when I saw you, I just couldn't leave." She frowned at Gerard. "Besides, I figured somebody ought to be keeping an eye out for you, since this shiftless father of yours wasn't doing anything to protect you."

Maggie sagged weakly against the headboard. Maybe this person had escaped from the state mental hospital Helena had told her about. But, no, she obviously was acquainted with the family. Who on earth was she?

Gerard and the woman were still grinning at each other, so it was a moment before they noticed Maggie's irritated stare.

"I'm Ernestine Carpenter, but most people call me Ernie." Her voice, dark and rich in tone, reminded Maggie of Lauren Bacall. "My mother and Gerard's grandmother were sisters, so that makes you and me cousins."

Cousin or no, the woman had given Maggie a good scare, and she wasn't quite ready to smile and hug this new relative. At least, not until Maggie had had her bath and several ounces of cold caffeine.

Ernie apparently realized that Maggie was slightly out of sorts at the moment, for she began pushing Gerard out the door. "We'd better get going so Maggie can get up," she said firmly. She smiled at Maggie. "I'll make my apologies later—

see you downstairs!" The door snapped shut behind them, and Maggie sank down on her pillows.

Now that her heart had resumed its normal rate, Maggie could see some of the humor of the situation. From what little she had seen, Gerard was fond of this cousin, and that was a good sign. She yawned as she pushed back the covers. As she was getting out of bed, she spied the key to the bedroom door on the bedside table where Ernie had placed it.

She was certain that she had locked the door before she had gone to bed. How, then, had Ernestine gained access to her room? Surely the woman didn't have a set of keys to all the rooms in the house. And from the way she had talked, no one had known she was coming upstairs to Magnolia's room, so no one would have furnished her with a key.

Shaking her head, Maggie wandered into the bathroom, where she looked blearily into the mirror. She was never at her best first thing in the morning, even after a good night's sleep. She was not one of those people who bounce perkily out of the bed each morning, eager to greet the new day. Getting up each morning was the low point of her day.

As she turned to begin running water into a bathtub that would easily have accommodated several Sumo wrestlers, her eyes saw something she had overlooked the day before whenever she had come into the bathroom. There was a door in the bathroom which gave access to the hallway. Maggie walked over to it and twisted the knob. It opened easily.

"Damn!" she said. She had lain there all night within easy reach of anyone who had wanted to enter her room. She couldn't blame Ernie for her own carelessness.

Half an hour later, after a steaming soak in the massive tub, with her hair nearly dry, Maggie dressed comfortably in a khaki skirt and navy blue polo shirt. Her stomach had begun to rumble, so she went downstairs in search of breakfast. It was after nine o'clock, so the rest of the family were probably already downstairs.

She found them all, except for Retty, in the dining room. One look at the tired, miserable faces around the table lessened Maggie's appetite somewhat. Ernie and Gerard, sitting at one end, were engaged in a reasonably cheerful conversation, catching up on two decades of news, but the rest picked at the appetizing food on their plates. She helped herself to scrambled eggs, biscuits, and bacon from the steaming dishes on the sideboard and took a seat next to her father. She poured herself a glass of water from the pitcher on the table, wishing instead for a Diet Coke.

Ernie interrupted her conversation with Gerard to apologize to Maggie for scaring her. Maggie, her sense of humor somewhat restored by several mouthfuls of the delicious food, waved Ernie's apologies aside. But to satisfy her curiosity, Maggie did ask whether Ernie had entered through the bathroom door.

"Yes, I did," she responded laughingly. "I remembered there was a separate door from the hallway, and since I needed to make a stop there anyway, I just went in that door. It wasn't until I had . . . er . . . finished, that I realized someone else had been using the bathroom. Then I peeked into the bedroom and saw you in the bed. The rest you know." She beamed at Maggie.

Maggie smiled back, then devoted her attention to her food as Ernie resumed her conversation with Gerard. While Maggie ate, she avoided looking at anyone except her father and Ernie. After Helena's revelations Maggie found it difficult to face any of them without recalling the secrets Helena had told her. Being privy to such knowledge might prove necessary, Maggie realized, but necessity did little to relieve her discomfort.

Adrian wandered in and out while they ate, checking the contents of the dishes on the sideboard, occasionally taking an empty one away. He ambled over to inquire whether she had everything she wanted. Maggie, her mouth full of biscuit and grape jam, swallowed quickly, then asked for a Diet Coke.

Flashing an amused grin, Adrian departed and returned scarcely three minutes later with a large glass of Maggie's favorite beverage. "Thanks!" She flashed him a shy smile.

The doorbell rang distantly, and everyone tensed. Maggie

could feel the change in the atmosphere immediately. Adrian left the room, returning soon after with Arthur Latham and someone Maggie had never seen, an elderly man whose sloping posture gave him the appearance of a tortoise.

"Good morning, everyone," Latham said briskly. "I'm sorry to trouble you again so early this morning, but, as I'm sure you'll realize, we can't afford to lose any time in a situation like this. We have a report from the coroner's office, as well as some additional evidence. I'd like to go over all your statements again." He looked around the table, noting the absence of one family member and the addition of one other. "Miss Carpenter, how are you? It's been a while." Not waiting for a response, he continued, "How is Mrs. Butler this morning?"

Sylvia smiled nervously. "She's still upset by all this, so I told her she should stay in bed. She wouldn't let me call the doctor." She frowned. "If you really need to talk to her, she might feel up to it by now."

Latham inclined his head. "I do need to talk with each of you, but there's no reason Mrs. Butler can't rest a while longer." He turned to his companion. "I guess y'all know Mr. Lyle Levering."

The elderly man frowned at them all from behind his horn-rimmed glasses. Dressed in a fashionably cut black suit, he reminded Maggie of the much younger businessmen one might see on the streets of downtown Houston. Mr. Levering waved a hand at them.

"We're all old friends here, Arthur, more or less." His eyes had fastened upon Maggie and Gerard with a puzzled look of semi-recognition. "Yes, old friends, I guess you'd say. Henry McLendon and I knew each other for over fifty years, ever since law school." He peered shrewdly around the room, taking a quick look at each face. "Henry called me last night, said he wanted to change his will, asked me to come over this morning. I came anyway, even though they said on the news that he'd been murdered."

Chapter Nine

AFTER THE LAWYER MADE HIS ANNOUNCEMENT, Maggie glanced around the room to see the expressions of her family.

Lavinia appeared insufferably bored with the whole proceedings, but Maggie was willing to bet that her great-aunt was much more interested than she let on. Helena and Harold were plainly curious. They kept looking back and forth between their plates and each other's faces. Adrian stood aloof from the family, while Claudine and Sylvia toyed with the food on their plates.

If Lyle Levering and Arthur Latham had hoped for some startling revelation after their surprise announcement, they were surely disappointed in the results of their stratagem, Maggie thought. These people were much too practiced in schooling their emotions to let such a clichéd trick unnerve them.

Ernie, Maggie could see, was highly entertained by it all. Patting her lips with the linen napkin, Ernie attempted without much success to hide her wide grin. She winked wickedly at Maggie when she caught the younger woman looking her way.

Latham cleared his throat. "Well, since most everybody's right here, I'd like to clarify, if we can, your movements last night. But, before we start, I do have one question. Miss Carpenter, I was just wondering, when did you get here? And why are you here, if I may ask?"

"Hello, Arthur, good to see you again, except for the circumstances. Well, I got here just a couple of hours ago, I guess. As to the reason I'm here, late last night I got a call from Cousin Helena, telling me what had happened, and I thought I should be here to support my family in this time of . . . of difficulty." She paused, making a move to push her chair back from the table. "I'll be glad to withdraw from the room, if you wish."

Latham sighed. "I suppose you might as well stay, now that you're here." Ernie grinned at him. He pulled one of the empty chairs from the table and sat down, motioning for Levering to do the same. "Now, about last night."

Maggie wondered what he was hoping to accomplish by this group interview. Did he think he would catch one of them in a lie? This could prove interesting. She sat back to watch, noticing as she did that Ernie was surveying the room, alert for anything that might happen.

The rest of the McLendons looked tentatively at one another, and then Harold spoke in his patient, well-modulated lecturer's voice. "Well, we usually dine at six-thirty, and last night was no exception. Everyone except Henry and Sylvia were at the table." He frowned, then turned his head to look at Claudine. "I believe Claudine came in just a few minutes after we had begun eating."

Aware that all attention had focused on her, Claudine took a deep breath before responding. "Yes, I was running a little behind yesterday." She looked steadily at Latham. "Yesterday was my evening off, and once Sylvia relieved me in the afternoon, I went shopping and to a movie. I got back a little later than I had planned, and I dropped by to check on Sylvia and Mr. Henry before I came down to dinner. Sylvia asked me if I'd mind staying with him while she went down to the kitchen to check on his dinner. Whoever's with him in the evenings," she explained, "has . . . er . . . *had* to bring up his dinner from the kitchen because the daytime help all leave at six-thirty."

Latham nodded encouragement, making a quick notation in his little book.

"That's about it, really," Claudine continued. "I was with him, oh, probably not even ten minutes, and then Sylvia was back, and I came on down to dinner, just a few minutes late." She frowned. "But we went through all of this last night."

"Yes, we did," Latham answered her firmly. "But sometimes it's necessary to go through everything several times."

He looked across the expanse of linen-covered table at Sylvia. "I believe that fits in with what you told me last night, right?"

Sylvia nodded. "I hated to ask Claudine to stay there on her night off while I went downstairs—ordinarily Uncle Henry was all right on his own—but he overdid it a little yesterday, and he was fussy last night. I just felt better having someone with him, and I knew Adrian would be busy enough down here."

She trailed off, then revived momentarily as another thought surfaced. "But by the time I came downstairs to watch the movie, Uncle Henry seemed to have settled down. I felt like I could leave him to rest, just like we always did. And I had my beeper, in case he needed anything." Her voice held a pitiable appeal. She was clearly upset at the thought that someone had murdered her patient while she had been enjoying a movie downstairs.

Claudine reached over to pat her hand reassuringly, and Sylvia smiled back.

"Right," Latham said. "Let's switch back to downstairs for the moment. How long were y'all at the dinner table?"

This time Adrian spoke. "We were all in here for close to an hour, I'd guess. I looked at my watch when we moved to the room where we watched the movie, and it was about seven-twenty-five then."

Seeing Latham's nod, Adrian continued his narrative. "Sylvia joined us there, and we talked for a few minutes until the movie was selected. Helena suggested that Maggie choose the movie, which she did. Then we settled down to watch the movie, which I believe runs something over two hours, say two-and-a-quarter, so that would make it roughly quarter to ten or ten o'clock when we finished it."

Latham consulted his notebook, flipping through several pages before he found what he wanted. "The call from this house to the police station was recorded at ten-oh-three, so that time frame sounds about right." He glanced around the table. "I think, if you don't mind, we'll go into the other room now so I can get a clearer idea as to what you all were doing." He stood up. "Miss Carpenter, if you wouldn't mind standing in for Mrs. Butler for a while, I'm sure the others will tell you just what to do."

Ernie beamed. "I'd be delighted, Arthur, to assist in any way."

A sound suspiciously like a snort came from Lavinia's direction, but everyone stood up just then, pushing chairs back from the table, so Maggie couldn't be sure she had heard it. Ernie cast a bland glance in Lavinia's direction but otherwise did nothing to acknowledge her. They trooped after the policeman and the lawyer who, Maggie noted, moved quite spryly for someone in his late seventies.

In the entertainment room Adrian rearranged the chairs so that the configuration was as it had been the night before. The small sofa where Maggie and Helena had sat was centered several feet in front of the large television screen. Directly behind the sofa by about six feet were three comfortable, high-backed leather chairs. There were three more chairs several feet to the left of the ones in the center and three to the right, forming a loose semicircle behind the sofa. Off to the right side were two larger sofas, positioned perpendicular to the small sofa. A small table with a lamp divided the two.

Arthur Latham and Lyle Levering stood to one side as the others assumed their places. Maggie twisted around to see where the others had been sitting the night before. Right behind her and Helena, Adrian sat in the middle chair with Sylvia to his left. To Sylvia's left, and several feet away, sat Lavinia. Next to her sat Claudine, with Harold on her left.

There was an empty chair on Adrian's right side, with some space to its right, followed by another empty chair. Ernie, taking Retty's place, sat next to the empty chair, with Gerard to her right.

Maggie attempted to memorize their positions. Glancing at her companion, however, Maggie was amused to see that Helena had pulled a small notebook from her running suit—electric lime this morning—and was surreptitiously making a diagram of the scene.

Latham moved to stand in front of the television screen,

while Levering sank into the cushions of one of the larger sofas. Latham looked right at Maggie and Helena. "You told me last night that neither one of you moved from your seats during the movie. Right?"

Maggie and Helena nodded an emphatic yes.

Latham then glanced at the others. "Everyone else, if I remember correctly from your statements last night, got up at some point and left the room."

Turning their heads, Maggie and Helena watched each of the others nod slowly in turn. Ernie, prompted by Gerard, nodded as "Retty."

"How clearly could those of you in the chairs see anyone else?" Latham asked.

Adrian spoke first. "Well, Helena and Maggie were easy to see, of course, because the only light in the room—from the television screen—was shining right on them. I could see Sylvia too, and generally the others on either side of us, but most of the time I wasn't paying attention to anything except the movie."

Sylvia concurred. "I got up once to go to the bathroom," she said. "I guess it was about halfway through the movie, and after I came back, I think Claudine went a few minutes later. Adrian had already gone, and when Claudine came back, none of the three of us left again." She shrugged. "I really didn't notice anyone else."

"Is that right?" Latham asked Claudine and Adrian. They agreed that it was.

Harold said that he had left the room twice, once during the first half hour of the movie and again toward the end. Claudine confirmed this.

Latham then turned to Gerard and Ernie-Retty. Gerard spoke for both of them. "I left the room only once, late in the movie. In fact, I met Harold in the hallway as I was coming back." He looked across at his uncle, who nodded. "Retty left once, about midway through the movie. Neither Maggie nor Helena ever moved from the sofa, unless they did so while I was out of the room, but I don't think they did."

The others agreed they had not seen either Maggie or

Helena leave the room. "As I said before," Adrian commented, "they were in pretty plain sight the whole time."

Latham nodded. "Yes, you've all made that fairly clear. Now—" he started to say, but Helena forestalled him, a triumphant note in her voice.

"And that means that only Maggie and I have alibis for Henry's murder. Doesn't it?"

Arthur Latham frowned in annoyance at Helena's remark. "Just why do you think that, Miss Helena?" he asked her in a tone that managed to be both repressive and somehow polite. Maggie marveled again at the Southern capacity for courtesy even under trying circumstances.

Slightly abashed, Helena subsided against the cushions of the couch. "Well, I don't really know, of course, but it just seems kind of reasonable that whoever killed Henry did it while we were all watching the movie. That would have been the best time."

Clearly she had brought up a point which he hadn't been ready to discuss, as he frowned in response. But now that the subject had been broached, Latham seemed inclined to answer Helena's question.

"The coroner finished his examination this morning. According to him, death occurred most likely within two to three hours of the discovery of the body. In other words, not earlier than about 7:00 p.m." Latham paused for a moment, glancing around at the faces of his audience.

"Of course, Miss Sylvia Butler claims that Mr. McLendon was alive when she left him around seven-thirty to come downstairs to watch the movie."

A small sound of protest came from Sylvia's direction. Latham waved a hand peremptorily lest someone interrupt him. "If it hadn't been for other evidence which has come to light, Miss Butler's situation might be a little more difficult. But, as y'all may remember, Mr. Levering here received a phone call from Mr. McLendon last night."

We'd all forgotten about that. Maggie grimaced. Her grandfather had wanted to change his will. Did that precipitate his murder? This question set her mind spinning onto various tangents.

Lyle Levering spoke from his comfortable seat at the side of the room. "Henry called me last night right around eight o'clock, told me he wanted to see me this morning about changing his will. And I do assure you that it was Henry McLendon I talked to." He smiled grimly. "Well, we talked only for about five minutes, then he hung up. But Henry was alive at eight o'clock last night."

"Thank you, Mr. Levering," Latham said. He turned his attention back to the family. "Now, as you see, we have a time frame that the murder has to fit into." He offered a small bow in Helena's direction. "And, as Miss Helena said, that frame does provide an alibi for her and Maggie, since by eight o'clock, y'all were already watching the movie."

Helena and Maggie both breathed small sighs of relief, but Maggie cast a worried look at her father. She knew he was innocent, but his position as the prodigal son might make things difficult for him. Helena, evidently intuiting the direction of her thoughts, squeezed her hand in reassurance.

"Maggie," Latham spoke quietly, but still Maggie started in surprise, "Miss Helena, and of course, Miss Carpenter, may now be excused for a while. The rest I'd like to stay here. Y'all made statements last night about your movements in and out of this room, and I want to go over all that again with you." He looked pointedly at Maggie and Helena. "Now, if you three ladies will excuse us."

"Certainly," Helena said, jumping up from the sofa and pulling Maggie with her. She motioned for Ernie to follow them. Turning back toward the policeman, she asked, "Shall I see if Retty feels up to joining you down here? Or would you rather wait to talk to her upstairs?"

Latham considered her gravely for a moment. "I'll be up to talk to her shortly, so there's no need to trouble her just now, thanks all the same." His tone indicated disinterest in further help from her, at least for the moment.

"Okay," Helena replied meekly. "Come on, girls."

The same young police officer who had watched over them the previous night was standing beside the door, but Maggie had never even noticed him. There was no telling how many men Arthur Latham had sprinkled around the house.

Helena led the way directly upstairs to her bedroom, down the hall in the opposite direction from Maggie's room. This room faced the back, as did Maggie's, and structurally it was similar, with the same large French doors leading out onto a balcony. The room was furnished eclectically. That was the kindest word Maggie could use to describe what she saw. She didn't know a lot about furniture, but it was obvious, even to her untrained eye, that the styles of the various pieces did not match. The one common quality, she felt certain, was the price tag. Mismatched as it was, this furniture looked expensive.

Helena plopped down on a brocaded sofa with claw feet and gestured for Maggie to join her. She pointed Ernie to a steel-and-leather chair nearby.

Ernie wasted no time. "Well, the family's in one hell of a mess this time." Her tone indicated that this was a state of affairs not likely to endure for long, and Maggie was delighted to hear the note of assurance in her cousin's voice. Ernie might be just what they all needed.

Ernie grinned at Maggie, who thought for a moment that the woman had read her mind. "Sorry about this morning," Ernie apologized again. "I never meant to frighten you, but once I came into the room and saw you sleeping there, so defenseless, I thought it wouldn't hurt to keep an eye on you." She grinned. "I bet you'll lock that bathroom door tonight."

Maggie grinned back. "You bet I will!"

Helena looked from one to the other, and Ernie quickly told her how she had surprised Maggie that morning. Helena joined in the laughter as Maggie described her reaction to Ernie's presence in her bedroom.

"Well, I suppose," Ernie said, once the laughter had subsided, "that we could spend the whole morning catching up with one another, but I guess we ought to discuss what we're going to do about Henry's death first."

Assuming that she could take their cooperation for

granted, Ernie continued before either Maggie or Helena could say anything. "I suppose the first thing we should do is figure out who actually had the opportunity to do it. Motive's important, of course, but if you don't have opportunity, motive's not much good." She glanced uncertainly at Maggie before turning toward Helena. "There are probably plenty of motives, once we start shifting through all the skeletons in the McLendon family closets—"

Helena interrupted her. "I've already told Maggie the worst, Ernie."

Maggie nodded. Her conversation with Helena seemed more like a bizarre dream now than an actual conversation. Fortunately for her peace of mind, she had been too busy thus far this morning to give much thought to what her great-aunt had told her in the small hours of the morning. Now, however, she would have to confront everything head-on.

"That's good, I guess," Ernie remarked, "although it's a shame for Maggie to have to hear the worst about the family before she gets to hear much of the good." She grinned again. "And believe it or not, there are some good things about this family. It may take us a while, but eventually we'll get around to them.

"Now then," she continued briskly, "let's talk about opportunity. From what I heard this morning, everybody in the house, except the daytime help—and that includes the cook—and you two, had the opportunity of sneaking out of the room while the movie was going on." She ticked the suspects off on her fingers. "Gerard, Lavinia, Retty, Harold, Sylvia, Claudine, and Adrian. That's seven—although I'm sure we can count Gerard out—but it's better for the sake of discussion not to leave any possibilities out."

Maggie hated talking about her father as a murder suspect, but Ernie was probably right. What mattered in the long run was getting to the truth, and Gerard would know his daughter couldn't really consider him seriously as a suspect.

Helena broke in before Ernie could continue. "I performed

a little experiment this morning." She looked slightly embarrassed. "I thought I'd time how long it took to run upstairs from the TV room and back down again." She swallowed hard. "And I estimated how long it would take to . . . er . . . do what the murderer did."

"Well?" Ernie demanded as her cousin stopped. "How long did it take?"

"I did it several times. The first time was as fast as I could, just like I thought a younger person could do it. It didn't even take five minutes. So, I suppose Gerard, Sylvia, Adrian, or Claudine could have done it in as much time—or less even— than I did. It takes that much time just to go to the bathroom. Lavinia, Retty, and Harold are all in pretty good condition for their age, but I think you'd about have to double the time for them. And that's still not an unreasonable length of time for someone to be gone during the movie."

Ernie was impressed with Helena's "experiment" and said so. "In that case, I guess any one of them could have done it without anybody really thinking much about how long they'd been gone from the movie." Ernie frowned. "But what about the weapon? Anybody have any idea what happened?"

Maggie felt sick to her stomach, because she was certain she knew the answer. Hearing her voice coming as if from far away, she explained as dispassionately as possible what she thought had been used.

"Dear God in Heaven," Ernie said, her face pale. "A baseball bat! Dear Lord above!" She closed her eyes for a moment, as if in prayer. Helena stared off into space.

Drawing a deep breath, Ernie went on. "Well, since a weapon was so ready at hand, it would take only a few seconds and then the killer could dash back downstairs."

"I agree with everything you've both said so far," Maggie remarked, forcing herself not to dwell on mental images of her grandfather's bludgeoned body, "but there are a couple of points which puzzle me, and I think they're important ones.

"First of all, how did the murderer know that there would be a weapon on hand? And second, what happened to make the murderer act so quickly? In other words, what made it necessary that the murderer act last night rather than today or tomorrow?"

Ernie nodded briskly. "Very good questions. And you're right—they are important." She looked at Helena. "Got any answers?"

Helena shrugged. "Well, the first one's easy enough. Henry had a pretty busy day yesterday. He talked to more of the family in that one day than he probably had the whole week before that." She turned to Maggie. "Lately, Henry was pretty quiet. He didn't encourage us to come by his room to chat, and honestly, none of us really felt the urge. If he ever wanted to talk to us, he would tell Sylvia or Claudine or Adrian, and we'd be summoned for an audience."

She scratched her nose. "Like I said, yesterday he talked to every one of us, I guess, except maybe Lavinia. He never wanted to talk to her if he could help it." She and Ernie smiled over this. "Anyway, Gerard had a long talk with him, and then, for some reason, Henry got a bee in his bonnet and had to talk to the rest of us. Me, Harold, and Retty. Claudine, Adrian, and Sylvia he saw every day anyway—they had the most contact with him."

"Then," Maggie said, in answer to her own question, "since you all talked to him after my father did, you would all have seen the baseball bat there near the bed." She had another queasy moment as she recalled stumbling over the thing the previous afternoon. *Steady now*, she told herself.

"Exactly," Helena said.

"So you had all seen the baseball bat there," Ernie repeated. "It would have been handy, but I daresay that, even if it hadn't been, there would have been something else that would have done the job just as well." She looked grimly at her companions, and Maggie was thankful not to be on Ernie's list of suspects.

"Let's move on to the second question, then," Ernie suggested. "What caused the murderer to act last night? Was it simply that a good opportunity had presented itself? Or did the murderer know Henry intended on changing his will?" She subjected Helena to a keen glance. "Do you have any idea about the provisions of Henry's will, Helena?"

Helena folded her arms across her chest and leaned back into the corner of the sofa before replying. "Despite all his other sterling qualities, Henry wasn't one of those who was always threatening to change his will every time he got irritated with one of us. And that was often enough, let me tell you. The last time the subject came up wasn't long after Henry's first stroke. I think he made some revisions then, and he told us all flatly that we didn't have anything to worry about—he'd made provisions for all of us. Even you, Ernie, because he's always been fond of you." She nodded in her cousin's direction. "I don't know exactly what the proportions are, but Henry gave the impression that he had pretty well divided things up among the family, with the major portion going to Gerard and Maggie, of course. He included Claudine and Adrian as well."

"So," Ernie concluded, "every one of us stood to gain by Henry's death." She chuckled. "That starts everybody off even with one motive in common—money. When we start adding up the other motives, we'll see who had the most motives."

Maggie had an objection. "You can't say that everyone had a motive just because of the will. I mean, sure, everyone would probably like to inherit money, but first you've got to prove that it would mean enough to one of us to kill for." At the moment she pushed aside thoughts of her own possible inheritance.

Ernie shrugged. "That's a good point, but the murderer wouldn't necessarily want the money right now. He or she was probably just thinking about the future, and being cut out of Henry's will might have been a prospect somebody didn't want to entertain."

Maggie nodded thoughtfully, then turned to Helena. "Just what would have made my grandfather cut someone out of his will? I mean, he seems to have been pretty tolerant in at least this respect. Most people in his position wouldn't have kept a so-called prodigal son in."

"Henry had strict notions about the money remaining in the family," Helena responded. "I can't swear what was in his will before his stroke—maybe he really had cut Gerard out before—but afterward he mellowed, and I guess he was thinking forward to a reconciliation." Her eyes glinted briefly. "Thank goodness he lived to see that," she added, her voice soft and sad.

Ernie shifted uncomfortably in her chair. "Well, then, what would have made Henry cut someone else out of his will?"

Helena frowned in thought. "I'm just not sure. Somebody would've had to make him awfully angry, and I can't think of anything one of us has done lately that would have brought on a reaction like that." She shrugged. "Sorry."

"I have an idea about that," Maggie said slowly, but before she could elaborate, a knock sounded at Helena's door.

"Come in," Helena called, and the door opened to admit Gerard, followed closely by Lavinia.

As Gerard greeted them, Maggie watched as Lavinia's eyes swept familiarly—and dismissively—around Helena's room. Obviously she found Helena's eclectic taste in furnishings questionable. Maggie caught the expression in the woman's eyes and felt a surge of annoyance. She then had to laugh inwardly at herself. *You hardly know the woman*, she thought, *yet you've already accepted Helena's and Ernie's assessment of her.*

Lavinia arranged herself comfortably on one corner of Helena's bed, while Gerard settled in a low chair at Maggie's elbow.

"What's going on now?" Ernie asked.

"The police have just finished grilling us about what we were doing last night during the movie," Lavinia said peevishly. "Can you imagine—Arthur Latham actually had the nerve to ask me how long I thought I took in the bathroom! I told him I had never timed myself and wasn't about to start now." She snorted in outrage.

Maggie didn't dare look at Ernie or Helena. Helena's shoulders quivered slightly, and rather than surrender to a fit of the giggles, Maggie managed to cough instead.

"It's all rather trying, I know, Lavinia," Gerard interjected soothingly. "But these are, after all, rather unusual circumstances, and Arthur is only doing his job."

Lavinia snorted again. "Asking a middle-aged woman how long it takes her to pee still seems odd to me. If I didn't know better, I'd have sworn he was enjoying it."

Maggie coughed loudly, followed in rapid succession by Helena and Ernie. Lavinia glared suspiciously at them but relaxed her gaze when they all stared blandly back at her.

Ernie cleared her throat. "Was Arthur able to figure out anything from what y'all told him about your movements last night?"

Gerard rolled his eyes. "Who knows? Arthur certainly isn't going out of his way to tell us too much. He's obviously told us about as much as he wants us to know for the time being, and that's that." He smiled. "That's a big change from the Arthur Latham I went to high school with. Back then the surest way of having the whole school know something you wanted to keep a secret was to let Arthur get wind of it. He couldn't keep his mouth shut for anything."

"Wonderful," Lavinia commented sourly. "And this is the man who's been asking me about my bathroom habits." She shifted on the bed, while the other women coughed, less noticeably this time. "The thing that really gets me in all this is that Henry was going to change his will. I wonder who he was going to cut out?" Her eyes glittered with malice.

"I don't suppose we'll ever know," Gerard commented, frowning in distaste. "Unless it turns out that that was the motive for the murder."

"Could be," Lavinia responded. "But old turtle-face Levering was awfully closemouthed. You notice he never said anything else about his conversation with Henry last night. For all we know, Henry might actually have told him who he wanted to disinherit and why."

Lavinia's air of smug satisfaction was for once justified, Maggie admitted to herself. Henry McLendon might have identified the object of his intended testamentary changes. This idea had escaped them all in the general excitement of the morning's happenings.

"But," Maggie objected as she thought of something, "if

they do know whom he intended to disinherit, wouldn't they have taken some action by now?" As quickly as she voiced her question, she answered it herself. "But such evidence would be circumstantial, I suppose, and wouldn't necessarily make the intended person the murderer. Unless, of course, he or she knew what he . . . er . . . my grandfather planned to do."

Ernie and Helena both nodded vigorously. "And I'd be willing to bet," Ernie said, "that's what they're waiting for. To get some indication, I mean, that the murderer did know about it." She frowned. "There must not be much physical evidence, if they're having to go for things like this." She turned toward Gerard. "Did Arthur ever say anything about fingerprints?"

He shook his head. "He told us that the . . . it had been wiped clean of prints. The murderer didn't even try to leave mine or anyone else's on there to try to incriminate someone."

"That brings us right back to opportunity and motive," Helena remarked. She glanced wickedly at Lavinia and then turned to her nephew. "We were discussing that before you and Lavinia came in, Gerard, and I have to tell you we decided that you certainly both had the opportunity."

Lavinia snorted and stood up from the bed. "I know you'd love for me to be the murderer, Helena McLendon, but I wouldn't have run up those stairs to bash in Henry's head. He wasn't worth the effort." She strode toward the door.

"Tsk, tsk," Ernie commented. "Still using that persimmon douche, I see, Lavinia." Her answer came as Lavinia slammed the door behind her.

Maggie and Helena were convulsed with laughter on the sofa. "I can't believe you said that!" Maggie told her cousin when she could finally stop laughing.

Ernie rolled her eyes. "I just never can resist taking those cheap shots at Lavinia. She's such an easy target, and the Lord only knows she gives you plenty of opportunities." She grinned. "You have to admit that the idea of her running upstairs is a mite ludicrous."

Helena snorted, in perfect imitation of Lavinia. "Are you kidding? That woman hasn't produced one iota of sweat since the Eisenhower administration. She wouldn't exert herself for anything." She paused. "I take that back. She would exert herself for one thing—money."

Ernie said, "Maybe," while Gerard remained silent. Maggie had noticed that he hadn't joined in their laughter at his aunt's expense. Now he was frowning at the three of them.

"Lavinia can be a bit much sometimes, I know," Gerard commented repressively, "but to think that she would have murdered my father for money . . ."

"I know it's difficult, Dad," Maggie responded softly, "but it has to be somebody in this house. I know it wasn't me, and it wasn't you, and it wasn't Helena or Ernie. That leaves six people, and Lavinia is one of them."

He sighed in resignation. "I know that, but it doesn't make it any easier to think about." He stood up. "I think I'll go wash up before lunch. That's really why Lavinia and I came up here anyway. Adrian said lunch would be served at one today."

He bent forward to touch Maggie lightly on the head. "And I think it would be a very good idea for you to stick close to Helena and Ernie or to me until all of this is settled. Okay?" Maggie nodded.

"Don't you worry about her," Ernie assured him. "I'm not about to let anything happen to this girl. You have my word on that!"

"Then that's enough for me," Gerard responded affectionately. "See you at lunch." The door closed quietly behind him.

Ernie consulted her watch. "We have about twenty-five minutes until lunch. Shall we continue our discussion, or shall we take a break until afterward?"

Maggie was about to say that she'd like to go back to her room to freshen up a little, but Helena forestalled her.

"I want to know," Helena said firmly, "before we go any further, just what it was Maggie was about to say when Gerard and Lavinia came in." She turned toward her companion on the sofa.

Maggie frowned as she tried to remember what she had said. There had been something, some thought, about the motive for the murder. "Oh, I know." She returned Helena's gaze with a decidedly curious one of her own. "Was there anything odd or suspicious about my grandmother's death?"

Chapter Ten

HELENA LOOKED BACK ODDLY at Maggie. "That's uncanny," she muttered.

"What do you mean?" Ernie asked. "Both of you."

Pointedly, Maggie waited for Helena to speak first. "That's mostly what Henry wanted to talk about yesterday," Helena responded, shaking her head. "I couldn't imagine why he wanted to dwell on a day we'd all just as soon forget, but he asked me to tell him what I remembered about that day." She nodded at Maggie. "Your turn."

"The second time we—my grandfather and I, that is—talked yesterday," Maggie answered, "was after he had spoken with my father. During our conversation, he made an odd remark. He said that, while he couldn't do much to make up for the years of estrangement, he could do something about my grandmother's death." She shrugged. "I thought it a strange thing to say at the time, but he was so obviously tired I didn't feel I could ask him about it. In the light of everything that's happened, though, it seems likely that maybe there was something suspicious about my grandmother's death."

Ernie frowned. "I suppose. Well, Helena, do you think there was anything fishy about Magnolia's death?"

"At the time, no," Helena replied slowly. "It was a terrible, tragic accident, or so we all thought. But now"—she threw out her hands in a gesture of frustration—"I'm not quite so sure. I told Henry everything I could remember about that day: I wandered by accident into the room where he and Gerard were arguing, but I got out of there the second I realized what was going on. I went into the library to read, and by the time I came out again, Magnolia was lying there, dead at the foot of the stairs."

"You aren't much help, then. I guess the only thing we can do is to question everyone about it. Who was in the house that day?" Ernie demanded of Helena.

Helena thought for a moment. "All of us, I guess. Henry, Retty, and I, of course, and Sylvia, who was about seven years old at the time. Harold was here, too. It was July, so he had the summer off from his university. Lavinia was here." She frowned. "Oh, and Claudine and her mother, of course. Claudine was probably eleven or twelve. The daily help we had at the time I think we can count out. Otherwise, that's everybody."

"Then we have our work cut out for us," Ernie said briskly. "I think Maggie had better try talking to Lavinia, don't you think, Helena? I doubt she'd take kindly to answering questions for either one of us. But she might talk to Maggie. The curiosity value alone might get something out of her." She stood up. "Do you mind, Maggie?"

"I guess not," Maggie answered with manifest reluctance. She, too, stood up. "But I think I'd rather try it on a full stomach."

"Good idea," Helena laughed. "I'll see y'all downstairs in a few minutes."

The mood of the family at lunch reflected the air of repressed tension that filled the room whenever they were all together. The cook was the only person in the house to have remained relatively unaffected by Henry McLendon's death. The food, as bounteous in quality as it was in quantity, Maggie found difficult to resist, although the waistband of her skirt informed her that she needed to eat lightly for a day or so if she wanted to appear clothed before the family. She refused a second helping of the delicious array of vegetables the cook had provided and firmly told herself that she could have only half a slice of the amaretto cheesecake.

The dearth of conversation at the table relieved Maggie of the necessity of trying to talk to Adrian, seated once more beside her. She glanced at Lavinia from time to time and was not encouraged by her great-aunt's forbidding expression as she munched her food. Lavinia had remained aloof ever since Maggie and Gerard had arrived the day before, and Maggie was nervous about approaching the woman who obviously had little interest in either her nephew or her great-niece.

After half an hour of subdued silence, broken only by occasional requests for the passing of a dish, the family members began pushing back their chairs. Maggie dabbed at her mouth with her napkin, steeling herself to approach Lavinia, who at that moment was also getting up from the table. As Maggie followed her great-aunt toward the door, she noticed Helena and Ernie moving toward their own objects of interrogation. Helena grasped Harold by the arm, while Ernie put a comforting arm around Retty's shoulders. Retty seemed grateful for the attention, because she actually looked her age for the first time since Maggie had known her. The death of her twin brother had affected her strongly, perhaps more-so than it had affected anyone else in the family.

Maggie caught up with Lavinia in the hall outside the dining room. "Lavinia," she called. The older woman, her impatience ill-concealed, stopped and turned to look at Maggie.

"Yes, what is it?" she asked when Maggie failed to continue.

"I was wondering," Maggie started, "whether you might feel like talking a little this afternoon. I mean," she hurried on, "you and I haven't had much chance to talk since my father and I arrived, and I'd like to, if you feel like it." Awkwardly she ground to a halt and waited for her great-aunt to respond.

For a long moment Lavinia regarded the young woman with an impassive face. Maggie feared that Lavinia would turn her down flatly, but to her great relief, Lavinia nodded.

"I generally rest a while in the afternoon," she said, her voice tart, "but I suppose this once it wouldn't hurt to talk instead." She turned toward the stairs, leaving a slightly flustered Maggie to follow.

Lavinia's bedroom was at the far end of the same wing of the house in which Helena's room was located. After glancing around Lavinia's room, Maggie had some appreciation for why Lavinia had metaphorically wrinkled her nose at Helena's room. Maggie could not place the period of the furniture, but everything was antique. The effect was somehow what she conceived of as Victorian, with ruffled lace skirts covering the legs of the chairs and tables, and shelf upon shelf of knickknacks and photographs in expensive-looking frames. Maggie felt sorry for the housemaid who had to dust Lavinia's room.

Waving an imperious hand, Lavinia pointed Maggie toward a large chair covered in beautifully detailed fabric, while Lavinia herself reclined on a chaise lounge covered in luxurious rose velvet.

What on earth am I going to say to her? Maggie thought as she settled into the comfortable chair.

Lavinia solved her dilemma for her. "What do you really want?"

Startled—yet somewhat relieved—by her aunt's directness, Maggie formed a reply. "I'd like to know more about you and my grandmother's family." She couldn't come right out and say, *I want to know whether you had anything to do with the deaths of my grandparents,* despite Lavinia's own directness.

"So you want a potted history of the illustrious Culpeper family?" Lavinia mused sarcastically. "Well, that shouldn't take long. The Mississippi branch of the Culpepers, originally from Virginia, of course, were quite the Southern aristocrats. The Culpepers were wealthy and cultured when the McLendons began building the basis of a small business empire. After the war"—here Maggie knew Lavinia was talking about the Civil War—"the Culpepers struggled to hold on to their various plantations while the McLendons just got richer."

Eyebrows arched sardonically, Lavinia continued the history which both she and Maggie knew that Maggie hadn't really wanted to hear, at least not at the moment.

"The Culpepers became successively more impoverished, to the point where you could actually call them *bourgeois.*" Lavinia's tone indicated what she thought of this label. "Fortunately for Magnolia and me, our father was one of the few

Culpepers graced with anything approaching financial acumen, so we never had to do without the basics. We just didn't get a lot of the frills." She waved her hand around the room. "Nothing quite like this style, that's for sure. Magnolia married well, just as she did everything else."

Lavinia raised one mocking eyebrow. "What else would you like to know?"

Lavinia had, in all her years of practice, elevated bitchiness to an art form. Or so Maggie thought in annoyance. No wonder Helena and Ernie disliked her so heartily. How was she ever going to find out anything if the woman persisted in toying with her?

Maggie decided to take the offensive. "And you never married?" Her tone was sufficiently commiserating to be insulting, and with some satisfaction she saw that she had scored. Lavinia's head stiffened.

"You do have claws after all," she commented, much to Maggie's surprise. Lavinia sat up a little straighter on her chaise. "There's more of Magnolia in you, then, than just the looks. She'd be proud of you." For once, Lavinia's voice had lost its almost-permanent sneer, and she laughed. "They used to call her the 'Iron Magnolia' at school, and nobody knew it better than I. You should have had to grow up in the shadow of a sister like her."

Maggie felt a brief flash of sympathy for her great-aunt. She sensed that, for the moment at least, the woman was speaking from honest emotion, and Maggie respected it as such. Whatever damage had been done to the relationship between the sisters so physically alike, Maggie could only imagine, but it had left a lasting mark for the worse upon Lavinia's personality.

"I'm not going to sit here," Lavinia continued, "and give you a long list of all the wonderful things about your grandmother." She smiled ironically. "You wouldn't believe me if I did, but then neither would you believe me if I started telling you about all the things we fought over for nearly forty years. I daresay most of them would sound pretty stupid, even to me now, but at the time they all seemed serious. Your grandmother and I never got along very well, and you could say the same for the family she married into. They accepted me only because I was her sister, and because they felt sorry for me for not having anything—any money or a family of my own."

Whew! Maggie thought. *I guess I couldn't ask for more honesty than that.* Yet, even as she thought this, she couldn't resist acknowledging the idea that Lavinia was once again toying with her. Just why, she couldn't say.

"What were you doing the day my grandmother died?" Maggie asked, hoping to startle Lavinia into an answer.

She succeeded to a small degree, because Lavinia's eyes narrowed in suspicion, and her face paled. But when she spoke, she had mastered her surprise—fear, Maggie speculated—at the inquiry.

Coolly Lavinia replied, "Minding my own business, of course." She smiled at the involuntary expression of annoyance which contorted Maggie's face. "I believe I spent most of the morning writing letters. I did spend about half an hour with Magnolia that morning. Claudine, who was always a thoughtful child, and I took turns reading to her while she was stuck in bed like that. I came downstairs for a while after that, and as well as I can remember I was sitting outside on the back terrace enjoying the sunshine when one of the housemaids came to tell me about Magnolia's terrible accident."

Well, Maggie thought, *I suppose that's that.* She rose from her chair, intending to thank Lavinia for talking to her. Lavinia forestalled her.

"Before you go," she said, "you might want to have a look at a few of my pictures." She waved her hand toward a nearby table.

Her curiosity piqued, Maggie stepped forward to take a closer look. The largest frame, which drew her immediate attention, contained a family grouping. She picked out her grandmother from among the five people. Judging from the clothes, the picture must have been taken in the mid-1940s. Magnolia looked about twenty-five, Lavinia and the boy seated beside her about fifteen years younger. Their parents, stiff smiles assumed only for the sake of the camera, looked uncomfortable as they stared into the lens. Lavinia and Magnolia looked much like their father, the boy favoring their mother. There was something oddly familiar about the boy, Maggie thought. Where had she seen his face before?

Holding out the picture toward Lavinia, she pointed at the boy. "Who is this?"

Lavinia smiled. "That's my twin brother, Lawrence. He was the black sheep of the Culpeper family—wine, women, etcetera. He had more charm than he ever knew what to do with—that was his problem. He died in a car accident about twenty years ago," she finished.

"Oh," was all Maggie could manage to respond. She looked again at the boy in the portrait, trying to remember where she had seen his face. Then it dawned on her. "He looks like Claudine!"

Lavinia laughed in genuine amusement. "You mean there's one family skeleton that Helena hasn't rattled at you yet?"

"What do you mean?" Maggie asked, startled, placing the picture back on the table with care.

Lavinia laughed. "Don't worry, this isn't a McLendon family secret—it belongs to the Culpepers. I'm surprised Helena hasn't told you already, since I'm sure she told you everything she could think of about the McLendons." She stretched back in her chaise. "Claudine is a Culpeper by-blow. My brother never could keep his hands off a pretty woman, especially one captive under his father's roof. Just one of many such outcomes, I'm afraid." She laughed again. "And Magnolia, of course, had to play Lady Bountiful and give the woman a job, so the child could grow up in a good home."

Trying to conceal her astonishment at Lavinia's disclosure, Maggie looked at the picture again. "I've not seen a picture of Claudine's mother, of course, but she certainly took after her father," she commented mildly.

"No," Lavinia replied, and the oddness of her tone made Maggie turn swiftly to look at her. "Claudine didn't take after her father very much. She looks more like my mother when she was young."

"Well," Maggie said, her tone brisk, "thanks for forgoing your nap time to talk. It's been interesting." She moved toward the door.

"And, I trust, instructive." Lavinia had regained her composure, waving a languid hand in dismissal.

And that, I suppose, Maggie told herself once she was out in the hall, *is what forty or fifty years of bitterness will do to you.* Instead of the annoyance she might have felt with her great-aunt, Maggie felt only pity. But she could understand the exasperation Helena and Ernestine felt toward the woman. After all, they'd had to spend a lot more time with her.

Maggie reached the quiet of her room, grateful for a brief respite. After a few minutes in the bathroom, she went out to stand on the balcony, staring out across the vast expanse of lawn behind the house. Over to the left, she caught the glint of sun off water, and by leaning forward over the rail and craning her neck, she could see a swimming pool near the opposite corner of the house. The early afternoon sun beat down upon her, and, heavy with humidity, the air around her clung to her skin. The pool looked more and more attractive.

Maggie went back inside her room, pulling the French doors shut behind her. The cool dimness of the room refreshed her. Jackson, she decided, could easily compete with Houston in the matter of summertime temperatures.

Time to move on in her quest for information. Out in the hall, she knocked on her father's door but received no answer. The hallway was eerily quiet as she made her way with hastening steps to the stairs. She hurried down to the first floor, her heels clicking on the marble steps. The drawing room was vacant, so Maggie next went to the entertainment room. She opened the door and walked in.

Claudine had her hand on Adrian's arm. "But why not?" Her tone was petulant.

"I said 'no,' and I meant it." Adrian, in turn, was exasperated. "Why can't you get it through your head—"

At that point both had realized another person was in the room. Maggie stood, rooted to the floor in embarrassment. "Sorry," she mumbled. "I have the wrong room."

"I'll say!" Claudine said, her voice sharp with annoyance. She glared at Maggie, then brushed past her on the way out of the room.

"I'm sorry," Maggie said, not knowing what to do or say. "I didn't mean to interrupt. I'm looking for my father."

Adrian offered a strained smile. "Try the library, two doors down."

Muttering her thanks, Maggie ducked out of the room and moved down the hallway to the door Adrian had indicated. *Wonder what all that was about?* she mused. *Looked like something personal. Oh, well, none of my business.*

Putting aside thoughts of Adrian and Claudine's odd behavior, Maggie stopped to stare once she had opened the door. This room was twice the size of her bedroom upstairs, and every wall was lined with bookshelves. Comfortable leather chairs with companion reading lamps were scattered around the room with a couple of desks mixed in. There were also a few low bookshelves standing away from the walls.

Seated in one of the leather chairs, Gerard looked up from his book and smiled a strained welcome to his daughter. He closed his book on one finger as he watched Maggie roam around the room, taking in the spectacle of some fifteen thousand books.

Someone had taken great pains over the family library, she realized, because the books were organized by category— European history, American history, gardening, cooking, fiction, psychology, law, medicine. The range of tastes represented by the books astonished her. In the history section she glimpsed the titles of several classics of medieval history, and in the fiction she found books by authors as diverse as Eudora Welty and Gunter Grass. Much to her delight, she found a collection of more recent mystery writers, such as Ruth Rendell, Martha Grimes, and Elizabeth Peters, to supplement the marvelous collection upstairs in her grandmother's bedroom.

"You see you came by your bibliophilia quite honestly," Gerard told her, his smile losing its pinched quality. He put his book aside and picked up his pipe from the table beside his chair. He began to fill it as he watched his daughter examine the contents of a shelf of books near his chair.

"It's amazing," Maggie laughed. "I thought you and I have a lot of books, but there must be four or five times that many here."

Puffing at his pipe until he had it drawing to his satisfaction, Gerard took a moment before he answered. "And these aren't all the books in the house, either. Harold and Helena have their own favorites in their rooms, and I believe Retty has quite a collection of Victorian novels in her room." He laughed indulgently. "I think practically everyone in the family has a personal set of Jane Austen—not to mention a few other favorites."

"Obviously a family of good taste, then," Maggie replied, determined to keep her voice light.

"At least in literature," he responded in kind.

With great reluctance she put back on the shelf an autographed copy of Eudora Welty's *Delta Wedding*. Putting off the questions she needed to ask her father wouldn't help solve anything, and she knew that they both would feel much better when the mystery of Henry McLendon's death was resolved.

Maggie sat down in a chair which faced the one in which Gerard looked so comfortable. "Dad," she began tentatively, resting her tired back against the reassuring firmness of the chair, "Helena, Ernie, and I have been talking things over—"

"I can imagine," Gerard interrupted wryly. "If we give Ernie time she'll have ferreted everything out and saved the police all the trouble of an investigation." He frowned at his pipe, which had gone out. He put it aside for the moment. "So now, I suppose, you've been deputized to ask me some questions. Right?"

Maggie nodded. "As a matter of fact, yes. I hope you don't mind, but I think we may be onto something."

He sighed. "I'm willing—God knows I want this to be over as quickly as possible. Though it's difficult for me to contemplate one of my family as a murderer, despite the cause my father may have given over the years."

"Well, it may be just a little more complicated than that," she hesitated in responding.

"What do you mean?" he demanded. He picked up his pipe again and lit it.

Waving her hand at the pungent pipe smoke drifting her way, Maggie wrinkled her nose in concentration before responding. "Yesterday, when I talked to Grandfather for the last time, he made an odd remark. I didn't ask him about it at the time, because I knew he was tired. Now, with everything that's happened, that remark seems more significant. He told me it was too late to do much about the years of estrangement, but that he *could* do something about my grandmother's death." An exclamation from Gerard startled her.

"It's okay," he said when she paused. "Go on."

"Well, when Helena, Ernie, and I were talking things over, I asked Helena whether there had been anything odd or suspicious in the manner of my grandmother's death, and Helena remarked that she hadn't thought so at the time. But she was beginning to wonder herself, because apparently Grandfather talked with everybody in the house yesterday, and the one subject he discussed with all of them was the day of my grandmother's death." Maggie clasped her hands together in her lap and stared at the intertwined fingers. "What do you think about that?"

Gerard took a deep pull on his pipe and expelled another cloud of smoke before answering. "You're right, it is odd. When he and I talked, though, it didn't seem odd, because that day was at the root of our problem. But by the time I left him, I could tell that he did seem somewhat excited. Perhaps something either one of us said had sparked a memory for him. Maybe he remembered something that looked odd with the advantage of twenty-five years' worth of hindsight." He shrugged.

Maggie leaned forward. "Would you mind talking about it all with me? Maybe that way we can figure out what it was that made him suspicious. I have an inkling as to what it may be, but the only way I can confirm it is to find out more about what happened that day."

In silence father and daughter regarded each other for several minutes. Maggie wasn't entirely comfortable with the topic of discussion, and she knew that her father wasn't, but surely he realized that only by delving into the past could they hope to understand the truth of what had led to Henry McLendon's murder.

"Okay," Gerard conceded. He smoked thoughtfully for a minute before he continued. "I tried very hard over the years to forget as much as possible about that day, but it never really worked. Some scenes from one's life remain vivid, I've found, despite the passage of time, while others fade quickly from memory. The day my mother died is definitely one of the former."

As he paused, struggling for a moment with the memories, Maggie did her best to relax.

"I came home that time hopeful that finally my father and I could reconcile our differences. We had been at odds so long it was difficult for me to remember a time when we weren't arguing over something. When I arrived, rather late in the evening, around eight o'clock, I visited with Mother for a while, showing her pictures of you and your mother, telling her all the inconsequential things that grandmothers want to know. She was recovering from the pneumonia but still very weak, so I left her when I saw her beginning to tire.

"That evening—what was left of it—I spent visiting with the rest of the family, again showing off your picture and regaling everyone with stories. Father was, as usual, reserved but not openly disapproving. I believe he quite enjoyed seeing your pictures, but he had little to say that night. The next morning I visited with Mother again. I left her after about an hour. She was going to rest a while, and then either Lavinia or Claudine was going to come in to read to her. She fretted a lot about not being able to be up doing something, so the family tried to keep her as occupied as possible while she was recuperating. Without exhausting her completely, of course.

"After my talk with Mother, I decided that I couldn't put off much longer a confrontation with Father, so I went downstairs looking for him. While Mother was ill and then convalescing, he spent as much time as possible at home. I found him in his study, and I told him I thought we should talk, but he put me off, saying that he had to finish something that morning. There would be plenty of time after lunch, he said, for us to talk."

Gerard paused, sucking at his pipe. Maggie squirmed a little in her chair and rubbed her arms. The temperature in the room was cool, and her bare arms were beginning to feel the bite of the house's efficient air-conditioning system.

"After lunch," he continued, "Father asked me to join him in the drawing room while the rest of the family went off to do whatever it was they usually did after lunch. For ten or fifteen minutes everything was going well. Father asked me for more details about you and your mother and your mother's family. I did my best to satisfy his curiosity, and to keep my temper while I was doing it. He seemed pleased with most of what I had to say. Then we began talking about my job. I told him a little about my teaching duties and my prospects for advancement. Then he wanted to know about my salary, the house we lived in, what kind of car I drove, whether Alexandra worked, and on and on.

"I knew what all these questions were leading up to, of course, and I tried hard not to let my resentment show. I could tell, though, that my answers certainly weren't pleasing him. It became increasingly obvious that he thought I wasn't doing a very good job of taking care of you and your mother financially. Finally he just sniffed—he had a horribly offensive way of sniffing to make a point—and remarked that I had indulged myself long enough and it was time now to consider someone besides myself. I had 'responsibilities,' and I should take a more practical attitude toward attending to them. The upshot of it was," he continued wryly, "that I should come back south, enroll in a respectable law school, then go to work for him after I graduated. I didn't quite laugh in his face, but I let him know that I found the idea offensive, and that set him off."

Pausing to lay his pipe aside, Gerard shifted positions in his chair. "My father never—well, almost never—raised his voice at me. That was one of the frightening things about him, he always had such control. We sat there for nearly an hour, talking quite heatedly, and he never once raised his voice. He always maintained that quiet tone because it sounded so frighteningly reasonable, I think, and made it even more difficult for anyone to argue with him.

"We went back and forth over the same ground we had covered countless times before, and neither one of us was willing to give an inch. I had hoped that, for Mother's sake, we could at least agree to disagree, but with him, it was all his way or nothing.

"I was sitting with my back to the door, and Father was facing it. Twice during the time that we talked, I heard someone open the door and come into the room. It's no wonder we were interrupted, because anyone standing outside the door couldn't have heard any sign of an argument in progress. Anyway, I don't know who came in, but Father naturally saw whoever it was, and both times he waved the person away without even pausing."

Maggie ventured a quick question. "Can you remember the timing of the interruptions?"

Gerard frowned in concentration. "Rather toward the end, I think. They weren't very far apart actually, and I believe the second person came in maybe ten minutes, maybe less, before I decided it was useless to talk any further." He shrugged. "Do you think that's important?"

Maggie nodded. "Yes, I'll tell you why in a moment. Please go on."

Again Gerard shrugged. "There's not much more to tell. Having had enough, I guess, I got up and told Father that I might as well leave, and I walked out of the room. He followed me and caught up to me near the foot of the stairs. He demanded that I come back, and I told him to 'Go to hell,' or some such nonsense, and that infuriated him. He grabbed me by the collar, and I actually think he was going to box my ears, when I heard someone cry out my name and ask me to stop.

"We both looked up, and there was Mother, standing at the head of the stairs, clutching at the baluster." Gerard frowned with the effort of remembering something so painful. "I shook Father's hand off and was going up to her, but she turned slightly sideways, as if to look over her shoulder, then she jerked forward. She was too weak to hold on to the baluster, and she pitched forward, striking her head hard against one of the steps. She just kept on rolling down, while Father and I watched, too stunned to move. When we did move, and got to her side, it was obviously too late. She had struck the marble so hard that she must have died almost instantly."

For a moment the two sat there, Gerard reliving the horrible moment of his mother's death, and Maggie visualizing it all too easily. After giving both of them a few minutes to regain their composure, Maggie felt she had to go ahead with her questions.

"Dad," she said, "there are several things about what you just told me that are curious, but the main thing is this: How did my grandmother know where you and your father were and that you were arguing?"

Chapter Eleven

"THAT," GERARD RESPONDED TENSELY, "is just what both Father and I wanted to know." He rubbed a hand across his eyes. "Witnessing Mother's death was such a shock that, for a long time afterward, I couldn't really bear to think about it. But as time passed, and I could look at it more or less rationally, I realized that it had to be more than mere chance that brought her out of her room. She was too weak to get out of bed, so she didn't just come wandering down the hall and happen upon the argument."

"Exactly," Maggie said, relieved that her father agreed upon the importance of this point. "Did you or Grandfather know whoever told her that you two were arguing?"

Gerard shook his head wearily. "No. We talked about it yesterday for the first time. Oddly enough, that one significant detail had escaped Father all these years. He told me yesterday that he had actually suffered a minor stroke that day, and I never knew it, because he ordered me out of the house and the only time I saw him after that was two days later at the funeral. By then he had recovered somewhat, but the stroke had affected his memory of that day." Gerard sighed. "He did seem a little excited when I asked him the very question you asked me, but he told me it was too late to worry about it now and that I should forget it. I see now that he evidently wasn't willing to do the same."

"And trying to find out who told her may have cost him his life," Maggie said.

"What do you mean?" Gerard demanded, his voice harsh.

"I think," Maggie answered slowly, "that it's very possible that your mother was murdered."

"Oh, no," he muttered. He shrank back in his chair as if

trying to distance himself from her.

"I'm sorry, Dad, but I really do believe it's possible." Maggie was stricken by her father's suddenly pale face, but she had to go on. "Think back," she urged softly, "to what you told me. Remember, you said that Grandmother, after she called out, seemed to glance back over her shoulder, then she jerked forward and fell."

Gerard nodded, his eyes screwed tightly shut, as if to ward off the vision of his dying mother. "Yes," he whispered. "She looked slightly puzzled as she turned back to look down at us, and then she fell. It was if her knees suddenly gave way." He opened his eyes. "Are you trying to tell me that someone pushed her?"

He flinched at Maggie's nod. "But why? Why?"

"I don't know," she replied. "I've thought a lot about that this afternoon, and it just seems like a very strong possibility. We know that someone had to have told her about your argument, someone who came in on you and Grandfather arguing. That someone went and told my grandmother to get out of her bed. Do you really think that that was done without malice? It seems to me someone was setting her up for just such an accident. The fact that you and Grandfather happened to witness it was probably luck on the murderer's part. Either way, it could have been—and was, until now—dismissed as a tragic accident."

"But no one hated my mother that much," Gerard protested weakly. "No one."

Maggie moved uncomfortably in her chair. "What about Lavinia?"

Gerard shook his head in denial. "I knew as well as anyone that Lavinia and Mother didn't get along at all, but Lavinia would never have done such a thing to Mother. I could almost see her doing something like that to Father—in fact I think she did push him down the stairs one day, Helena told me—but I don't think she hated Mother enough to do something like that."

"But would you say she was malicious enough to go to your mother and tell her about the argument?" Maggie persisted.

Reluctantly Gerard nodded. "Probably so." He threw up his hands. "I just don't know. Even after all these years away from them, I thought I knew my family, but now . . ."

"I know this is awful for you," Maggie said as she moved from her chair to kneel in front of her father's chair. She clasped his hands in hers and squeezed tightly. "And I hate dredging all this up, but if Grandmother really was murdered, then I think that the same person must have murdered Grandfather. He must have revealed something to his killer, or somehow made the killer suspicious. Otherwise, why the sudden decision to change his will?"

"You're probably right," Gerard agreed, gently disengaging her hands before standing up. He retrieved his pipe from the table and stuffed it in his shirt pocket. "It all makes rather macabre sense. If Father had decided he knew who was responsible for Mother's death, he wouldn't have waited to do something about his will. He told me yesterday that everyone in the family was well provided for, so I've no doubt he intended to cut someone out. Just what he planned to do after that we'll never know."

Maggie had stood up with him, and now she encircled his waist with one arm. "The murderer obviously didn't want to wait to find out. Although," she mused, "Grandfather probably couldn't have proved anything and would have had to settle with disinheriting whoever was responsible and kicking him or her out of the house."

Gerard nodded. He moved toward the door, and Maggie followed. "I'm going up to my room for a while, I think. What about you?"

"I'm going to find Helena and Ernie, I guess."

"Well, just be careful, all three of you." So saying, Gerard ambled tiredly away from her. With concern, Maggie watched him go, wishing she could do something more to console him and silently castigating herself for not approaching the topic of her grandmother's murder with a little more tact. But how else could she have done it?

As Gerard disappeared around the foot of the staircase, Maggie at a slow pace followed in his footsteps until she stood at the foot of the graceful, but solid marble structure. Gazing up, she forced herself to visualize a figure standing upon the top step, leaning against the baluster. On either side of the head of the staircase were waist-high balustrades of marble, each about ten feet long. These ran flush against the walls of the corridors which ran the length of the house on either side. Hidden from the view of anyone below, someone could easily have crawled along the floor and hit Magnolia McLendon in the knees, causing her to jerk forward and then fall down the stairs. Only a slight blow would have been necessary to topple the woman from her weak hold of the baluster.

Hurriedly Maggie turned away from contemplation of what she was convinced was the scene of her grandmother's murder. Her reconstruction of it, though circumstantial, seemed horribly plausible.

"Maggie."

She whirled around to face Adrian Worthington. Though he had spoken softly, nevertheless he had startled her. "Sorry!" He grinned at her, and Maggie's irritation faded.

"It's okay," she assured him. "I've still got eight lives left."

Adrian grinned again, and she wished she could think of something else amusing to say. He had a most attractive grin, especially when it was directed at her.

"About what happened a little while ago," he said.

For the moment, Maggie had forgotten the tense scene she had interrupted. The memory of it made her uncomfortable. It had been a private moment, and she was embarrassed that she had intruded upon it, even inadvertently.

"Don't worry," she said, embarrassment making her voice cooler than she intended, "it's really none of my business."

"Oh," Adrian said, his own face coloring slightly, "well, I just wanted to tell you Helena's out by the pool, and she thought you might like to join her. I believe she expects Ernie to join you, too."

"Sounds good to me," Maggie responded in a voice that was too bright. "I haven't been outside the house at all since I got here."

"Then follow me," he said abruptly as he turned away.

Feeling even more awkward, she followed him down the hall and into a short corridor on the west side of the house. At the end of the corridor was a small room—Maggie had already decided that, with this house, "small" was always a relative term—which Adrian called the "sunroom." He pointed toward several doors on one side of the room near the outside door and explained that these were changing rooms which were also accessible from the outside. "Every convenience," he assured her at his most polite.

Opening the door, Adrian ushered her out onto a large patio. Straight ahead of them was an Olympic-sized pool. Scattered around the expanse of the pool were wrought-iron chairs and chaise lounges, all covered with gaily colored, water-resistant cushions. Sitting comfortably beneath a large beach umbrella whose fabric matched that of the chair cushions was Helena. She waved a languid hand at Maggie, who skirted one corner of the pool to join her.

Maggie turned to speak to Adrian, but he was heading back into the house, the door closing upon him even as she turned. *It doesn't really matter,* she told herself. *Just forget about it.* So she sat down in the chair Helena indicated and poured herself a glass of iced lemonade from the pitcher on the table.

"This is nice," Maggie commented after taking a long sip from her glass of lemonade. She cast approving eyes at the scene around her—gently sloshing, sparkling water in the pool, neatly trimmed lawn around the patio, a breeze with a more-than-welcome hint of coolness, and ample protection from the hot sunshine. "Nice," she repeated.

"It certainly makes a pleasant change," Helena agreed. She shifted in her chair so that she could look directly at her grandniece. "This wasn't the sort of homecoming we had planned for you." She shook her head dolefully. "Jackson is a lovely little city, and there are places I wanted to show you and people I wanted you to meet, but the time really isn't right for all that now."

Maggie patted her hand in a consoling manner. "I know."

Helena squinted into the sunshine as they heard the door

to the sunroom close with a slight bang. "Here's Ernie," she announced, and Maggie turned to smile a welcome at her cousin.

"Lord, it's hot," Ernie grumbled as she plopped down into a chair beside Maggie. She moved her chair a little farther into the shade of the umbrella. "I feel like jumping into the pool. Anyone want to swim?" she asked hopefully.

Smiling, Helena and Maggie shook their heads. "Maybe later," Maggie said.

"You're right—we really should get down to business." Ernie sat up straight in her chair and nodded at Maggie. "Let's hear your report first."

Suppressing the urge to salute, Maggie did as requested, giving the other two women a detailed outline of her conversation with her father.

Helena gasped and Ernie narrowed her eyes when Maggie repeated her theory that Magnolia's death was murder, rather than accident. She gave her reasons for thinking so and was relieved when Helena and Ernie nodded vigorously at her conclusions.

"That explanation makes sense of a lot of things," Ernie said, "although it raises a whole nother set of questions."

"We may not have to look too far for some answers." Helena's eyes gleamed as she looked back and forth between her companions.

"All right, give," Ernie ordered. "What have you found out?"

"Well," Helena said in an arch tone, "I talked to Harold after lunch today, and I asked him what he was doing the day Magnolia died. He told me that Henry had asked him the same question, just as we thought. Anyway, Harold had spent most of his time that day in the library. He came out for lunch, but he went back right afterward. He said he knew Henry and Gerard looked like they were spoiling for a fight, and Harold's policy was to stay out of Henry's way as much as possible."

"Get on with it, Helena!" Ernie urged as Helena paused to take an unnecessarily long sip of her lemonade.

Helena grinned. "Okay. Harold did come out of the library once that afternoon before Magnolia's accident. He was going up to his room for some notes or something, and as he was about to come around the foot of the stairs he saw someone coming out of the drawing room. Before the door closed he heard a snatch of the conversation and knew that Henry and Gerard were still in there, arguing. Harold had stopped where the person coming out of the room couldn't see him, but he could see who it was who had just come out."

"Who?" Maggie and Ernie demanded in unison.

"Lavinia!" was the joyfully malicious answer.

Chapter Twelve

MAGGIE EXPELLED THE BREATH she had been holding. "I knew it!" She slapped a hand down on the table, nearly overturning her glass of lemonade. She steadied the glass before it emptied its contents across the table.

"I'm not surprised," Ernie admitted. "But we know that two people stumbled into that argument—rather," she corrected herself, "we know the argument was nearly interrupted twice. Though I suppose it would be slightly odd if the same person had stumbled in twice. So there must have been two people. Right?" she demanded of her companions.

"I can put your minds at rest on that score," Helena said wryly. "I was the other person. I knew Henry and Gerard had gone into the drawing room to talk, but I'd say at least half an hour had passed by the time I went to the door. If I'd been paying much attention, I guess I'd've heard them talking as I opened the door. But I wasn't paying attention, so I just blundered in. Henry just waved me away, and Gerard had his back to me, so he didn't even know who it was."

"What about the timing?" Maggie asked.

Helena cocked her head to one side and thought for a moment. "According to what Harold told me, Lavinia must have gone into the room *after* I did. He stood and watched her go back upstairs, then he followed and went to his room. About fifteen minutes later, when he came out of his room, he walked down the hall to the stairs where he found Henry and Gerard bending over Magnolia halfway down the stairs." She shuddered. "Anyway, as near as I can recall, it must have been about thirty minutes after I walked in on that argument that Retty called up to my room to tell me to get downstairs because something had happened."

Ernie sat back in her chair, letting her shoulders slump against the plump cushion. "What do we do now? Confront Lavinia, I guess." She looked from Maggie to Helena and back again. "Who wants to volunteer?"

"I'm not doing it by myself this time," Maggie protested. "I vote for a committee of three."

"Yes, I think so," Helena agreed. "She'll have a harder time denying it if all three of us talk to her together." She stretched her arms out in front of her, then over her head. "I know *I* didn't run upstairs to tell Magnolia that Gerard and Henry were arguing, so Lavinia must have done it. And we'll make her admit it." She picked up the pitcher. "Lemonade anyone?"

Both Maggie and Ernie held out their glasses for a refill. As she poured out the remainder of the lemonade, Helena asked, "Well, Ernie, what did my big sister have to say about all this?"

Ernie took a long swallow from her lemonade before she replied. "The whole conversation was kind of strange," she finally remarked. "I wouldn't be completely surprised if Retty had suffered some sort of mild heart attack, because I've never known her to be so dithery." She looked sideways at Helena.

"Unlike me, you mean," Helena supplied without rancor.

"Well, yes," Ernie admitted. She laughed softly. "You haven't always been the most direct or decisive person in the world, while Retty has. That's why it disturbed me to see her this way." She sighed. "But I guess age just catches up with all of us sooner or later."

Ernie took one final, long drink from her glass, then put it aside. "But that's not really what you wanted to hear about. Anyway, it took me a little while to get Retty to the point, because she kept letting herself wander off on tangents the whole time we talked. I finally got her to talking about the day Magnolia died, and she wasn't very helpful—just mentioned what we already knew. That Lavinia and Claudine had been taking turns reading to Magnolia while she was recovering. Retty didn't see anything that day, because she spent most of the afternoon in her room writing letters. She didn't know anything had happened until Sylvia came tearing in to tell her about it."

"That's when Retty called me," Helena reminded the other two.

"What about Sylvia?" Maggie asked suddenly. "Where was she while all this was going on? And how old was she?"

Ernie answered first, frowning slightly. "According to Retty, Sylvia had been in her own room, playing, but she was leaving her room to go outside to play, when Claudine came running down the hall. Claudine told Sylvia something had happened to Magnolia, then Sylvia went to her grandmother, then I guess Retty went to Helena?" She looked at Helena for confirmation.

Helena shrugged. "That's correct, as far as I know. But I hadn't ever given much thought to where Sylvia was during all this, because I guess she was only about seven or eight at the time. And Claudine is only about five years older than Sylvia."

"That accounts for everybody, then," Maggie said, running over the list of people in her mind. Suddenly she stopped. "No, there's one other person we haven't mentioned." She looked questioningly at Helena and Ernie, waiting to see whether they'd come up with the name.

The two older women traded interrogative glances, then faced Maggie again, shaking their heads. "Claudine's mother," she reminded them. "Where was she while all this was going on?"

"Lorraine!" Helena cried. "You're right! We'd forgotten all about her." She frowned, thinking furiously. Then her face cleared. "But she wasn't here that weekend. One of her elderly aunts was in the hospital in Memphis and wasn't expected to live, so Lorraine had gone up there to be with her."

"Then that's one less suspect to worry about," Maggie replied. "Although we know she couldn't have murdered my grandfather, and I'm convinced that the same person murdered them both." She fingered her glass for a moment. "Now, when do we want to talk to Lavinia?"

After a brief discussion they agreed to wait until after dinner that evening before they accosted her. Secretly Maggie was relieved as she made her way upstairs; she wanted to postpone the moment for a while. Now that they were approaching what seemed like a solution, she was oddly reluctant to press ahead with their rather amateurish search for the truth. The family as a whole would be vastly relieved to have the matter settled, and having Lavinia as the guilty party would make things that much easier. *Still,* Maggie thought, *I don't relish having to corner her.* As far as she was concerned, Lavinia's bark was probably just as bad as her bite, and either one could be painful.

Sitting out in the afternoon heat had left Maggie feeling less than fresh, so she decided to soak in the huge bathtub for a while before getting ready for dinner. As she relaxed in the warm water, her mind wandered lazily back over the afternoon's conversation with Helena and Ernie.

Everything seemed to suggest Lavinia as a culprit in Magnolia's death. The important point, however, was this: Had Lavinia told her sister about the argument simply out of malice, knowing that the woman would be distressed by it, or had she done it in order to maneuver Magnolia into a vulnerable position where murder might easily be concealed as a tragic accident? Did someone else come along and take advantage of the opportunity that had presented itself, after Lavinia had done her dirty work?

In other words, thought Maggie, *to what degree is Lavinia guilty?* They were perhaps being careless in their reasoning by assuming Lavinia guilty without more than the woman's own waspish personality as evidence, admittedly circumstantial. But who else would have, or could have, told Magnolia about the argument?

Helena could have, she thought abruptly. What she knew of her great-aunt argued against her doing such a thing, but it was within the realm of possibility. The time factor, however, was important. Magnolia had to have had time to make it down the hall to the head of the stairs after someone told her about the argument. *How weak had she been?* Maggie wondered. *Was she moving so slowly that it had taken her twenty minutes to reach the top of the stairs? In that case, Helena would have to have been the one who told her.*

But then Harold or Lavinia would probably have seen Magnolia in the hallway when they went up. She sat up quickly in the tub, causing the water to splash around the sides. She reached for a washcloth to scrub her face as she considered the implications of a new idea.

Harold had gone upstairs right after Lavinia. He admitted to knowing that Gerard and Henry were arguing. What if he had been the one to go to Magnolia? He could have done it as easily as Lavinia. Neither Helena nor Ernie had mentioned this possibility, and Maggie hadn't thought of it at the time. Was Helena protecting her brother by focusing their line of questioning upon Lavinia? Maggie wasn't sure, but she thought it important to question Harold at some point herself, after they questioned Lavinia.

Maggie stared vaguely at the water draining out of the tub. Finally she roused herself to reach for a towel and dried herself. Slipping on a robe, she unpinned her hair and brushed it out with vigorous strokes. The bath had refreshed her body, but her mind still buzzed with the urgency of the questions she wanted answered.

Twenty minutes later, dressed in a comfortable and flattering dark green cotton dress, Maggie knocked at her father's door. Receiving no reply, she made her way downstairs to the dining room, where she found the rest of the family beginning to wander in. Quickly she sat down between Gerard and Ernie, noticing as she did so an empty space beside Adrian. She thought he looked slightly disappointed as he glanced her way. Her stomach gave a queer little lurch, but she would have felt awkward moving now. She stayed where she was, turning to offer a belated greeting to Ernie.

Lavinia and Claudine, the last to arrive, came in a few minutes later. Claudine claimed the empty seat next to Adrian. Maggie watched as she leaned toward him and whispered something to him. Then Maggie turned her head, staring down at her plate, as Adrian looked her way, his eyes unreadable.

As hands moved to begin passing dishes of steaming vegetables, Retty cleared her throat loudly to gain everyone's attention.

"Before we begin," she said, her voice quavering, "I have an announcement. Gerard and I have consulted with Arthur Latham, and Henry's body has been released for burial. We've arranged the funeral for tomorrow afternoon at two. After the service, we'll return here for the reading of Henry's will. Lyle seemed to think we might as well go ahead with it, the . . . um . . . investigation notwithstanding." Her announcement finished, Retty turned her attention to her plate. Her fork clinked shakily against the china.

The desultory conversation which had been going on before Retty's announcement seemed suddenly to dry up. In silence they all passed dishes back and forth, and even the normally irrepressible Helena and Ernie had little to say. Gradually, however, the tension eased, and quiet conversation resumed. Maggie and Ernie discussed Maggie's interest in the history of medieval women, and, blotting out the rest of the family, they talked comfortably for the remainder of the meal.

Eventually Retty stood up from her place at the head of the table. Ernie broke off in the middle of a point she had been making about Eleanor of Aquitaine when Retty cleared her throat to make another announcement. The other conversations ceased as everyone looked at the self-appointed head of the family.

"I'm spending the rest of the evening in my room," she said. "You may all watch a movie, or do whatever you wish. I'll see y'all in the morning." Turning to her granddaughter, she said, "Sylvia, if you don't mind, I'd like you to come up with me for a while." She moved from the table toward the door with Sylvia trailing in her wake.

After the door shut behind the two women, the rest of the family pushed their chairs back from the table. "Well?" Claudine asked. "Is anyone in the mood for a movie?" Her tone indicated that she didn't think much of the idea.

Seeing the general disinterest, she smiled tiredly, shrugged, then disappeared through the door, followed in quick succession by Harold and Gerard. Maggie looked suspiciously at Helena and Ernie as they moved toward Lavinia, who seemed disconcerted by the abrupt departures of the men. Maggie wondered whether either her cousin or her aunt had engineered the quick disappearing act of the men. Adrian had already departed unobtrusively for the kitchen. The four women were suddenly and efficiently alone.

"Lavinia." Ernie spoke quietly, yet Lavinia's head jerked sharply toward her. "We'd like to talk to you about something. Why don't we go somewhere we can be a little more comfortable." She grasped Lavinia's arm and led her toward the door. Maggie and Helena followed behind.

Maggie had expected Lavinia to put up a fuss, but for whatever reason, she was going along with them docilely enough at the moment. Ernie steered them toward the entertainment room, which was smaller than the drawing room and better suited for their intended discussion.

She motioned Lavinia to one of the sofas at the side of the room and seated herself beside the object of their inquiry. Maggie and Helena moved two of the comfortable chairs close to the sofa so that they were all seated close to one another.

"Well, what's this all about?" Lavinia snapped suddenly. "I don't imagine you want to know my opinions on the state of the economy. What do you want?"

Ernie had apparently decided to take on the role of chief inquisitor. "We appreciate your directness, Lavinia, and we'll return the favor. We want to talk about what happened in this house twenty-five years ago."

"You mean Magnolia's death?" Lavinia asked incredulously before Ernie could continue. "What the hell has that got to do with anything?"

Ernie replied, "We're just a little curious about what went on that day, and we'd like to ask you some questions. Okay?"

Lavinia's nose wrinkled in distaste, and with a slight shock Maggie recognized a gesture she herself used when she was irritated by someone or something.

"Go ahead," Lavinia responded grudgingly. "Although Maggie has already put me through one inquisition today."

"Yes, we know." Ernie was curt. "But what you didn't tell Maggie was that you walked in on the argument Gerard and Henry were having the day Magnolia died."

"So?" Lavinia's tone was irritatingly dismissive. "Henry and Gerard never were together more than five minutes before they started arguing about something. That wasn't any different."

"Yes, there was a difference." Ernie in her turn was triumphant, and Lavinia's eyes narrowed in suspicion. Maggie and Helena watched the other two women with all the intensity of spectators at a wrestling match to see who would land the telling blow first.

"It was a little too much of a coincidence, don't you think," Ernie went on smugly, "that Magnolia just happened to come out of her room at that time and then fall down the stairs. She was weak, and the only way she would have gotten out of her bed was if someone had told her that Gerard and Henry were having a huge row again."

Lavinia's face turned a mottled red. "And I guess you three think I was the one who allegedly told her?" Seeing the answer only too clearly in the other women's faces, Lavinia stood up in disgust. "I've had about enough of this." She stepped between Maggie and Helena and headed for the door. No one made a move to stop her. Maggie couldn't summon the nerve to say anything, and Helena and Ernie both seemed at a loss as well.

Halfway toward the door Lavinia whirled around. "So what if someone did tell her that Henry and Gerard were arguing? What was the harm in that?"

Helena replied tartly, "Because we think whoever told Magnolia about the argument made her fall down those stairs."

Lavinia moved a few steps closer to the other women. Her face had drained of color, and for a moment Maggie feared the woman was going to faint. "You mean to tell me you think Magnolia was murdered?" She laughed weakly, unable to muster the scorn she obviously intended, when Helena nodded. "And I'll bet you think I was the one who pushed her." She advanced menacingly a step toward Helena, some of her strength returning. "I ought to yank your hair out, you bitch."

Helena stood up angrily. "Just you try!"

The two women faced each other without flinching. Maggie looked nervously at Ernie, hoping her cousin would intervene. Ernie, however, sat on the sofa, watching the proceedings with great interest.

"What the hell is going on here?"

A new voice from the direction of the doorway made them all look around. Claudine stood there, a frown on her face. "What is going on?" she repeated as she moved toward Lavinia and Helena.

"Lavinia was just answering a few questions," Ernie replied coolly. "Nothing to get worked up about."

Claudine grimaced. "It doesn't look that way to me." She took Lavinia's arm. "I think you'd better go upstairs now. Your blood pressure doesn't need to get any higher." She then looked sternly at Helena. "And I think you ought to calm down a little, too." She herded the docile Lavinia toward the door as Helena, her anger deflated, sat down in her chair.

"I'll be back in a few minutes," Claudine promised from the doorway, "and then I want to know what the hell's been going on here." The door slammed behind her.

The Grand Inquisitor and her two assistants looked warily at one another.

Chapter Thirteen

"WHEW!" MAGGIE SAID in as light a tone as she could muster. "I'm not so sure I want to stick around."

Ernie snorted. "That was real helpful! We never did get anything out of Lavinia, except that she more or less admitted she did know about the argument."

Helena threw up her hands. "Even so, you can't convince me Lavinia didn't tell Magnolia. She acted pretty funny about that. I won't go so far as to say she was the one who did the pushing, but I wouldn't be surprised."

Maggie shrugged that aside for the moment. "Before Claudine gets back, I want to know something. Are she and Lavinia particularly close?"

Helena wobbled her head back and forth in such an odd manner that Maggie couldn't tell whether she was indicating "yes" or "no" to the question. "Sort of," she finally said.

"That's a helpful answer," Ernie commented tartly. "Would you like to go into a little more detail?"

Helena rolled her eyes. "Well, Maggie, I guess I'd better let you in on another family secret, so to speak. One of the few I didn't tell you, because I didn't think it was all that important."

Maggie held up her hand. "It's okay. Lavinia's already told me about Claudine's father."

Helena's eyebrows arched. "Really? Quite an honor, I should think. Anyway, the fact that Lavinia is Claudine's aunt has made them a little closer than they would have been otherwise, I suppose." She frowned. "Claudine was always such a contradictory child. She has this nurturing instinct. She always seemed to know before anyone else when someone in the family was going to be ill, and she delighted in helping take care of anyone who was sick. That's why none of us was surprised when she wanted to be a nurse, and that she's such a good one. But at the same time, she's so independent and—well, *prickly* I guess is the best word for it. She knew the truth about who her father was when she was pretty young, and that's what made her the way she is. She's never really let any of us get that close to her—even Lavinia, as far as I can tell, although they do seem to get along pretty well."

"As well as anyone can with Lavinia, you mean," Ernie added wryly.

"It strikes me as a little odd," Maggie said reflectively, "that my grandmother would have taken the mother of her niece into this house as a *servant*." Placing a slight emphasis on the last word, she looked inquiringly at Helena.

Helena shrugged. "It was a strange situation at first, but you see, Magnolia didn't really know about Claudine—the truth of her parentage, I mean—for nearly a year, I guess." She shifted in her chair. "Lorraine had left the Culpeper family about the time she found out she was pregnant. I think the Culpepers sent her to stay with some relatives in Louisiana. Lavinia had just gone to New York for eighteen months to visit her maternal grandparents—she's half Yankee, by the way, which maybe explains some of her cussedness—and Lawrence and Magnolia didn't get along too well. She disapproved of him mightily because he wouldn't settle down to anything."

As Helena paused for breath, Maggie laughed. "This sounds like a soap-opera plot." Ernie quickly joined in her laughter.

Helena acknowledged their laughter with a wave of the hand. "Yes, it does, but it happens to be true in this case. Anyway, no one had bothered to tell Magnolia that Lawrence had gotten Lorraine pregnant. Old man Culpeper might have told her, but he died about a year before all this happened, and Mrs. Culpeper adored Lawrence and wouldn't do anything to get him in bad with his big sister. Lorraine showed up one day, looking for work, when Claudine was about nine months old, and Magnolia took her in. It wasn't till about a year later, when Claudine was nearly two, that we found out the truth of her parentage. By then she and Lorraine were practically part of the family, and nobody really minded, to tell the truth."

"Ain't this a grand family?" Ernie asked Maggie whimsically.

Maggie had to laugh. The two of them were making somewhat light of the issue, but surely it couldn't all have been as easy as they made it out to be. The McLendons and the Culpepers definitely had their fair shares of closets rattling with skeletons, and she had the feeling that it might take her quite some time to find all the keys to the various closet doors. At least the search shouldn't prove dull.

Ernie scowled at her watch. "I'm not going to wait all evening on Claudine. Where is she? It's been nearly twenty minutes since she stormed out of here with Lavinia." Her foot tapped impatiently on the carpet.

"Maybe Lavinia's taking longer to tuck in than she thought," Helena suggested, smiling at the idea.

No one seemed to have an answer to this remark, so they sat for about ten minutes more, each mulling over her own thoughts. Then Ernie consulted her watch and announced that she was going up to her room. "Claudine can wait until tomorrow if she really wants to talk to us. I'm tired. I got up awfully early this morning." She yawned.

Both Helena and Ernie stood up. "What about you?" Helena asked Maggie.

Maggie gestured with a listless hand. "I guess I'll go up in a minute."

Helena bent to kiss her on the cheek, and Ernie did the same as the two older women wished her good night. Maggie sat there for perhaps five minutes, thinking Claudine might appear. Maggie was curious to talk to her, but maybe Claudine had decided that she didn't want to talk to any of them after all.

Maggie stood up, deciding that she would go to the library to seek out something to read herself to sleep. She wasn't in the mood right now for Pollock and Maitland and the complexities of medieval English law, nor was she in the mood for one of the mystery novels in her bedroom. Maybe something else—a nice big book with pictures.

Absorbed in thought, Maggie opened the door of the library and stopped in the doorway as she heard the swell of music coming softly from somewhere within the room. She recognized a Telemann violin concerto about the same time she recognized the figure seated in one of the leather chairs. Pipe in mouth, smoke swirling about his head, and book in hand, Adrian Worthington looked up when he heard the door open.

"Hello," he said, laying his book aside as he stood up. "This is an unexpected pleasure."

Thankful that the light near the doorway was dim, Maggie blushed, not at the casual gallantry of Adrian's greeting, but for the sincerity she heard in his voice.

"Thank you," she replied. "I'm sorry to disturb your reading. I just wanted to get a book to put myself to sleep with." She still felt awkward with him but didn't know what to do about it. She burned with curiosity about the scene earlier that day with Claudine, but unless he brought it up first she wasn't going to mention it.

"Help yourself," he said at his most polite. "You have quite a collection to pick from." He resumed his seat and put his pipe aside as Maggie wandered to the section of shelves which contained the history books.

"You don't have to put that out on my account." She waved toward his pipe. "I'm used to it, believe me. My father rarely has one out of his hand."

Adrian laughed and picked up his pipe again. "Okay, but you really shouldn't encourage me, you know. I've been trying to give it up, but I'm too lazy to break the habit."

"There are worse things you could do," she commented as her fingers roamed lightly over the spines of books until she found something suitable—a coffee-table book on the stately homes of England and Ireland. She pulled it off the shelf and turned back toward Adrian to find him watching her intently. He looked down at his book as her eyes caught his.

Taking a deep breath, Maggie walked over to a chair near his and sat down. Adrian turned toward her as he was relighting his pipe. "We haven't had much chance to talk," Maggie said, hoping her voice wouldn't betray her nervousness. She started to say that Helena had refused to tell her anything about him but caught herself up short. "How long have you . . . um . . . been with the family?" *Lord*, she thought, *please tell me that didn't sound patronizing.*

Evidently it didn't, for he turned his attention from his pipe to her and smiled. "Almost four years."

He's not going to make this too easy for me, she thought. *Oh, well, plunge ahead!* "Do you enjoy being a butler?" *Now that did sound patronizing!* Maggie winced.

Adrian lit his pipe before answering. "Well, there are other things I'd rather do, to be honest, but my job here has been interesting, to say the least." He paused to blow out a long plume of smoke, and they both watched it swirl away. "Actually I've enjoyed myself a lot, because despite what you may have heard to the contrary, your grandfather was a good man to work for. He was demanding, I'll admit, but he was always fair with me."

"I'm glad to hear that," Maggie said. Sadly she continued, "I didn't have much of a chance to get to know him."

Adrian nodded in sympathy. "I know." He struggled for a moment over something, then seemed to come to a decision. "I guess I should tell you that Helena told me the reasons your father and your grandfather were estranged."

She shrugged. "Well, I guess it's really no big secret. Except from me, of course." She laughed somewhat bitterly, then took herself firmly in hand. "But that's certainly not your fault. I'm happy that I had the chance to meet him and talk to him, at least briefly." *Although*, she thought, *the things I've learned about him don't make those memories completely comfortable.*

Adrian must have sensed something of her turmoil. "Your grandfather was no saint. From some of the stories I've heard, and not just from Helena, he could be pretty ruthless when he thought it was necessary." He paused reflectively. "But I can't really judge him on those standards. I have to consider my own dealings with him, and in that respect he was always very fair. Demanding, but fair." He puffed on his pipe for a moment. "And I don't know whether it's any consolation to you—or whether consolation's even the right word—but he was tremendously pleased about seeing you after all this time. Your visit meant a lot to him, even though he couldn't swallow his pride earlier and just ask your father to come for a visit."

Adrian watched her for a moment, his eyes curiously blank, and Maggie returned his gaze. Finally she remarked, a little stiffly, though she was sincere, "Thank you for telling me this. I've learned quite a bit about my grandfather over the last two days, and some of it is difficult to absorb. But what you've told me will help me sort things out."

"Then I'm glad, too," he responded.

To lighten the mood a little, and also because she was still very curious, Maggie asked, "How did you come to work for my grandfather?"

Adrian smiled impishly as he took a long draw on his pipe before answering. "My fellowship ran out four years ago, and I badly needed a job. The timing was right, so I applied, and I got it."

"Fellowship?" she inquired nonchalantly.

His impish smile widened into a wicked grin. "Yes, I was taking longer than I had planned to finish my dissertation, so I had to go to work."

"Dissertation?" Maggie tried to keep her voice from squeaking in surprise but wasn't quite successful.

Adrian assayed a half-bow from his chair. "Dr. Worthington at your service, ma'am."

She grinned back at him, vowing silently that she would wring Helena's neck the first chance she got. "Glad to meet you, Doc." She bowed back.

"Thank you. I hear you're a masochist, too."

Maggie had to laugh. "Oh, yes, but I'm a couple of years at least from having degree in hand." She grimaced. "But that's something I prefer not to think about too often. What's your degree in, and what's your dissertation about?" She leaned back in her chair and assumed an earnest expression.

"English lit," he replied, "and I wrote about Jane Austen."

He's gorgeous, and he likes Jane Austen! Maggie sighed inwardly. "The immortal Jane," she finally managed to reply, forcing herself to concentrate on something besides his face. *Did that sound flippant?* she wondered hastily.

Adrian drew on his pipe and she was afraid she had offended him, because he didn't say anything for a long moment. "I thought," he said mildly, "you'd ask me why I'm not teaching somewhere."

Relieved, Maggie shrugged. "Well, I know what the academic job market is like, especially in English, so it's not really surprising that very talented scholars are finding jobs elsewhere."

"Thank you for the compliment," Adrian laughed, "but you ought to read some of my work before being so generous. You're right, though. Taking this job while I finished writing the dissertation was literally a godsend, because it allowed me to move back home from the East to be near my family. Your grandfather, oddly enough, was very understanding, because many of my duties aren't that demanding, and I could often get things done during the day that I might not have with a less flexible job. I finished writing the thing fifteen months after I came to work here, defended it, and promptly returned to work here." He waved his pipe in the air. "I applied for academic jobs, but I decided I'd rather write than teach, and working for this family paid well and allowed me to write."

Maggie was impressed and said so. "What are you working on now?"

Adrian's eyebrows arched quizzically. "Fiction, mostly. I tried my hand at a novel. I've got one manuscript making the rounds with the publishers, and I'm working on some short stories now." He grinned again. "If you're not careful, I'll give you a copy of my book, so you'll have to read it and say polite things about it."

She laughed. "If you're not careful, I might just take you up on it."

They both sat, quiet, Adrian smoking, Maggie staring at

the book in her lap.

Adrian broke the silence. "There's one other thing I think you should know." His tone was odd, she thought, devoid of any emotion.

"What's that?" she asked, looking at him.

"The way I found out about the job here." He stumbled to a halt.

"Was there something odd about it?" she prompted him.

Adrian shrugged. "Depends on the way you look at it, I guess. I found out about it from Claudine."

"Oh," Maggie said. Her fingers tightened on the book. "So you knew Claudine before you came to work here?"

"Briefly." He fidgeted with his pipe. "Look, I know this is going to sound bad, but there's really not that much to it. I met Claudine in a bar while I was visiting friends here on spring break. We got to talking, and we went out a couple of times. Nothing really came of it, though. We're just friends."

Maggie watched him through lowered eyelids. *What is it he's really trying to tell me?* she wondered. "Thanks for telling me." She stood up reluctantly. "Well, I guess I'd better go on upstairs."

Adrian stood up beside her, and for a moment their bodies were nearly touching. She breathed in the scent of mingled aftershave lotion and pipe tobacco and stepped back involuntarily as she started to take another deep breath. Feeling the blood rush into her face, she spoke quickly. "Well, good night. See you in the morning."

As she made a less-than-eager move toward the door, Adrian stretched out a hand to detain her, and Maggie's pulse raced a little faster. She turned back to face him. "Don't go just yet," he said, his voice low.

They were standing very close, almost touching. Hesitantly Adrian pulled her closer, and his face reached down. Pushing all her doubts aside, she met his lips with hers. As they kissed, somewhere in the back of her mind she admitted that this was something she had been wanting to happen ever since she had laid eyes on the man.

Maggie's book dropped to the floor, and her arms wrapped

around Adrian's back as she kissed him with even more enthusiasm. After a long and very enjoyable interval, she pulled away reluctantly.

"I've been wanting to do that for quite some time," he told her softly.

"So have I," she replied mischievously, surprised at her own boldness. She was usually much more reserved with men. "Let's not wait so long next time."

Adrian laughed and pulled her back for another, briefer kiss. "You have my word on that," he said as he released her.

Breathless, Maggie stooped to retrieve the book she had nearly forgotten. Clutching it firmly at her side, she said, "See you in the morning." Suddenly shy, she turned and almost ran out of the room.

"Good night, Maggie," Adrian replied. "Sleep well." He gave her one last, long look, which she failed to see as she slipped out of the room, closing the door jerkily behind her.

Her thoughts whirled as she ran up the stairs and down the long hall to her bedroom. *What was I thinking?* she chastised herself. *Girl, you're an idiot!* She sat on the bed and tried to catch her breath.

She had been in her room only a few minutes when someone knocked on the door and interrupted a very pleasant reverie. Hastily checking her face in the mirror over the elegant dresser, Maggie was relieved to see that her lips were only slightly redder than normal. Hearing another knock, she quickly went to the door. "Who is it?" she asked, her hands on the lock.

"Claudine" was the briskly offered answer. Maggie opened the door, and Claudine strode in without an invitation. From the middle of the room she turned to face Maggie.

"You and I need to talk," Claudine announced flatly. "It's time someone told you the truth about your dear grandmother."

Chapter Fourteen

"WHAT DO YOU MEAN?" Maggie demanded, closing the door behind her. She leaned back against the door and contemplated her visitor with ill-concealed curiosity.

"I mean," Claudine replied slowly, "that your grandmother wasn't the little plaster saint that everybody's been telling you she was." She sat down in one of the chairs near the French doors and motioned for Maggie to join her. After a momentary hesitation, Maggie complied with Claudine's imperious gesture.

"Well?" Maggie inquired when Claudine failed to follow up her statement right away.

"Look," Claudine said, "I just spent nearly an hour trying to calm Lavinia down, and my temper's a little frayed. I certainly don't mean to take it out on you, but this idea of yours—and Helena and Ernie who damn well ought to know better!—that Lavinia murdered your grandmother is a little too much. Lavinia's awfully upset. She has a problem with high blood pressure, and scenes like I saw tonight don't do her any good."

"No one really accused her of murdering my grandmother," Maggie pointed out in a mild tone. "I regret that she became so upset, but we were merely asking her some questions about the day of my grandmother's death. Did she tell you about that?"

Claudine nodded. "Yes, she did. Now I grant you, Lavinia and Magnolia didn't always get along too well. I was only a kid at the time, but I can remember overhearing some of their arguments. You wouldn't have thought two supposedly refined southern ladies knew such language." She leaned forward in her chair. "The point is, Magnolia and Lavinia weren't that much different. That's why they never got along too well. Your grandmother was strong-willed and didn't like it too well when someone didn't do just what she wanted."

At the moment Maggie was neutral, despite the angry tenor of Claudine's remarks. Perhaps she should have been hurt by what Claudine was saying, because, thus far, no one else had offered her such a view of her grandmother and she had built up a different mental picture from the one Claudine was forcing on her. Everyone else had talked about how well-loved Magnolia McLendon had been, with nary a whisper of ill-feeling toward her. But neither had anyone, as far as Maggie could remember, attempted to convince her that her grandmother had been, in Claudine's words, a "little plaster saint."

"Okay," Maggie replied, "so she was strong-willed and liked to have her own way. What of it?"

Claudine uttered a quick grunt of irritation. "The point I'm trying to make here is that Lavinia wasn't the only one who couldn't get along with your grandmother, despite what Helena probably told you. Before you start casting Lavinia as chief villain in your little drama, you ought to check out the rest of us."

Still cool, but definitely intrigued, Maggie replied, "I'm willing to listen, so why don't you keep talking? But I do want to ask one question—why are you so determined to defend Lavinia?"

Claudine laughed sourly. "Lavinia's capable of conducting her own defense if she can ever get past feeling sorry for herself over all this 'persecution.' I'm not really doing this for Lavinia's sake, but you just can't expect to pop into this family one day and hand out judgments without knowing the whole story—or stories, as the case may be."

"Fair enough," Maggie responded equably, though her temper was beginning to fray around the edges. "Like I said, I'm willing to hear the other stories. Are you willing to tell them?"

If Claudine was disconcerted by Maggie's forthright approach, she concealed it well. She shrugged. "Might as well, I guess, at least what I know." She challenged Maggie with a direct look. "Am I right, though, that Helena's the source of most of your information?"

Maggie nodded, and Claudine smiled in amused satisfaction. "Then we might as well start with her. Helena did get along with your grandmother pretty well, because Helena always did exactly what Magnolia told her to. Until your grandmother died, Helena wouldn't've gone to the bathroom by herself unless someone told her it was okay. She's a lot different these days—practically liberated in comparison—but as long as your grandmother was alive, Helena was the meekest creature on earth. She never spoke until someone spoke to her, and even then she had very little to say. Your grandfather didn't have much patience with her, so he let Magnolia run her life for her, and believe me, back then someone needed to. If Helena had been left on her own, she would have messed things up royally."

Does Claudine know about the pregnancy and the child given up for adoption? Maggie wondered. *Could this be what she referred to? Surely she must know,* she argued to herself. *Everyone in the family seemed to know everyone else's secrets, so why should Claudine be any different?*

But, in case Claudine didn't know, how could she ascertain this without giving away Helena's secret? Then an appalling thought struck her. Suppose Claudine meant that it was actually Magnolia, rather than Henry, who had insisted upon Helena's giving up the baby for adoption?

For the first time during this discussion, Maggie's pose of detachment began to falter. The thought that her grandmother might have connived at, or even instigated, the horrible deception practiced upon Helena sickened her.

"What do you mean by that?" Maggie demanded. "How would Helena have messed up her life?"

Claudine's lip curled. "The only man she ever got up the nerve to talk to turned out to be a con man, and Helena let things go too far and ended up pregnant. Naturally it wouldn't do for a McLendon to have an illegitimate child—at least one that everyone in Jackson knew about—so your grandfather arranged for the baby to be given up for adoption. He packed Retty and Helena off to Boston without telling anyone what his real plans were. Your grandmother was furious when she realized what had happened, because she could have persuaded Helena to think it was her own idea all along, and Helena would have been happier with the way things turned out. She could talk Helena into anything. As it was, your grandfather just made her really bitter against him."

Relieved, Maggie drew a shaky breath, causing Claudine to peer at her suspiciously. "Didn't Helena already tell you all this?" she asked.

Maggie nodded. "But, as I'm sure you'd agree, it's necessary to hear confirmation from other sources. After all, that's your purpose, isn't it?"

"I suppose so," Claudine conceded, clearly uncertain whether she ought to be offended by the tartness of the remark.

"What about some of the others?" Maggie continued. "Harold, for instance."

Claudine laughed. "This has never been a real liberal household, so I bet you can guess how much your grandparents loved having a homosexual in the family. Your grandfather could never even bring himself to acknowledge the fact that his only brother was 'queer'—I think it was completely beyond his comprehension. Magnolia was usually more forward-thinking than your grandfather, but not on this issue. They didn't exactly refuse to allow Harold to come home, but they certainly didn't throw out the red carpet either. After Magnolia died, Henry just didn't seem to care anymore, and we saw Harold a lot more after that."

Claudine's revelations convinced Maggie that it was even more important now to have a long talk with Harold. What Claudine had told her didn't convince her that Harold had had a strong motive to murder his brother and sister-in-law. But hearing his recollections of the past would certainly offer a different perspective on the two deaths, and every bit of fresh insight into the problem might lead that much more quickly to a solution.

"Anybody else who had a reason to dislike my grand-mother?" Maggie asked.

"Retty." Claudine stretched in her chair. "Retty's husband died when I was still a small child, and he didn't leave Retty and their son too well off. Retty's son, Lionel Junior, hadn't been married very long then—he got married while he was still in college. When Lionel Senior died there wasn't enough money left for Lionel Junior to finish college, much less support a wife, so Henry stepped in and took over. Lionel finished college and went on to law school, and Henry took him into the law firm when he graduated. Retty had to sell her house, so Henry insisted she move back in with the rest of the family here.

"Retty has always been the exact opposite of Helena. She's got at least two opinions on everything, and she'll tell you what they are without any prompting. Back when she first moved in here permanently, she was also used to running her own house, and it didn't set too well with her to have to step back and be a permanent guest in someone else's house. She kept trying to interfere with the way Magnolia ran the house, always bringing up her 'little ideas' for improvements. She nearly drove Mother crazy, trying to get her to do things behind Magnolia's back. Finally, your grandfather put his foot down when Retty and Magnolia had it out one day after a Ladies' Guild luncheon here. From that point on, Retty barely spoke to Magnolia."

Thus far Claudine had talked about Lavinia, Helena, Harold, and Retty. Sylvia, of course, had been much too young at the time to be considered seriously as a suspect in Magnolia's death. Sylvia's parents had died about a year before Magnolia, if Maggie remembered correctly what Helena had told her. That left two people unaccounted for.

"What about my grandfather?" Maggie asked.

This time Claudine was disconcerted and showed it. "What do you mean?"

"Just what I said," she responded impatiently. "What about my grandfather? Was he as devoted to my grandmother as everyone has said?"

Claudine nodded emphatically. "That's the one thing you could bank on. He was as strong-willed as she was, and they had their arguments, mostly over your father, but they adored each other."

"Okay," Maggie replied, impressed by the force of Claudine's assurance. "That leaves us with one person—you. How did you get along with my grandmother?"

"Oh," Claudine laughed uneasily. "I was the poor little bastard child, grateful for crumbs from the family table." She looked impishly at Maggie, registering the distaste she saw in her cousin's face. "Yes, cousin dear, I had a delightful childhood. Kinda like one of those Victorian governesses in those books your grandmother was always having me read. They never really could decide, your grandparents, just how I fit into the family. I was family, but my mother was an uneducated servant, of all things, so they settled on tolerating having me around, as long as I didn't overstep any boundaries." She laughed again and couldn't quite keep the bitterness out.

Maggie didn't know how to respond. Claudine had spoken flippantly, but underneath the indifferent exterior the woman obviously spoke from long-harbored feelings. Commiserating with her would probably seem patronizing, Maggie thought, so she said nothing at the risk of seeming insensitive.

Abruptly Claudine stood up. "One more little bit of advice, cousin. Though I don't think you're going to appreciate it."

"What's that?" Maggie said.

"Stay away from Adrian. He's gorgeous, and he's a smooth talker." Bitter self-reproach twisted her face into an ugly mask. "I should know. Oh, he'll be interested in you, no doubt about that. You're attractive, and now you're probably going to be rich, once they've read Henry's will. Just the way Mr. Smooth Talk likes them."

Stunned, Maggie stared up at her.

"You and your father are real happy now, I guess." Claudine bared her teeth.

"What do you mean?" Maggie asked, her teeth clenched.

"All the money you're going to inherit," Claudine said. "Money that you didn't earn, like the rest of us did, living here year after year, taking orders from that old tyrant."

"Get out," Maggie said. Cold rage swept through her. If Claudine remained in her room a moment longer, Maggie didn't know what she would do. She thought of several nasty things she could say, but she restrained herself. The whole episode had sickened her completely.

Claudine backed away as Maggie stood. Slowly she walked toward the door, opened it, then pulled it shut behind her.

Trembling now from the aftereffects of the confrontation with Claudine, Maggie walked with shaky steps toward the door and locked it. Then she went into the bathroom and checked to make sure that the door there was locked as well. Suppressing the urge to vomit, she instead made her preparations for bed, her mind numb for the moment.

Once the room was dark and she was snuggled into the bed covers, she tried to relax. She felt as if she'd been stripped naked. Part of Claudine's hateful remarks she recognized for what they were: jealousy. But a small part of her couldn't stop acknowledging that Claudine just might be right about Adrian's interest in her. Why else would such an attractive man display such an obvious interest in her, and at a time like this? And she had played right into his hands. She called herself all kinds of fool, holding the tears back with fierce determination. Finally, she willed herself to think about something else.

Instead, she focused on the other things Claudine had told her. Claudine's information gave her a more rounded view of the people in the household at the time of Magnolia McLendon's death. But Claudine's evidence, if one could call it that, needed verification. Maggie was reluctant to approach Helena for this purpose. She decided Ernie might be more frank with her.

Desperately though she tried, Maggie couldn't block Claudine's words from her mind. Her mind leaped back and forth from question to question. Other people besides Lavinia had disliked Magnolia, if Claudine was to be believed, and

Maggie had to admit now that Lavinia had had no more compelling motive to murder her sister than had other members of the household. Or had she?

Restless, Maggie wiggled around in the bed, never getting quite comfortable. She spent a miserable night, occasionally dozing for a brief spell, but always coming out of the doze before it turned into restful sleep. She gave up as the dawn began to penetrate into her room. Glancing at the clock, she saw with dull eyes that it was barely six o'clock. Pushing aside the bed covers, she decided she might as well get up and get dressed. The idea of an early morning walk appealed to her. Just getting out of the house for a little while would be refreshing.

Dressed in jeans, jersey, and tennis shoes, Maggie left her room and headed for the staircase. "I hope I can get out the front door without setting off an alarm," she muttered to herself in the eerie, early-morning silence of the vast house. The hall was dimly lighted, but the light grew stronger as she approached the stairs. The sun coming through the large glass panels on either side of the front door would offer more than enough light for her to make her way down the stairs.

At the head of the staircase she jerked to a stop. The rising sun had indeed illuminated the stairs. Soft, glowing light poured in upon a scene which Maggie desperately wished were a bad dream. Moving carefully and quickly down the stairs, she stopped to kneel beside a nightgown-clad figure lying near the bottom. The lifeless head lay at a drunken angle on the bottom step.

Lavinia Culpeper was dead.

Chapter Fifteen

THE BLOOD POUNDED BLINDINGLY in her head as she stooped over Lavinia's lifeless body, and for a moment Maggie feared she would faint. She sat down on the stairs next to the body and put her head between her knees. Her feelings of panic began to subside, and she lifted her head again, praying—vainly, she knew—that there would be no dead body in view.

Hastily Maggie averted her gaze from the eye which glared at her, even in death. Shaky, she stood up and moved down the stairs and around the body. Somewhat disoriented, she couldn't think what to do next. "Phone," she muttered aloud. There was a phone in the entertainment room.

Underneath the phone she found a list of house extension numbers similar to the one in her bedroom. Scanning the list, she found Adrian's number and punched in the two digits, not stopping to analyze why she was turning to him, rather than to her father in this moment of crisis. The phone buzzed three times in her ear, then he answered with a gruff "hello."

"Adrian," Maggie said, her throat so dry she had to struggle to form the words. "Lavinia's dead."

"What the hell?" Adrian squawked into her ear. "Where are you?"

"She's at the bottom of the front stairs. Can you come?"

"Of course! Be right there." The phone clicked in Maggie's ear.

She wanted to wait for Adrian where she was, but she chided herself for being foolish. She had nothing to fear from a dead body. Still, once she neared the stairs, she stayed to one side, where she wouldn't have to look at Lavinia's body.

Though the interval seemed much longer to Maggie, barely

a minute passed before Adrian joined her. He came from somewhere behind her, and not down the stairs, so his room must be, she thought inconsequentially, in the back of the house. His hair rumpled, he was dressed in jeans and an old jersey which sported an Ivy League logo.

He knelt beside the body and felt for a pulse on the side of the neck. Getting no response, he stood up and walked back to where Maggie stood, around the corner of the stairs. The grim expression on his face frightened her a little. "This is insane!" he muttered.

Maggie nodded, and Adrian pulled her into his arms. But as she stood there, his arms around her, hers around him, she heard Claudine's voice in her head. Awkwardly, Maggie pulled away, not looking at him.

"I'd better call the police," he said, watching her in puzzlement. "Will you be okay?" Silently, she nodded. He moved toward the entertainment room, and she followed, unwilling to remain alone with the body. She waited nearby while he called the police.

After a brief conversation Adrian replaced the receiver in its cradle. "They'll have someone here in a few minutes, and they'll notify Latham also."

Maggie shivered. "I hope no one else wakes up for a while. I wouldn't want anybody else to walk into it the way I did."

"Lavinia was usually the only one up this time of the morning." Adrian shook his head. "She got up every morning at five-thirty. I think she liked to have the house to herself in the morning. I'm not usually up until six-thirty, and nobody else makes it down before seven-thirty or eight most mornings." He made a move in her direction, but she stepped back, casually, and he stopped in his tracks.

"So," Maggie said, forcing herself not to give in to the slightly hurt look on his face, "everyone knew she was always up early, and that this would be the perfect time to push her down the stairs without waking anybody else."

"We don't know that she was pushed," Adrian pointed out gently. "Maybe she fell." His voice trailed off as he observed the skeptical look on her face.

"An accident would be just too much of a coincidence right now, don't you think?"

"You're right, I guess," Adrian conceded. "You need something warm to drink. Let's go to the kitchen, and I'll make you some hot chocolate, or coffee, or whatever you want."

"Thanks," Maggie replied. "That sounds like a good idea." She followed him out of the room, seeing his shoulders slumped. She wanted nothing more than to reach out to him, to pull him close for comfort, for both their sakes, but Claudine's poison had done its work.

Miserably, she trod down the hall behind him. She tried not to gape at the sight of the kitchen, which was three times the size of her own kitchen in Houston. Adrian seated her at a small table on one side of the room while he rummaged in the pantry for the instant hot chocolate mix, since Maggie expressed a preference for it rather than coffee.

The mix found and the water put on to boil, Adrian was about to sit down with her when a bell rang somewhere nearby. "Front door," he explained, then insisted that she remain to fix her chocolate while he admitted the police.

Left in the solitude of the kitchen, decorated in cheerful yellow and pristine white, Maggie began to feel some distance from her grisly discovery. Once she left the warm confines of the kitchen, the oppressive feeling of fear would return, but for now she was determined to enjoy her few minutes of calm.

The water was boiling, and she stirred the powdered chocolate into a mug of the steaming liquid. The warmth of the mug comforted her, and she blew into it, taking a tentative taste. For a few precious minutes she sipped at her drink, letting the warmth spread through her body. Then Adrian appeared in the kitchen doorway and motioned for Maggie to follow him.

She caught up with him in the hallway. "Latham is on his way," he told her. "The officer who's in charge at the moment wants us to wake everyone and ask them to come down to the kitchen by the back stairs. Latham wants to question everyone as soon as possible." He led her to the back stairs, which she had not known existed.

Emerging from the staircase on the second floor, Maggie paused for a moment to get her bearings, then realized that they were at the opposite end of the long hallway from her bedroom.

"I'll wake Harold and your father," Adrian said. "Why don't you wake Ernie first, and ask her to help you with the others?" He pointed out Ernie's bedroom. Maggie nodded and he left her.

Ernie answered Maggie's knock promptly, unlocking the door to admit her young cousin. Maggie tried not to goggle at the elaborate silk kimono Ernie was wearing, but the garishly bright colors distracted her momentarily. Then, collecting her thoughts, she launched into a brief explanation, and Ernie, much to Maggie's relief, didn't waste time with needless questions. She offered to waken Retty and Claudine, while Maggie went to rouse Helena and Sylvia, Ernie having pointed out where the latter's room was.

Some fifteen minutes later, the family had gathered in the kitchen. Shock, distress, distaste—these were some of the emotions Maggie identified in faces as she observed her family members. But no real sign of grief anywhere. Retty seemed to be taking it hardest of all. Her skin was chalky white, and Maggie feared she would collapse at any moment. Sylvia sat next to her grandmother at the kitchen table, gently rubbing one of the old woman's hands in her own and urging her to drink the hot chocolate Maggie had provided. With trembling hands Retty lifted the cup to her lips and drank while her eyes darted around the room.

Gerard stood over the burbling coffeemaker. Maggie reached an arm around his waist. "Are you okay?" she asked.

He smiled grimly. "I should be asking you that. I'm still in such a daze I haven't even stopped to think how you're feeling." He returned her hug, so strongly that Maggie had to pull slightly away from him. As she looked into his face, she saw tears in his eyes.

"Lavinia could be a great aggravation," he whispered, "but she didn't deserve that." He drew a shaky breath. "When I was a child, she'd play games with me for hours on end. Later on, we grew apart, but I've never forgotten how much I loved her when I was small."

Maggie felt tears prick at her eyelids. Thus far she had managed to avoid thinking about Lavinia's death in personal terms, but now that someone was demonstrating actual grief at the woman's death, the sadness of the situation touched her. To die with so little regret expressed at one's passing was very sad indeed.

Arthur Latham chose that moment to appear, and the first person he wanted to question, naturally, was the one who had discovered the body. Maggie followed him out of the kitchen, casting a shy glance back at Adrian, who smiled uncertainly at her.

Latham had chosen Henry McLendon's study again as his base of operation. He motioned Maggie into a chair and, with no preliminaries, asked her to describe the events of the morning.

"Well," she began slowly, "I didn't sleep very much last night, so when I could see that the sun was coming up, I thought I might as well get up and get dressed. I glanced at the clock and it was just a minute or two past six. It took me only a couple of minutes to get dressed, and then I headed for the stairs. I was going to go out for a walk around the house—anywhere, so long as it was out." She drew a deep and steadying breath. "When I reached the top of the stairs I looked down, and there was a body lying sprawled across the steps near the bottom of the staircase. For a moment I was so shocked I couldn't focus, and I didn't realize who it was—except that it was a woman—until I got closer."

Latham nodded as Maggie paused. She clasped her hands together in her lap and continued. "I knelt down beside . . . her, and I could tell that she was dead, her head was at such a strange angle. Then I thought I was going to faint, so I sat down beside . . . beside the body and put my head between my knees. When the dizziness passed I got up and tried to think what to do next. The only thing I could think of was 'phone,' so I went into the entertainment room and called Adrian. He came and looked at the body, then we went back to the phone to call the police. After that, we waited in the kitchen until some of your men arrived. Adrian said that Lavinia was usually the only one up this early, so we just left everything the way we found it . . . er . . . her till the police got here."

"You didn't hear anything? Nothing—a scream, say—woke you up?" Latham asked.

"No," Maggie replied. "That's the strangest thing about it all. I wasn't sleeping very soundly. But my room is quite a way down the hall from the staircase. Even if she had screamed, I might not have heard anything."

"You're probably right. Well, we certainly do appreciate your presence of mind for not disturbing anything," Latham responded. "Although I know it would have been a terrible shock for anyone else to come along and stumble across what you yourself did." He stood up. "I think that will do for now, Miss McLendon. We may ask you to sign a statement later, of course."

Maggie remained seated, and Latham eyed her curiously. "If you don't mind, sir, I have a question."

Frowning, he sat down. "Okay, but there's no guarantee I can—or will—answer it."

She nodded impatiently. "Of course. My question is this— is there any way that Lavinia's death was nothing but an accident?" She herself didn't believe it, but she wanted to hear an expert opinion.

Latham watched her for a moment before answering. "There's always a chance in a situation like this, but from what I saw I think an accident was highly unlikely."

"Why?"

Latham shrugged. "The gown she's wearing is only ankle length, so I doubt she tripped over it. Ditto for the short housecoat she's wearing. Her slippers have the kind of soles that don't slip too easily on any surface. Now, she could have lost her balance somehow. I know she suffered from high blood pressure, and maybe she suffered a stroke at the top of the stairs." He shrugged again. "That's a distinct possibility, and we won't know for sure until the coroner takes a look at everything. But it just doesn't look like an accident to me. Satisfied?"

Maggie ignored the ironic tone of his question. "Do you think she was murdered?" she asked.

Latham clearly didn't quite know what to make of her insistent questioning. With exasperation in his voice, he replied, "It's a distinct possibility, I'd say, since one murder has already taken place in this very house. Do *you* think it was murder?"

Uncomfortably she nodded. The moment she had been anticipating had come. "Yes," she responded flatly, "I do."

"And why, pray tell?" Latham was rapidly losing patience with her, but Maggie's answer quelled his unrest.

"Because my grandmother was murdered in the same way twenty-five years ago."

"What?" Latham nearly leaped out of his chair. "I think you have a little explaining to do." He settled back in his chair to listen.

Tiredly, patiently, Maggie outlined the theory which she, Helena, and Ernie had devised to account for the murder of Henry McLendon. For the moment, however, she did not divulge the various family secrets she had learned, stressing instead the unusual circumstances surrounding the death of Magnolia McLendon twenty-five years before. Latham could probe for the reasons later if he decided that their theory of the murders was the correct one.

Once Maggie had finished her recital, Latham regarded her in silence for perhaps two minutes. "That's a very plausible theory," he admitted with grudging respect. "Very plausible. But now your chief suspect is dead and, as you pointed out, died in the same manner as your grandmother. What now?"

"I think you are in a better position to follow that up right now," she pointed out with gentle irony.

Latham stood up again. "Right you are. Send Worthington next, will you? And for now, please remain in the kitchen with everyone else—but don't talk about our conversation. This shouldn't take too much longer."

Thankfully Maggie left him and made her way back to the

kitchen. As she pushed open the door, she was surprised to hear the sounds of slightly raised voices. Claudine was standing over Retty, still seated at the kitchen table. "Well?" Claudine demanded angrily. "Are you going to tell us or not? What were you and Lavinia arguing about last night?"

For a long moment no one moved or spoke, and Maggie watched silently from the doorway. As she observed the direction of Claudine's gaze, Maggie realized that Claudine had been speaking to Sylvia, and not to Retty.

"I think you're forgetting yourself!" Retty spoke in a sharp voice, anger bringing animation and color back into her face. "You have no right to speak to my granddaughter like that!"

"It's not likely I could forget myself," Claudine said mockingly. "You've never let me, in all the years I've lived in this house! But your precious granddaughter has some explaining to do, so let her get the hell on with it!"

Retty wilted at this onslaught, and everyone waited to hear Sylvia's answer.

The expression on Sylvia's face betrayed her wretchedness. *What on earth can be the matter?* Maggie wondered. *What does she know?*

"Well?" Claudine demanded impatiently. "Answer me!"

Sylvia expelled an angry breath as she stood up to face Claudine. "If you really have to know, we were arguing over medicine. Lavinia called me last night about ten-thirty and asked me to come to her room. I went, and she told me she was having a terrible time getting to sleep. Her nerves were completely shot, and she wanted me to give her something to help her sleep."

"So what was the argument about?" Claudine asked less forcefully when Sylvia paused.

"Lavinia insisted," Sylvia continued, "that I give her a whole bottle of tranquilizers. I had offered her one of the mild ones the doctor prescribed for me, but she wanted a whole bottle, God knows why. When I kept on refusing to give it to her, she got angrier and angrier and started shouting at me. I finally just put a couple of tablets on her bedside table and left. There wasn't anything I could do with her, the state she was in. I figured if I left, she'd settle down a little, take the two pills, and have a good night's sleep." She sat down again, her last words thrown defiantly in Claudine's face.

"Thanks," Claudine said laconically, but Maggie could tell from Claudine's expression that she was disturbed by Sylvia's answer. Maggie was disturbed also. What had Lavinia wanted with a whole bottle of tranquilizers? Had she intended to commit suicide? Maggie shuddered, then had to stifle a scream when a hand fell heavily on her shoulder.

Turning swiftly, she saw that the offending hand belonged to Arthur Latham. "Sorry," he muttered, none too contritely, as she scowled at him. "I didn't mean to startle you, but I've been waiting for Worthington. What's going on?" He moved past her into the kitchen.

Latham looked around the room, but no one volunteered an answer. Sylvia stood up. "I guess I have something to tell you." She shrugged. "I don't know whether it has any bearing on what happened, but that's for you to decide."

"Well, then, if you'll come with me, we'll try to figure that out." Latham spoke calmly enough as he turned to leave the kitchen, but from the telltale redness in his face, he seemed more than a little irritated, Maggie thought.

Once Sylvia had followed the policeman out of the room, Maggie moved to stand beside Ernie. Retty, Maggie was glad to see, had regained something of a more normal color in her face, but she still seemed shaky after her outburst. Helena had taken Sylvia's place beside the older woman, and she spoke to her sister comfortingly. The others remained silent. Claudine stood somewhat to one side, aloof from the rest, a frown of deep concentration between her brows.

Ernie gave Maggie a welcoming smile which quelled some of her jitters. "How was it?" she asked in an undertone. "With Arthur, I mean?"

Maggie shook her head lightly. "Not so bad, really. He was very interested in some of the things I had to say."

Ernie cocked her head interrogatively to one side. "Such as?"

Maggie grimaced as she glanced around the room. "I can't

really go into it all right now, but I'll tell you more about it later. Okay?"

"Okay, I guess, but you've sure made me curious."

"What are you two whispering about?" Gerard asked as he came to stand beside his daughter. His tone was light, but Maggie knew he wanted a serious answer.

"Oh, Ernie was asking me about my 'interrogation,' and I told her that it wasn't too bad," Maggie replied. More than this she didn't want to say, because she didn't want to involve her father more than was necessary at this point in her theorizing about the murders.

Gerard raised one eyebrow skeptically, a gesture that many of the undergraduates in his English literature survey courses found devastating, but Maggie wasn't intimidated. She gazed back at her father unrepentantly, and he sighed. She wondered idly where the cook and the daily help were, then realized that Adrian, or someone, had probably called and told them not to come in today. *Not that any of them probably wanted to,* she thought dispiritedly.

Thereafter very little conversation disturbed the quiet of the room as each waited his or her turn to be called for questioning at varying intervals. After Adrian returned from his interview, he busied himself by cleaning up around the kitchen. Occasionally someone moved to the stove or to the refrigerator to replenish a cup of coffee or a glass of orange juice.

Gradually the family left the room, one by one, Latham having decided that they could return to their rooms, until only Gerard was left with Maggie and Adrian. Still they remained quiet under the watchful gaze of the policeman Latham had stationed in one corner of the kitchen. Ernie returned to give Gerard his summons. As he left, she turned to Maggie and Adrian.

"I don't know about you two," she said briskly, "but I have a feeling the rest of the family might be interested in a little breakfast pretty soon. And even if they're not interested, we all need a good, hot meal."

Adrian nodded. "You're right. I suppose it's okay with the

police?"

Ernie laughed. "I expect Arthur Latham wouldn't turn up his nose at some scrambled eggs and bacon right about now, so I don't think we'll have any problem with the police." She started looking through cabinets and drawers, hunting for suitable pans and utensils. "Well? Are you two just going to stand there, or don't you know how to cook?"

"Yes, ma'am!" Adrian saluted smartly, then guided Ernie to the hiding place of the cooking utensils she sought. In only a few minutes the three were busily engaged in brewing more coffee, scrambling eggs, frying bacon, and toasting bread. Half an hour later, when Adrian went to the kitchen phone to begin summoning the rest of the family to the breakfast table, Maggie's mouth was watering. She hadn't really expected to be hungry, but she was.

The rest of the family, once they had assembled in the dining room, made no demur about tucking into the plain but hearty breakfast that the three chefs had assembled. Keeping their mouths full obviated the necessity of having to talk about Lavinia's death, and no one seemed anxious, at least for the moment, to delve any further into that particular mystery. Maggie from time to time glanced furtively around the table, and several times she caught Ernie doing the same thing, but for the most part everyone kept eyes firmly focused on plates.

Retty was first to break the silence. "Does anyone know," she asked, her voice old and small, "what effect this all is going to have on the funeral this afternoon?"

"I can answer that, I believe," Arthur Latham said from the doorway. He and his men had declined the offer of breakfast. He advanced into the room, fully aware that he had everyone's attention.

"Well?" Gerard spoke tersely, eyeing his old friend in none too friendly a manner.

Inclining his head in Gerard's direction, Latham spoke. "I think you ought to go right ahead and hold the funeral and everything as planned."

"Right." Gerard stood up, throwing his napkin down on his

empty plate. He stalked out of the room, and Maggie stared after him in astonishment. What had happened that morning—besides Lavinia's death, of course—to make her father behave this way? Normally, he kept his temper under better control, but obviously he was annoyed about something.

Latham watched Gerard's departure sardonically, then turned back to the rest of the family.

Maggie pushed her chair back from the table, determined to find out what was bothering her father. Hastily she apologized to Ernie for not staying to help clear the table.

"It's okay," Ernie assured her. "You go see what's wrong with Gerard."

Maggie made her way to the back stairs, not feeling quite up to returning to the scene of Lavinia's death yet. She tried her father's bedroom first, and with some relief she heard a gruff "Who is it?" in response to her knock.

She opened the door and stuck her head inside. "Just me. Can I come in?"

Gerard turned from his rigid stance in front of the French windows and replied tersely, "Of course. What's up?"

"That's what I wanted to ask you," Maggie said as she closed the door behind her.

"Oh, not much," he responded in a bitter tone. "Except for the fact that Arthur thinks I murdered my father—and Lavinia, too, by the way."

Maggie sank down on Gerard's unmade bed. "Why does he think you're responsible?" she managed to ask calmly.

"Because," he said tiredly, "Father told me that afternoon that he was going to change his will." Bemused, he shook his head. "All those years, even though we were estranged, he left me in the will as his chief beneficiary, but he had changed his mind and was going to make someone else the chief heir. And Arthur just happened to know that."

Chapter Sixteen

MAGGIE STARED WORDLESSLY at her father. He stared back, looking defeated.

"Let's get this sorted out," she managed to say, motioning for Gerard to sit beside her on the bed. "Grandfather told you, the afternoon of the day he died, that you had been his chief beneficiary, but that he had changed his mind and he was going to make someone else his principal heir?"

He nodded confirmation.

"Well, then," she continued, "did Latham tell you how he happened to know about this?"

Gerard grimaced. "Apparently he and Lyle Levering have been holding a few things back—only natural under the circumstances, I suppose. I assume from what Arthur told me that Father did tell Levering during their phone conversation what changes he wished to make in the will—at least in broad detail—so that Levering would be prepared to discuss it all with him the next day." He rolled his shoulders tiredly. "And that's about all Arthur told me. I'm certain there's more to it than that, but obviously I wasn't in much of a position to argue for more information."

"Did he come right out and accuse you of murdering Grandfather? And Lavinia?" Maggie had to admit that the threat of disinheritance would be a hell of a motive—for someone besides her father. He might not mind having extra cash around, but he certainly wouldn't murder his own father to get it. And what motive could he have for murdering Lavinia?

"No, he never really came right out and said it, but he sure as hell suggested it," Gerard replied bitterly. "He talked about how difficult it must be to send a daughter to graduate school on a professor's salary and the costs of living in the big, expensive city." He grinned suddenly. "I think if I'd actually told him just how much I make a year, he might have backed down a little. I haven't been teaching twenty-seven years for nothing."

"Maybe you should have done it. Although the almighty dollar sign that all this represents"—she waved her arm around vaguely to encompass the whole house—"must surely seem like a prime motive to him." She frowned. "That would explain Grandfather's death, but what about Lavinia's?"

Gerard snorted in disgust. "I have you to thank for that one. Arthur seemed rather taken with your theory about Mother's death, and he has somehow worked out that Lavinia was responsible. The way Arthur sees it, once I realized the truth about Mother's death, I pushed Lavinia down the stairs for revenge."

Appalled, Maggie stared back at him. Finally she managed to sputter, "But that's insane!"

"Not from Arthur's point of view!" Gerard contradicted her. "And you have to admit that it makes a certain mad sense."

She shook her head. "I suppose it does, but we both know it's not the truth." She took a deep breath. "I'm sorry my theorizing has made things difficult for you, Dad, but I do think I'm right about your mother's death. Lavinia's death only confirms it. It's too macabre otherwise." She shivered suddenly, and Gerard stretched an arm around her shoulders. They clung together for a few minutes.

"I'm not keen on being Arthur's chief suspect," he admitted, "but until this hellish mess is settled I guess I'm stuck. I don't know whom else he's going to find to fit the ticket."

"Doesn't it seem slightly odd to you, then," Maggie said slowly, "that Latham hasn't made any move toward arresting you? God knows I'm thankful that he hasn't," she added hastily as Gerard frowned, "but with the motive he can ascribe to you—and the opportunity—you'd think he'd have done something by now."

"I've wondered the same thing myself," he admitted, "but I think there must be something else about Father's conversation with Lyle Levering just before he died that Arthur knows and that we obviously don't. There's something holding Arthur back—certainly something other than our old friendship—and that's the only thing I can imagine it would be. Unless, of course," he added thoughtfully, "there's some scrap of evidence they found."

"Well, we definitely aren't going to leave you as his only choice for murderer," Maggie stated in defiance. "Somehow or other we're going to figure this out, and soon."

Then she thought of a question she should have considered earlier. "If Grandfather was going to replace you as his chief heir, who was going to take your place?" She looked at her father expectantly.

He shrugged. "Father didn't tell me specifically, but I gathered from his hints that it was probably going to be you."

"Oh," Maggie responded, taken aback. This was a possibility she hadn't considered—at least not too strongly. She thought furiously for a moment.

"But I should think that would dilute the strength of your alleged motive, wouldn't you say? I mean, the money would still be in the family, right?"

Again Gerard shrugged. "That's the way I'd look at it, but right now I think Arthur simply wants to have someone to ride hard, and I'm his best choice at the moment. Like I said, there's something he's holding back. What it is, and why, I don't know."

"Well," she responded, "like I said before, we're not going to let you be his only suspect." She gave her father a fierce hug.

Gently disengaging himself from Maggie's embrace, Gerard stood up. "It's nearly noon, so we'd better stop speculating and start getting ready for the funeral. Did you happen to bring anything suitable to wear?"

Her nose wrinkled in distaste. "I have that charcoal gray suit I usually wear to give papers in—I guess that'll have to do." She knew that her father would be suitably attired. He favored dark suits anyway, and more than likely he had brought a black or navy one with him. Standing up, she said, "I think I'll go take a bath." She kissed Gerard on the cheek.

"See you downstairs about one-thirty, then," he responded.

Some ninety minutes later, feeling slightly restored by her bath, Maggie met the rest of the family, all still subdued from the events of the morning, in the drawing room downstairs. There were two large and imposing black Lincolns to drive them to the church where Henry McLendon's obsequies would be held. Adrian ushered Maggie and Gerard, along with Ernie and Helena, into the car that he would be driving. Claudine drove the second car.

The church—Baptist, Maggie saw from the sign in the churchyard—was noticeably grand. Her mind was so busy chasing tangents that she observed little of the ceremony which followed. She had attended few funerals in her life since the death of her own mother, and she always attempted to block out whatever was going on around her. Today was no exception, and afterward she could recall nothing of what the minister had had to say about the life of Henry McLendon.

Once the service had ended, the Lincoln transported them to the cemetery for the interment. The day was a beautiful one, as if in denial of the grim occasion. The heat of the sun was welcome after the chilly air of the church. Again, once she was seated under the capacious tent near the graveside, Maggie resolutely thought of other things until her grandfather was at last laid to rest. Though she endeavored to keep her mind occupied elsewhere, she finally was unable to hold at bay the waves of sadness. She began quietly to cry, reaching out to her father beside her, seeking comfort from his nearness.

Emerging from under the tent, Maggie retrieved her sunglasses from her handbag. The bright sunlight cared little for the fact that her eyes were sensitive from crying. Clasping Gerard's hand once again, she walked with him back to the car, where they waited patiently for Adrian and the others to join them. A few people came up to Gerard to offer their condolences. Those he recognized he introduced to Maggie, who could never afterward remember any of their names.

There were also a number of reporters in attendance, and a couple of them accosted her and her father, asking incredibly insensitive questions. Adrian, with the help of a couple of Latham's men, got them out of the way very quickly.

When Maggie thought her nerves could stand no more, Adrian ushered them all again into the car, and in restful silence they drove home.

A sleek and powerful foreign sports car followed the two Lincolns into the driveway of The Magnolias. As the family began to mount the front steps, the sports car pulled up quietly behind the second Lincoln, and Lyle Levering emerged from the passenger side of the car. With a polite nod of greeting he followed the family into the house.

In the hallway everyone turned to look at the elderly lawyer, clearly waiting for instruction. Clearing his throat discreetly, he spoke. "As you know, I am here to discuss the provisions of Henry's will. If you will all return to the drawing room in about fifteen minutes, we'll get started."

Without waiting for their acquiescence, Levering then moved to the drawing room as the family began to drift up the stairs to their bedrooms.

By the time Maggie returned downstairs, Adrian had rearranged the chairs and small sofas in the drawing room to provide a more comfortable grouping for listening to Levering, seated at the head of the group behind a small secretary desk. Adrian had also thoughtfully provided a large pitcher of water, in addition to the drinks tray. Maggie helped herself to a glass of water before joining her father on one of the small sofas.

Almost everyone else was there. Levering fussily consulted his watch every few seconds as they waited for Helena, the last to arrive. Finally she slid guiltily into the room, casting an apologetic glance toward Levering, who remained unappeased.

"Now we may begin," he said in a pompous tone. He peered at them through his glasses, and Maggie was reminded once more of a cranky old turtle. "I'm not going to sit here and read it to you word for word, because there's no need. Any one of you who wants to may examine this later, but I can assure you—and you certainly ought to know this as well as I—that

Henry knew his own mind and the business of will-making. As do I."

He cleared his throat yet again, and Maggie wondered whether the will would prove controversial from the family's point of view. Levering's prefatory remarks had given her that impression, but then she hadn't been present at many will-readings before. Except, of course, in the pages of mystery fiction.

"First," Levering said, "Henry made arrangements for the law firm. He had an agreement with his chief partner, Terence Lackey, that Terence would, upon Henry's death, buy Henry's interest in the firm. Henry arranged it this way, since there was no family member interested in a career in law. Had he had someone to whom he might bequeath his interest in the firm, he doubtless would have done so." Here Levering glared pointedly in Gerard's direction, but Gerard returned the malicious glance with one of boredom.

"Well," the old lawyer continued with a snort, "the rest of the bequests are fairly straightforward. To Adrian Worthington, for 'his outstanding organizational abilities and his knack for always convincing me that the best ideas were my own when they were, in reality, his, and in hopes that he will pursue his literary career, the sum of one hundred thousand dollars,'"

A gasp came from somewhere in the room, and Maggie thought it might have originated with Adrian. She didn't quite have the nerve to turn around to catch the look on his face, fearing that he wouldn't appear surprised, only satisfied.

Levering continued. "To Claudine Sprayberry, niece of the late Mrs. Henry McLendon, he left also the sum of one hundred thousand dollars. To Sylvia Butler, granddaughter of his sister Henrietta, also the sum of one hundred thousand dollars. To his siblings—Henrietta, Harold, and Helena—and to his sister-in-law Lavinia, now unfortunately deceased"—here Levering peered at them with some distaste over his glasses— "Henry left the right to live in this house for as long as they live, should they so wish. He arranged that each of the aforementioned four would have access to a generous monthly income for other than the normal household expenses already provided for." Levering looked up from his papers. "Henry set aside funds for the maintenance of this house and for the continued management of the estate. And he directed that you, Mr. Worthington, were to continue in your present position as the estate and household manager for as long as you should wish." He consulted his papers again.

"In addition to providing for his siblings, Henry also stated that both Sylvia and Claudine could remain here, but upon the death of his last surviving sibling, the possession of the house should devolve upon his only son, Gerard McLendon, and in the event of Gerard's predeceasing his aunts and uncle, possession would then devolve upon his only grand-child, Magnolia Amelia McLendon."

Somewhat in shock, Maggie ignored the use of her full name, which under normal circumstances made her cringe. She had been expecting this, more or less, since her conver-sation that morning with her father, but hearing it read aloud still was surprising.

"The bulk of the estate is left to Henry's only offspring, his son, Gerard, except for the sum of seventy-five thousand dollars to the aforesaid Magnolia Amelia McLendon. This money is to be used to enable Miss McLendon to travel to European archives for research, either for her dissertation or for later projects." Levering let the papers fall lightly onto the desk. "And that is that."

Maggie found herself short of breath. Seventy-five thou-sand dollars. Seventy-five thousand dollars! She couldn't believe it. And all to be used on research trips. Why, she could spend six months, or even a whole year, in England if she wanted. The realization was staggering. It was impossible at the moment for her to sort out her feelings, but she found it somewhat difficult to reconcile such generosity with the insensitivity and even cruelty which had been imputed to Henry McLendon. A nasty little voice inside her whispered that redemption has a price tag just like anything else.

Lyle Levering stood up, shuffling his various papers

together before stuffing them in his briefcase. Slowly the family left their seats and began to move toward the door. From what Maggie could see, everyone seemed reasonably satisfied with Henry McLendon's will.

And the murderer must be satisfied, because he or she had definitely forestalled disinheritance. Of course, when the murders were eventually solved, as Maggie knew they surely must be, the murderer would have gained no benefit from the crimes. But she was convinced that the murderer's chief motive had not been a desperate ploy to avoid being disinherited. Rather the murderer had killed to avoid being revealed as Magnolia McLendon's killer.

If only I knew what my grandfather had told Lyle Levering during that fateful phone conversation! Maggie thought. The fact that Arthur Latham probably did know only frustrated her further. Having that missing bit of information would help her put a lot more of the puzzle together.

As she frowned and nibbled at the cuticle of her right thumb, she gradually realized she was alone in the drawing room. She could hear a conversation in progress as she approached the door.

". . . remarkably generous, I must say," Retty was telling Sylvia, who was guiding her grandmother toward the stairs. "Certainly more than I had expected, but then Henry really had mellowed a good bit in the last year. Ten years ago he would have left everything to fund a scholarship or to some obscure charity, and to hell with the family. Despite the way he always carried on about how important family was." Sylvia nodded silently, more intent on seeing her grandmother safely upstairs than on discussing the will.

Where did everyone else go so quickly? Maggie wondered. Sylvia and Retty, moving steadily up the stairs, were the only others present in the hall. She decided to go in search of a Diet Coke and headed for the kitchen, realizing on the way that she had never had lunch and that she was surprisingly hungry.

So, as it turned out, were the rest of the family. Adrian and Ernie were busily making sandwiches while Claudine and

Harold fixed glasses of iced tea for everyone. Gerard and Helena desultorily prepared the table.

Adrian sent Maggie into the pantry for potato chips, and soon the impromptu meal was ready. Sylvia had appeared by then to prepare a tray for her grandmother and herself. She departed quietly upstairs while the others were devoting their attention to the food.

As they ate, no one mentioned the will. In fact, apart from requests to pass the bowl of potato chips or the tea pitcher, they ate in relative quiet. Once they had finished, Adrian insisted that they all leave the kitchen to him, and no one argued.

Harold, Claudine, and Gerard left at once, but Ernie rather pointedly indicated that Maggie and Helena should follow her.

Ernie led Maggie and Helena out onto the patio near the pool. Ignoring Helena's protests that she really must change out of her black silk, Ernie motioned the other two women to seats beneath one of the huge umbrellas.

"Now we can get back to business," she said briskly. "Why do you two suppose Lavinia wanted to commit suicide?"

Chapter Seventeen

"GUILTY CONSCIENCE?" Maggie responded in a mild tone to Ernie's provocative query.

"Probably," Ernie snorted in reply. "But the important question is, what exactly was she feeling guilty about?"

"Well," Helena said, "it could have been any number of things, I suppose. Maybe she was the one who told Magnolia that Gerard and Henry were arguing. And even if she didn't push her down the stairs, she might have felt morally responsible for Magnolia's death." She squinted into the afternoon sunshine. "Of course, if she was the one who pushed Magnolia, and maybe killed Henry too, then I guess that would be enough—if she was feeling remorseful." Her tone indicated that she thought the idea of a remorseful Lavinia was a trifle far-fetched.

Ernie smiled grimly in agreement. "I think it was more likely," she mused, "that Lavinia intended to use those pills on someone else."

Maggie shook her head in doubt. "Granted you two both knew her much better than I, but from my impression of her, I wouldn't have thought she'd've been dumb enough to think she could get away with it. The pills would have been too easily traced."

Ernie and Helena nodded. "You're right," Ernie concluded reluctantly. "Lavinia was sharper than that. I guess my head needs a little clearing today, because I should've thought of that one myself."

Maggie shrugged. "Maybe so—but that leaves us with the suicide theory again. Would you have ever thought of her as the suicidal type?"

Helena spoke up quickly. "No, because she was always

too self-centered. I don't think she would've done anything like that unless she was pretty desperate."

"So we're firmly back to square one," Ernie muttered. "Was she, or wasn't she, a murderess?"

"When you say 'desperate,'" Maggie queried, responding to Helena, "do you mean because she was afraid of being convicted of murder?"

Helena nodded. "Probably so. I don't think Lavinia could've faced the thought of prison, first because of the shame, but also because of the lack of all the physical comforts she was used to."

"This is all really a moot point now, I suppose," Ernie reflected. When Maggie and Helena shot pointed glances her way, she had the grace to laugh. "Yes, I know I was the one who brought the whole thing up, but we had to talk about it at some point."

She leaned back in her chair and crossed her legs comfortably at the ankles. "I'm sure she was murdered," Ernie continued, "so we should probably concentrate on that. Though, mind you, I think the possibility of her having contemplated suicide is important."

Maggie nodded in agreement. "I think it's probably an important point, too, but for now we need to concentrate, like you said, on the fact that she was murdered."

Helena surprised both of them with a loud sniff.

Maggie noticed that her great-aunt was suddenly having trouble holding back her tears. "What's wrong?" she asked gently.

With an effort Helena regained her composure. "I'm sorry, but I was just thinking how sad it all is. Lavinia and I grew up together, did you know that?"

Fascinated, Maggie shook her head, while Ernie waited calmly to hear what Helena had to say. Maggie nodded her encouragement, and Helena continued.

"Well, our family and the Culpepers had been friendly for a long time. Lavinia's father was a businessman, though he wasn't a particularly successful one. My father, and Henry in his turn, served as old man Culpeper's legal advisors.

Lavinia and Lawrence and Harold and I all went to the same school. I was a year or so younger than the Culpeper twins, and Harold was a couple of years older. He and Lawrence were really good friends, and Lavinia and I got along pretty well—all those years ago." Helena sniffed again, and a solitary tear escaped her tightly clinched eyelid.

"Lavinia was a lovely girl, but of course Magnolia was always there, older and prettier and more vivacious. Lavinia fell in love with Henry, just like her big sister. At first I thought she was carrying on about Henry only because she wanted to annoy Magnolia, but I think she really must have meant it. She never married, after all." Helena shook her head wonderingly. "It's hard to believe—or maybe it's not—that the lovely young friend I used to have turned into the malicious old maid I couldn't stand."

Maggie reached out to pat her great-aunt's hand as Helena added, "Now I wish our friendship could have survived the way Harold's friendship with Lawrence did." Abruptly she stood up. "I think, if y'all will excuse me, I'm going to lie down for a while. I just don't have the stomach for this right now."

Ernie and Maggie murmured soothingly, and Helena left them. Ernie turned to Maggie with a sigh, once Helena had entered the house. "She always was too tenderhearted, but I have to admit it's good to see somebody mourning poor Lavinia. At least a little bit." She shook her head.

Maggie had no response to this, and for a few minutes the two women sat, staring into the gently lapping waters of the pool, stirred by a mild breeze which offered them brief respite from the late afternoon heat.

Maggie broke the comfortable silence first. "My father told me something I think you should know." Ernie's eyebrows arched in curiosity, and Maggie continued. "He says Arthur Latham thinks that Dad is responsible for both murders." Ernie snorted in derision, but Maggie kept talking. "Grandfather told Dad that afternoon that he was going to replace Dad as the chief beneficiary in his will, and Latham thinks—naturally enough, I guess—that gives Dad the best motive for murdering Grandfather. And Grandfather apparently told Mr.

Levering that he intended doing so."

"But what about Lavinia's death?" Ernie protested. "Why does he think Gerard would've killed her?"

Maggie fanned her face dispiritedly with her hand as the breeze died down. "Revenge—for having killed my grandmother."

"That makes a mad sort of sense," Ernie admitted, "but it's a little too mad to be true."

Maggie had to laugh, though not quite in amusement. "That's about what Dad said."

Ernie sat up straight in her chair. "But that means Henry could also have told Levering whom he meant to be his new chief beneficiary and whom he meant to cut out."

"Exactly." Maggie agreed. "Dad thinks that Grandfather had intended to make me his chief beneficiary, and of course I think that would lessen the motive in Dad's case, but Dad says Latham just wants somebody to 'ride hard,' and for the time being he's stuck with that."

"I suppose so," Ernie responded. "If only we could find out who it was Henry intended to cut out of his will—besides Gerard, that is," she complained. "That's got to be who the murderer is."

"You're probably right," Maggie agreed. "But unfortunately I don't think Latham is going to come running to us with the information." Her tone turned speculative. "I'd almost be willing to bet that Latham knows who the killer is, but he doesn't have any conclusive evidence that he's right."

Ernie nodded emphatically. "You just might be right."

"We'll have to keep at it the hard way—in the dark," Maggie said, "if we're going to figure this out ourselves." She leaned forward in her chair and stared into her cousin's face. "Now, there are some other things I'd like to talk to you about without Helena here."

Ernie looked suitably interested in Maggie's remark. She leaned closer in an encouraging manner. Maggie gave her a quick outline of her conversation the previous evening with Claudine. "So," she concluded, "was Claudine telling me the truth? Did everyone besides Lavinia have motives for murdering my grandmother?"

Ernie slumped back in her chair, wiping a few beads of moisture from her forehead. She took so long to answer that Maggie feared she had somehow offended her cousin.

"Frankly," Ernie said at last, "Claudine soft-pedaled it more than I would have expected her to."

"Oh?" was the only response Maggie could manage.

Ernie nodded slowly, tiredly. "I'm afraid so. I was very fond of your grandmother, my dear, but there's no denying that she was a very strong personality. Things got so bad between her and Retty that they hardly spoke to each other for five years before Magnolia died. And Helena really didn't have much of a spine in those days. She did pretty much every-thing Magnolia said. Maybe the worm finally did turn."

"What do you mean?" Maggie asked quickly.

"Well, just look at Helena these days," Ernie responded vaguely. "Nobody would call her exactly spineless these days, now would they? After Magnolia's death, she changed, became more self-assured, started offering her opinions in conversations—which she never used to do." She shrugged. "Magnolia's death liberated her, though that sounds a little extreme."

"Do you seriously think Helena might have murdered my grandmother?" Maggie asked. "We know she couldn't have murdered my grandfather; and unless we're talking about two murderers here, I don't think she's a suspect."

An odd look flitted across Ernie's normally placid counte-nance. "I don't know, but there's someone we're forgetting here. Harold."

"True," Maggie said. "What about Harold?"

"I hate to say this, because it's the one thing I disliked most about Magnolia, but she and Henry treated poor Harold pretty shabbily most of the time. She wouldn't have Harold around too much, except when there were lots of the family here, because she didn't want him to have much contact with Gerard. She was afraid, God knows why, that Harold would try something with him." Ernie's voice evinced her disgust at the thought. "Harold adored Gerard and would never,

never have done anything to harm him, but your grand-mother had a blind spot on that one issue. She could be really hateful about it, too."

"That's so sad," Maggie whispered. "That kind of willful misunderstanding is difficult to deal with."

Ernie snorted dismissively. "Call it that if you want, I call it just plain prejudice. And ignorance! Magnolia and Henry were both intelligent people, but sometimes they were damn stupid."

Maggie couldn't argue with Ernie's more honest assess-ment of the situation. "Well," she asked, "do you think Harold resented the way he was treated enough to murder?"

"Possibly" was Ernie's terse response.

"What is it?" Maggie asked, after a few moments' silence. "What's wrong?"

"Nothing, really," Ernie answered, "but I just had the most appalling idea."

Chapter Eighteen

"WHAT IS THIS APPALLING IDEA OF YOURS?" Maggie spoke more sharply than she had intended when Ernie failed to follow up her remark with an explanation.

Ernie shifted in her chair as she looked at Maggie. "Helena has always been protective of Harold, and the only times I know of that she ever crossed Henry or Magnolia were on his account. I remember hearing about an almighty fuss she stirred up one summer when Harold wanted to come for a visit before Gerard was going to be packed off to some camp. Magnolia didn't want Harold here until Gerard had left, but Helena carried on so that for once Magnolia gave in."

Puzzled by the import of this reminiscence, Maggie remarked, "That's very interesting, but I'm not really following your point here."

Ernie grimaced. "It was what you said about two murderers a couple of minutes ago. It just struck me as possible that Helena and Harold could be covering up for each other. Maybe Harold was responsible for both murders, and Helena's been protecting him." She squirmed again in her chair. "Or Helena could have killed Magnolia all those years ago, and then Harold killed Henry, and either one of them could have pushed Lavinia down those stairs. They knew her habits as well as anybody."

Maggie's mind worked busily as Ernie fell silent. True enough, Harold could be the killer. After all, he had readily admitted to having heard the argument between Gerard and Henry the day Magnolia had died. And, although he claimed to have seen no one else when he went upstairs to his room, he could easily have gone to his sister-in-law's bedroom to inform her of the argument in progress downstairs.

Or he just as easily could have told Helena about the argument, and then she could have gone to tell Magnolia, followed her back down the hallway, and then pushed her down the stairs.

Frowning, Maggie looked at Ernie. "It's certainly possible that either one of them could have killed my grandmother. But Harold would have to have been the one who killed my grandfather, because Helena didn't leave my side during the time when he must have been murdered."

Ernie sighed tiredly. "This is pretty revolting, having to think these things about my own family. But we know that one of them is responsible. I guess we just keep digging until we find out who."

"I have a funny feeling there's got to be something else, something we don't know about, that may be the key here." Maggie shook her head doubtfully. "I've heard various reasons people had for hating my grandparents, but so far I'm not really convinced by any one of them. From what I've heard, Helena certainly had the strongest motive to kill my grandfather, but we know she couldn't have. I still think the important thing is finding out who had the most reason to want my grandmother dead."

Ernie nodded slowly. "I agree with you, but I'm afraid you already know all the family secrets I know. There're bound to be others, but whose they are, and who'll tell them to us, I don't know." She rolled her head back on her neck, attempting to ease the tired muscles. "Helena and Harold have always been close, but I'd be willing to bet there are things they've never told each other, and Retty's pretty close-mouthed, too. The same with Claudine and Sylvia. I just don't know that much about them."

"Do you think it would do any good for you to talk to Helena?" Maggie asked.

Ernie's eyes rolled back. "I don't know, but I suppose I can try."

"If you'll talk to her, then," Maggie said, standing up, "I'll try Harold. We can tackle Retty together."

Ernie waved her agreement as Maggie started walking

toward the house. "I'll be there in a little while," Ernie called after her.

Maggie was glad to exchange the humidity for the air-conditioned comfort of the house. She hadn't realized how warm she had become until she stepped into the dark coolness of the house. She decided she needed liquid refreshment before she attempted to coerce Harold into sharing further family secrets with her. She headed first for the kitchen. She found Sylvia, Claudine, and Adrian seated at the table and chatting idly about some documentary on Mississippi history which Sylvia had seen the previous week.

Nodding a quick and smiling greeting in the general direction of the others, Maggie opened the refrigerator door and searched for a Diet Coke. As she was about to give up and settle for water, she spotted a glint of silver and red behind several jars of jelly and triumphantly pulled her prize from the back of the refrigerator.

Diffidently she turned toward the three at the table. Brandishing her Diet Coke, she said, "This seems to be the last one. Anybody mind if I take it?"

Adrian flashed a brief smile. "Go right ahead. There's a case in the pantry. I just need to put some in the fridge." He stood up. "Might as well do it now. If I don't start moving around, we'll never have dinner on time." He looked at Maggie, as if expecting something.

"Need some help?" Claudine asked quickly. "You know I'm not much of a cook, but I can slice, dice, peel, or whatever." She smiled. "I'm a good assistant.

"Sure." Adrian said. He smiled, but to Maggie he looked disappointed. She felt awkward. Had Adrian wanted her to offer to help? Should she offer to pitch in now?

But, she told herself sternly, *you've got to talk to Harold, and you can't put it off any longer.* She was torn, but she decided that she'd be better off talking to Harold.

"Anybody know where I might find Harold?" she asked before Sylvia made it to the door.

"He's probably in his room," Adrian answered her. "He likes to read in the afternoon. I'm sure he wouldn't mind an interruption, if you want to talk to him."

"Thanks, I do," Maggie replied with a smile. "See you later." She followed Sylvia out the door as Adrian and Claudine began inspecting the contents of the meat drawer of the refrigerator.

Sylvia said nothing as Maggie quietly followed her to the front staircase. Observing the look of intense concentration on her cousin's face, Maggie was loath to disturb her thoughts, but she was concerned—and curious—to know what was exercising Sylvia's mind.

"Sylvia," Maggie said hesitantly as they began mounting the stairs. She had to repeat her cousin's name in a louder tone to catch her attention.

"Sorry," Sylvia smiled, tiredness making her look even more fragile than usual. "I'm afraid I'm not very good company right now." She halted where she was, about halfway up the stairs, and Maggie paused beside her.

"Are you worried about your grandmother?" Maggie queried in sympathy.

Sylvia nodded. "She's taking all this pretty hard." She grimaced. "I guess we all should, but to be honest, I was never that fond of either Uncle Henry or Lavinia. Grandmother wasn't either, most of the time, but Uncle Henry was her twin brother, after all."

Maggie squeezed Sylvia's arm comfortingly. "I'm glad she's got you to look after her. She's in good hands."

"Thanks," Sylvia smiled wanly. She started again up the stairs. "I know we'll all feel a lot better when this is settled. I just wish it were over now. I'm not sure how much more Grandmother can take."

I wonder, Maggie thought slowly, *whether Retty knows who the murderer is, but can't bear to do anything to convict her brother or sister as a murderer. Or,* her thoughts continued, *she's terrified that she's going to be found out herself.*

At the top of the stairs Maggie quickly asked Sylvia to point her to Harold's room, and Sylvia obliged. "It's the room right across from Lavinia's."

Sylvia knocked gently at the first door on the left, her

grandmother's room, while Maggie continued slowly to the end of the hall to Harold's room. She gave an involuntary shiver as she looked toward Lavinia's door. Resolutely she turned her back and knocked firmly on Harold's door.

In the ensuing silence Maggie began to think that Harold was after all downstairs somewhere, but then the door swung inward without warning, and Harold peered out at her.

His face cleared when he recognized his visitor. "My dear," he exclaimed, as he swung the door wide open, "this is a pleasant surprise. Do come in." He stepped aside to allow her to enter.

"I hope I'm not disturbing you," she said, half hoping he would tell her that she was.

"Not at all. Not at all!" Harold ushered her farther into the room and seated her in a comfortable chair near the window. He sat in the companion chair on the other side of a small table standing between them. He pushed a small crystal coaster toward her, and she set her Diet Coke can down on it.

Maggie glanced around the room, registering with approval the quiet good taste with which it was furnished. Here there was no suffocating Victoriana like she had seen in Lavinia's room, nor the bizarre eclecticism in Helena's, but a cool and stylish simplicity which gave the room an air of space and a surprising amount of comfort. She liked the subdued colors of cream, brown, and gold, livened here and there with touches of a vivid green.

One wall, as in her room, was lined floor to ceiling with bookshelves. As always, Maggie itched to inspect the books, but for now she had to concentrate on the point of her visit.

Harold had been watching patiently, smilingly, while she let her eyes roam around the room. "Retty is responsible for the decor," he said. "Do you like it?"

"Very much," Maggie replied. "It's certainly different from Hel—" she trailed off awkwardly, realizing what she had almost said.

Harold laughed. "I would never let Helena decorate my room for me, if that's what you're thinking. I do love her, but she has no taste when it comes to furnishing a room." He laughed again, and Maggie joined him.

"I'm very happy," Harold continued, and his voice assumed a serious tone, "that you and Gerard have finally come home. But I certainly wish the circumstances could have been happier."

Maggie indicated her soft drink. "Would you think me rude if I drink? I've been sitting outside talking with Ernie, and my throat's a little dry." At Harold's quick nod, she took a sip from her drink. Then she addressed Harold's remark.

"It has been very distressing, I must admit, because I knew practically nothing about all of you before now, and these certainly aren't the best circumstances for getting to know the family." She paused, and Harold smiled his encouragement at her. "But I think something—not necessarily murder, though—was bound to happen once my father came home."

"What do you mean?" Harold asked, startled.

Maggie took another sip from her drink before replying. "Has Helena told you anything about the theory that she, Ernie, and I have come up with?"

"That Magnolia was murdered, and that her murderer is responsible as well for Henry's death?" At Maggie's nod, Harold continued. "We've talked about it, and I admit the idea is plausible, but it's pretty horrifying."

"Yes, it is," she agreed. "From what everyone has told me about my grandmother, I find it hard to believe that anyone hated her that much. I understand that she could be difficult at times—and perhaps overbearing—but to such an extent that someone wanted to murder her? Nothing I've heard so far has convinced me of that." She took a deep breath. "What do you think?"

Harold shifted uncomfortably in his chair. "You realize you're asking the wrong person, don't you?"

"Helena told me something about the way my grandmother treated you, and I regret that. It bothers me, because I guess I just thought any grandmother of mine should have been more enlightened than that."

Harold regarded his fingernails as he replied. "I've lived

with that particular prejudice quite a long time, and I suppose I've gotten used to it, after a fashion, but it rankles all the more when it comes from one's own family." He looked straight at Maggie, disconcerting her with the intensity of his gaze. "Being homosexual in the South when I was growing up was just as bad as, or maybe even worse than, being black. Being black was at least an act of nature, albeit a cruel one, but being homosexual was unnatural. And of course it was an unnatural choice—why would anyone want to behave in such a way?"

He spoke in a bitter tone, and Maggie at first was at a complete loss to reply, but then she realized that he didn't expect this of her. She simply nodded encouragement, and he continued.

"Helena has always accepted me just the way I am, and Retty more or less so, once I had explained it all to her. She was shockingly naive for a married woman." There was a hint of amusement in his voice for the moment. "Even so, I was always expected to be excessively discreet and to play a part—mustn't do anything to disgrace the family, you know."

There was no trace of self-pity in his voice, yet Maggie could sense the frustration behind the coolly uttered words. But had this frustration caused him to murder three members of his family?

She drained the last of her drink and set the empty can once more on the crystal coaster. The conversation had progressed rather rapidly in the direction she had wanted, but now she was uncertain how to push it further.

"I don't know," she began slowly, "whether my father has told you this, but Arthur Latham considers Dad his prime suspect right now."

Harold snorted in derision. "Arthur's just stuck without any real evidence, so he's clutching at the handiest straw available, and that's Gerard."

"Still, it's a pretty scary clutch he's got," Maggie pointed out. "And that's why I'm trying to do what I can to figure out who the real murderer is. Will you help me?"

"I'll try, certainly," Harold responded, sounding surprised

that she should doubt his willingness. "But I'm not sure what I can do." He waved one hand in the air.

Here goes nothing, Maggie thought. She plunged in. "So far I've been told a number of family secrets, and I've been trying to make sense of the whole mess, sorting out who's got a motive to do what to whom, if you follow." Harold nodded, and she continued. "Someone told me why you would have a motive to murder my grandmother—namely, that she didn't want to have you around the house with my father when he was younger. I don't really think that's much of a motive, do you?"

"Of course not," Harold laughed uneasily. "But, as I told you before in another context, you're probably asking the wrong person."

"That's as may be," Maggie commented drily. "Anyway, I'm just not convinced that it's so simple. Why, for example, was my grandmother so worried that you would . . . er . . . behave badly? Was it really sheer prejudice, or misunderstanding, on her part? My impression was that she was a little smarter than that, but nobody's saying anything."

Harold's face had lost color. Maggie sensed there was something he could tell her, something that might prove important, but what else could she say to encourage him to tell her? Stymied, she decided to wait.

"For your sake, and for your father's," Harold said at last, his voice low, "I'll tell you something that not even Helena knows. In fact, it's something no one else in the family knows. Henry probably did, but no one else, I'm sure. I'm not certain how useful this information could be, but the way things have been going the last few days, I simply don't know anymore. You can either eliminate me entirely from your list of suspects, or move me to the number one position."

Maggie waited, scarcely breathing, for Harold's revelation.

"Magnolia didn't trust me around Gerard," Harold said wearily, "because she held me responsible for seducing her baby brother."

You wanted to know, Maggie told herself sharply, *and now that you know, what do you say?*

Harold took pity upon her embarrassment. "It's quite all right, my dear," he said gently. "I think perhaps the time has come to talk about this with someone. I've kept it to myself for a long time. I've never even told Helena. Probably I should have, but I was so used to keeping some things secret that I just couldn't bring myself to tell her." He sighed deeply.

"Do you think it has any bearing on what has happened here?" Maggie asked.

Harold shrugged. "Perhaps. I don't really know. I've thought about it, and I've realized that there may be a connection. Let me tell you my story, and I'll see if you reach some of the same conclusions."

Maggie nodded.

Harold launched into his story. "Lawrence and I had been friends, as were Lavinia and Helena, in our youth. We all attended the same school, as Helena probably told you. But I was a couple of years older than Lawrence, and I went away to college while he was still in high school. At the time I had feelings for him, feelings I didn't completely understand, because I just didn't understand much at all about what I was. I was shockingly naive, though perhaps that sounds silly these days."

"Not at all," Maggie said. "It's perfectly understandable."

"In college," Harold continued, after a brief smile, "I soon discovered that I was not the only person like that, that I wasn't isolated and alone. That was incredibly liberating, I'm sure you can understand. When I would come home to the family again, during holidays, though, I felt out of place, maybe even more than before. Consequently, I made fewer and fewer visits home.

"Lawrence had also gone away to school, and I rarely saw him. When I did, I was much too shy to approach him, to tell him of my feelings, because I was so afraid of his reaction." Harold took a deep breath. "Then came the Korean War. Lawrence went into the Air Force, and I was in the Army. We didn't see each other for several years because of the war."

Fascinated, Maggie imagined a younger and more dashing Harold in uniform. Almost as if sensing her thoughts, Harold pointed toward a shelf. "There's a picture of me, taken during the war." She got up from her chair and walked over to the photograph. A young face, remarkably like her father's, peered out at her. She noted the lines of strain in the face, but the eyes were keen and alert, the body poised for action.

"Very handsome," she commented, turning with a smile to her great-uncle. "Then and now."

"Thank you, my dear," he said, his face alight with pleasure. Maggie resumed her seat, and Harold continued.

"After the war, I went back to graduate school, and Lawrence went back to college and then on to law school. Again, our paths rarely crossed. We both became caught up in our careers. I was teaching at a small university in the East, and Lawrence set up practice here in Jackson. Then old man Culpeper died, and a day later, my father died. So I came home for the funerals. The night of my father's service, Lawrence and I sat up late talking. I suppose we'd both had a bit too much to drink, and I said something. Now I can't even remember what, but then we were confessing how we'd always felt about each other. I was stunned, and thrilled, as you might imagine. We agreed to meet the next afternoon."

"What happened?" Maggie asked softly, when Harold had fallen silent.

"There's an old summerhouse out by the tennis courts," he replied. "Have you been out there yet? No, I guess not, you haven't had much time. Anyway, that's where Lawrence and I met that day. No one else in the family was much interested in tennis, and he and I did genuinely like to play. But it was a convenient site for us to meet. That day," Harold sighed, "we were just careless, so caught up in each other that we weren't thinking clearly. Magnolia walked in on us. She was looking for Gerard, who had just had yet another argument with his father about something. Gerard was fourteen or fifteen, and he and Henry were always butting heads, it seemed. Magnolia didn't find Gerard, but she did catch me and her brother in a compromising situation. That was the point at which she wanted me out of her house for good."

Harold laughed, bitterly this time. "It did no good for Lawrence to tell her that he hadn't been coerced, or even seduced. For pity's sake, we were both around thirty at the time! She wouldn't believe that her only brother was 'like that.' She blamed me completely. Years later, I think she eventually understood and perhaps forgave me, although she never really trusted me again."

"That must have been very painful for you," Maggie said, feeling inadequate.

"It was horrible," Harold said. "I had already noticed that Magnolia and Henry were having some problems. They had always seemed so happy together, but that summer, something was definitely wrong. Magnolia was angry with everyone just then, and Henry did nothing to make it better. Evidently he'd had a brief fling with someone, and Magnolia had found out about it. It took them quite a while to work through that, but they did eventually."

"Sounds like it was hell on the rest of the family, too," she observed.

"Yes," Harold smiled wryly. "Neither Magnolia nor Henry were ever ones to suffer anything alone. Anyone around them had to feel the effects, one way or another."

"What happened with you and Lawrence after that?" Maggie asked, after a brief pause.

Harold shook his head. "After that, and Magnolia's tirade, Lawrence was terrified. I know it's difficult for you to imagine, but your grandmother had such a strong personality. Lavinia would stand up to her, or at least try, but Lawrence never could. Magnolia told him what to do, and he did it. I tried to talk him into coming back east with me, but he refused. We kept in touch, but things were never the same after that."

"And only my grandmother knew about what had happened between the two of you?" Maggie asked.

Harold nodded slowly. "It wasn't something she wanted everybody to know. She told Henry, of course, but other than that, she kept quiet about it. And I never even told Helena. She may have suspected, but she's not said anything to me in all these years about it, and I didn't bring the subject up, even after Lawrence died."

"What about Lavinia?" Maggie asked, remembering that her great-aunt had told her how Lawrence couldn't keep his hands off a pretty woman. Had she known the truth about her brother?

"I don't know that Lavinia knew the truth about Lawrence and me, but she did know Lawrence was homosexual, if that's what you're asking." At Maggie's nod, Harold continued. "Both Magnolia and Lavinia found it difficult to accept, so they encouraged stories about Lawrence being a scandalous womanizer. In his letters to me, he would laugh at them behind their backs, but it didn't really bother him that much. It was useful camouflage. He never tried dating a woman. He just let the two of them talk about him as if he had. That was enough, and he went his own way."

"But what about Claudine, then?" she asked as an important point occurred to her.

"That's a good question," Harold responded, nodding approvingly. "Whatever Lavinia or Magnolia thought, Lawrence most definitely was not Claudine's father. He told me that himself."

"Why would they all have pretended he was for all these years?" With a sudden flash of insight, Maggie thought she knew the answer, but she wanted Harold to confirm it for her.

"For one thing, it gave a ring of truth to those stories Magnolia had been telling for so long about Lawrence. She'd much rather have had to tell people, albeit shamefacedly, that her brother had gotten a servant in the family way than to tell them that he was a queer." He laughed bitterly. "Lawrence didn't live very long after that for it to matter much to him."

"Who was Claudine's father, then? She certainly looks a lot like Lawrence. I saw his picture in Lavinia's room. Although," she continued, thinking back to the conversation, "Lavinia did say Claudine looked more like her own mother, Claudine's grandmother."

Harold shrugged. "To tell you the truth, back then I never

cared that much about it. I just assumed that old man Culpeper's brother was responsible, and that he had gotten poor Lorraine Sprayberry in the family way. She was very pretty, and he was the one who had trouble keeping his hands off a pretty woman, not his nephew. But nobody's ever said. As far as I know, even Claudine thinks Lawrence was her father, though she uses her mother's name, Sprayberry."

Maggie mulled this over for a moment. Harold waited in silence.

"If Lawrence wasn't her father, but there's definitely a Culpeper family resemblance, then I think that leaves one other possibility," she said slowly.

Harold nodded.

"Lavinia must have been her mother, then."

"That's what I've been thinking," Harold said.

"But who, then," Maggie wondered aloud, "is her father?"

Harold cocked his head to one side, waiting.

"Good lord!" she said, stunned, as the answer hit her. "You really think so?"

"Yes, I do," Harold said.

"That changes everything!" Maggie was flabbergasted.

"When Henry was murdered," Harold said reflectively, "I honestly hadn't given this aspect of it much thought. Just about any one of us could have murdered him, he gave us all enough cause over the years. But after Helena told me what you were thinking about Magnolia's death, I got to thinking. Then with Lavinia's death, I thought maybe it had all fallen into place."

"What were you planning to do?" Maggie said.

"Keep my mouth shut, for the moment," Harold said, making a face. "I didn't want to give anything away and get my head bashed in or get pushed down the stairs." He laughed, a bleak sound which gave Maggie a momentary chill.

"That's not going to happen again," she said firmly. "Now that you've told me all this, we can put an end to it."

"Yes, my dear, I know you will."

Maggie stood up and moved in front of her great-uncle's chair. "Thank you," she said softly as she bent down to kiss his cheek.

He sat quietly in his chair as she, empty soft-drink can in hand, left the room.

Reaching the solitude of her room, Maggie thought to check her watch. Nearly time for the evening meal. She tossed her empty can into the wastebasket in the bathroom before running a brush through her hair. After washing her face and hands, she went back into the bedroom and sat down on the bed.

She was pretty sure now that she had figured out who the murderer was, and why. But how to prove it?

It wasn't really her job to do that, of course. That was up to the police. Perhaps she should just call Arthur Latham and tell him. Let him figure out how to prove it.

That was the crux of the problem. As far as she could see, there wasn't much but circumstantial evidence linking the killer to the crime. She had no idea what evidence the police might have, however. Maybe they had something which could link the killer with the crime.

What to do?

She consulted the list of telephone extensions, figured out which room Ernie was in, then punched in the number.

She held her breath until Ernie answered.

"Ernie, it's me, Maggie. Don't ask me why, but can you call the police and get Arthur Latham here? I think we can get this over with."

Ernie squawked a bit, but she soon agreed to do what Maggie asked. "You know you're killing me with curiosity, don't you?" she grumbled at Maggie before hanging up.

"I'm trying to keep any more of us from being killed," Maggie replied. "And hopefully this is the way."

She hung up the phone and checked her watch. Just about time for dinner; she might as well head downstairs.

A few minutes later she pushed open the door to the dining room. Adrian and Claudine were standing at the sideboard. Adrian was saying, "No, for the last time, no. Forget about it, once and for all."

In their brief acquaintance, Maggie had never heard him

sound so annoyed. *What had Claudine said or done to him?* she wondered.

She cleared her throat to announce her presence.

Turning, Claudine scowled at Maggie. "What do you want?" she asked. One hand reached up nervously and plucked at the brilliantly colored scarf around her neck.

"Of course!" Maggie said, then was disconcerted when she realized that she had spoken aloud. She was so stunned by the revelation she'd just had, she lost sense of where she was and who was listening to her.

"What is it, Maggie? Are you okay?" Adrian moved toward her.

She nodded her head. "I'm fine, really." She flashed them a nervous smile. "I'm just wandering around in a daze, as always. Pay no attention to me."

"Was there something you needed?" Claudine asked pointedly.

"Dinner," Maggie pointed out, her tone as mild as she could make it. "I thought it was about time for dinner."

"Oh, right," Claudine said. She turned and walked away, through the door which led to the kitchen.

"Everything will be ready in just a few minutes," Adrian said. "Would you like something to drink while you wait?"

"Yes, thanks, don't mind if I do," Maggie said, approaching the sideboard. She helped herself to a glass of iced tea, then took it around to her accustomed place at the table, and sat down. "Okay if I wait here?"

"Certainly," Adrian smiled at her. "I'll be back in a tick, and surely the others will be down for dinner any minute now." He followed Claudine back to the kitchen.

Alone in the dining room, Maggie sipped at her tea. She had figured out what had been missing, and now she just had to steel herself for the confrontation to follow.

Chapter Nineteen

MAGGIE HAD DRUNK ABOUT HALF of her glass of tea by the time other members of the family began trickling in for dinner. Gerard came first, followed soon by Ernie and Harold. Helena came with Sylvia, who announced that her grandmother was resting in her room and wouldn't join them for dinner that night.

Just as well, Maggie thought. Retty was the one who'd likely be the most upset by what she was planning to do.

Adrian and Claudine came back from the kitchen with the last serving dishes, and soon everyone was filling plates with a variety of vegetables and cold cuts. Adrian apologized for the odd fare, but Helena assured him that this was fine.

Maggie had decided to wait until everyone had at least had a few mouthfuls of food before she put her plan into motion. Shortly after taking her seat at the table, Ernie had assured her with a quick nod that the police were on their way. Now all she had to do was settle her stomach a bit and get going.

Putting aside her fork, Maggie cleared her throat loudly. "Excuse me, everyone. If I could have your attention for a few minutes, there's something I'd like to say to you all."

Conversation ceased, and everyone looked at Maggie. She focused on Ernie's face, and her cousin's calm visage gave her courage.

"Coming home," she began, "has been much more of an ordeal than either my father or I ever expected. I've been wondering, if we had stayed in Houston, would things have happened differently? Would two lives have been spared? Maybe." She took a drink from her tea glass, pausing for time.

"This homecoming was joyful, at first. My father and my

grandfather were reconciled, after a long separation. They were each doing their best to put aside past differences, and I'm happy that I was able to meet my grandfather, however briefly, before he was so brutally murdered."

She shook her head. "I'm sorry, I know this all probably sounds unbearably pompous and self-indulgent, but there is a point, if you'll just bear with me. The thing is, in a very short period of time, I've learned all sorts of things about my family. Other than Helena, I never really knew anything about any of you before my father and I came here. And now I've learned maybe more than I wanted to know about the McClendons and the Culpepers. But I guess, like any family, we all have things we'd rather forget, secrets we'd just as soon keep out of sight forever.

"The trouble is, sometimes secrets can be dangerous. Secrets can cause resentment, and resentment can get really ugly. Even deadly. Just like it happened here. One member of this family finally couldn't stop the resentment from boiling over, and the result was that two people have been murdered."

"Are you telling us you're about to accuse someone?" Gerard demanded.

"Yes, Dad, I am," Maggie said.

"Who?" Helena asked, looking around the room.

"Yes, who, Miss McLendon?" Arthur Latham startled them all. Ernie must have left the front door unlocked for him, Maggie realized, and he had come right in and no one noticed his presence. He advanced into the room and stood at the head of the table, behind Retty's chair.

"Someone who had better cause than most to resent my grandparents and poor Aunt Lavinia," Maggie said. "Someone who was treated like a servant all her life, but who really was a part of the family, by blood. Someone whose real parents never acknowledged her, as far as I know. At least, not publicly."

"Claudine?" Helena's voice rose an octave in amazement.

All eyes in the room turned on Claudine, who sat coolly at her place at the table.

"What wonderful little fairy tale have you cooked up, Maggie?" Claudine said. "Trying to come up with a story so some other member of the family won't get the blame? Pin it on me, instead?" She shook her head. "Honey, I don't think you're nearly as clever as you think you are."

Maggie smiled, deliberately. "Maybe not. But then neither are you, *honey.*"

"Maggie, what is this?" Gerard said. "How is Claudine supposed to be a member of the family? You mean because Uncle Lawrence was her father? How does that have anything to do with this?"

"Yes, Maggie," Claudine said. "How does that have anything to do with the murder of your grandfather and my aunt?"

"For one thing," Maggie said, taking a deep breath, "Lawrence Culpeper wasn't your father."

The silence in the room was absolute.

"Why on earth would you say something like that?" Helena said impatiently. "Everyone knows he was a womanizer! Magnolia always said so. I can't remember how many times she was telling me about little scrapes he was getting himself into over some woman."

"That was deliberate on my grandmother's part, Helena," Maggie said. "She was trying to mislead you and everyone else about her brother, because she didn't want them to guess the truth."

"What on earth are you talking about?" Helena demanded.

"Lawrence was gay, like me," Harold said quietly. "He wasn't interested in women. As Maggie said, Magnolia made up all those stories because she didn't want anyone to know the truth. You can take it from me, Lawrence was not Claudine's father."

"Good lord!" Helena said. Everyone else, with the exception of Harold and Claudine, looked as stunned as Helena.

"Then who was Claudine's father?" Gerard asked. "There's no denying a family resemblance. I mean, it's clear that she's related to the Culpepers."

"That came from her mother," Maggie said, watching

Claudine closely.

Claudine sat stone-faced.

"You mean Lavinia?" Ernie asked, her voice almost squeaking in disbelief. "Good heaven above."

"Yes, Lavinia. Do any of you remember a time when Lavinia was away for a while, visiting family and friends back east?" Maggie asked.

Helena nodded emphatically. "I sure do. And if I remember correctly, it was during the time when Claudine would have been born."

They all stared now at Claudine, but still she sat, refusing to acknowledge any of them.

"Then who was her father?" Gerard asked.

"I also found out," Maggie said slowly, "that about this same time, my grandparents were going through a bad time in their marriage. They weren't getting along, and it seems that it was because my grandfather had been having an affair. My grandmother discovered it, and between them, they apparently made everyone around them miserable."

"Oh, my," Helena said in a faint voice. "I knew Lavinia was always after Henry, but I never knew she caught up with him. Heavens to Murgatroyd!"

Claudine broke her silence by laughing. "You sure have been busy. *You* should be writing fiction, instead of Adrian here. You've got a real potboiler going, you know that? This is ridiculous!"

"No, it's not," Maggie said. "I'm sure a simple blood test will help resolve this. And maybe a look at the original birth certificate."

Claudine shook her head. "Amazing. Why are you trying to pin this on me?"

"Because everything fits. You had the opportunity, and you certainly had the motive. You killed three people in cold blood."

"Three people?" Claudine remained amused. "My, you certainly do have an active little imagination, honey. And here I thought you were supposed to be an intellectual, like your father. But you're not very smart, after all, are you?"

Maggie refused to be baited. Instead she decided to push Claudine as far as she could. "You see what a lifetime of jealousy can do to someone. All her life Claudine's been eaten up by it, because neither one of her parents ever acknowledged her publicly. Instead, she lived like a servant in her own father's home. You might say they eventually caused their own deaths by the way they treated her, because the worm finally turned." She stared straight at Claudine. "The poor little bastard child had to settle for second- or third-best all her life, because neither one of her parents wanted to own up to the truth."

"You vicious little bitch!" Claudine said, her cool demeanor finally deserting her. She stood up. "You and your father waltz in here after twenty-five years, with not a single word to anyone in the family, and you get treated like royalty. While the rest of us stayed here, putting up with that old bastard and his every whim, and what do we get for it! I worked my ass off for him, and what did he ever do for me?"

"I'm not going to argue that one with you, Claudine," Maggie said. "He treated you monstrously, as far as I'm concerned, and you had every right to be upset with him over that. But if you hadn't pushed my grandmother down the stairs twenty-five years ago, you might have stood a better chance of winning his affection and public recognition as his daughter."

Claudine laughed. "There's no way anyone can prove that I pushed Magnolia down the stairs. Don't be absurd!"

"No, you're right," Maggie said. "No one can prove that you did it. But I know you did it, and I notice you didn't deny it, just now. They probably won't prosecute you for my grandmother's murder, you're right about that, but it's a different story with my grandfather's murder. They'll be able to find proof linking you to the murder weapon, and you're not going to get out of that one."

"What do you mean, 'proof'?" Claudine asked.

"I have to say I admire your guts, Claudine. I don't know that I've ever met anyone who's as cool as you are. I mean, look at you, you're wearing the evidence around your neck.

That takes guts."

Claudine's left hand reached up, convulsively, to the scarf around her neck.

"I didn't catch on to it, at first," Maggie explained to the others. "It wasn't until a little while ago, in the kitchen, that I remembered. Seeing you with the scarf again reminded me. You were wearing it that night, at dinner and when we went in to watch the movie. But I suddenly realized that you weren't wearing it when Sylvia came downstairs and told us my grandfather had been murdered. I'm not sure what you did with it in the meantime. You probably washed it, but I doubt it came completely clean. I'm sure when the police examine it, they'll find some traces of my grandfather's blood on it, and maybe even some of that flaky varnish, from where you used it to grip the baseball bat when you beat him to death."

Claudine didn't flinch from the brutality of Maggie's words.

"You don't know what it was like, living in this family and being treated like a piece of furniture, most of the time. I deserved better."

"I think you'd better come with me, Miss Sprayberry," Latham said, coming around the table to where Claudine stood, still defiant.

"McLendon," Claudine said. "Not Sprayberry." Head held high, she went quietly out of the room with him.

Two mornings later, Maggie was in her bedroom, packing her suitcase for the return trip to Houston. She and her father had tickets for an early afternoon flight. Ernie and Helena were there, chattering away, discussing coverage of the murders in the local newspaper, while she worked.

"Lord have mercy," Helena groaned, shaking the paper in front of her, "Henry and Magnolia must be rolling in their graves because of this!"

"'Pride goeth before destruction,'" Ernie intoned in a deep voice.

"Pride got them both murdered, I guess," Maggie said, pausing for a moment in her packing.

"Yes, it did," Ernie sighed loud and long. "But back then, they did what just about anyone else in their position would have done. Covered it all up, pretended Claudine was someone else's child, just like they did. Heaven forbid that they should admit that she was really Henry's daughter, and by his own wife's sister! You can't imagine what a scandal there would have been in Jackson back then."

"And Magnolia couldn't have stood that," Helena said. "It was one thing to have people whisper behind her back about her brother, I guess, but she would have been mortified to show her face anywhere, if people knew her husband had been having an affair with her sister—and got her pregnant, to boot!"

"I don't suppose she would have considered divorcing my grandfather," Maggie observed.

"Divorce! Good grief, no," Ernie laughed. "That would have been even worse. Besides, despite everything, she and Henry still loved each other, no matter how it must look."

"Lavinia and Claudine didn't stand a chance against Henry and Magnolia, that's for sure," Helena said. "Talk about iron will."

"Claudine seems happy enough now to be dragging the family's name in the mud," Maggie said, gesturing toward the paper in Helena's hands. The headline ran LAWYER'S SECRET FAMILY PROVES DEADLY."

"I still can't believe how cold she was about everything," Ernie said. "Then, I guess, revenge is a dish best taken cold. Didn't someone say that?"

"But that's the way she always was, poor girl. Cold," Helena said.

"Poor girl!" Ernie snorted. "That 'poor girl' murdered three people, and might have murdered more, if Maggie hadn't caught on to her."

"You weren't around her much as a child," Helena said, making a token protest. "You didn't know her very well." She paused. "Well, I guess I didn't know her very well either, come to think of it. But what I mean is, she was always a bit reserved. Kept things to herself. She was always there in the background. If you asked her to do something, she'd do it, never say much about it. That's the way she was."

"And none of us ever had any idea who she really was." Ernie was still marvelling over the facts of Claudine's parentage.

"To think that she had such hatred inside," Helena said. "That's what I can't get over! Where did it come from?"

Maggie turned from her packing and pointed toward the portrait of her grandmother. "There, for a start."

"What do you mean?" Helena asked. "Your grandmother wasn't to blame for all this. She was the injured party!"

"Was she?" Maggie said, walking toward the portrait. She stared at the face so like her own. How much was she really like her grandmother—on the inside?

She turned back to face Helena and Ernie. "I've heard so much about my grandmother these last few days, it's hard to sort everything out. But I've heard time and again that she and Lavinia had a difficult relationship. Lavinia was always jealous of my grandmother. Okay, that happens. But did my grandmother do anything to try to counteract that jealousy? Did she do anything to help her sister grow out of those feelings? Or was it all Lavinia's fault?"

Helena sighed. "Well, I have to admit, you've got a point. Magnolia seemed to enjoy rubbing Lavinia's nose in it. Oh, I grant you, she usually did it subtly, but she did it just the same. No wonder Lavinia was so bitter."

"And she fed that bitterness to Claudine, I expect," Ernie said.

Maggie nodded. "She must have, over the years. I guess Claudine never really had a chance. It would have been better for her if she had been given up for adoption, so that some nice normal family could have reared her and given her a happy childhood. She can't have been that happy here. With Lavinia around, telling her who-knows-what, filling her head with all sorts of things."

"You really think Lavinia told her, early on, who her real parents were?" Helena asked.

"It's the only answer that really fits," Maggie said. "Think about it. Why else would Claudine have pushed Magnolia down the stairs like that? I imagine she thought that, if she could just get Magnolia out of the way, Lavinia and Henry would be free to marry, and then Claudine could have everything she ever wanted."

"But surely you don't think Lavinia encouraged Claudine to push Magnolia down those stairs!" Helena said.

"No, I don't think she did," Maggie said. "I don't think Lavinia was that bitter, or that twisted. I think she was probably appalled by what happened, though of course at the time she just thought it was a tragic accident. When we confronted her with our theory about what happened, I think she finally put everything together and realized what her daughter had done, and why."

"And maybe," Ernie said softly, "that's why she wanted those pills from Sylvia. She was going to kill herself."

"Maybe," Maggie said. "Or maybe she was going to kill her daughter, then herself. But Claudine found out and struck first, to protect herself, in case Lavinia planned to expose her."

"So much damage done," Ernie said. "So many lives hurt, or ruined completely." She gazed at the portrait.

"Yes," Maggie said. "Maybe it's just as well I never knew her. I can love her, because she was my father's mother, and he loved her. Dad and I had a long talk about this last night. For his sake, I can love her. But I wonder if I would have liked her." She went back to her suitcase. Turning to face Ernie and Helena, she said, "I'm sorry, I know I sound impossibly judgmental and prissy. I don't really mean to be. But, well, I just don't know. It's going to take me a long time to sort this all out and come to terms with it."

"I know what you mean," Helena said. "Only too well, I'm afraid. I loved her dearly, but sometimes she just wasn't a nice person. Oh, dear." Tears rolled down her face.

"There, there," Ernie said, patting Helena on the knee. "She was human, like the rest of us. Just like Henry. For all the bad things they did, they also did some good things." She paused. "Give me a while, and I'll think of a few." She made a face.

A knock sounded at the door. Maggie went to answer it.

"Hello," she said. "I'm almost done packing, if you came for the bags."

"Not exactly," Adrian said, coming into the room. He stopped when he saw Helena and Ernie. "I'm sorry, I didn't realize you had someone with you." He turned to go.

"We were just leaving," Ernie announced, standing up. "Weren't we, Helena?"

"What?" Helena said, wiping her eyes. "Oh, yes, got a thousand things to do." She followed Ernie out of the room, after giving Maggie a quick hug.

The door shut behind them. Maggie stood awkwardly by the bed, wishing she could crawl inside the suitcase and close the lid over her head.

"I've been hoping for a chance to talk to you," Adrian said. "Things have been rather crazy the last couple of days, and I haven't had much chance."

"No," Maggie laughed nervously, "after my big Jessica Fletcher act the other night, things have been a bit busy here."

"You handled it very well," Adrian said.

"Thank you."

"Look, Maggie," he said, in a very determined tone, "I think I finally figured out what went wrong."

"What do you mean?" she said, though she knew what he was talking about.

"I mean, between us," Adrian replied. "It took me longer than it should have to realize that Claudine must have said something to you. That's what it was, wasn't it?"

Maggie nodded. She couldn't bring herself to repeat what Claudine had said, and she hoped he wouldn't ask.

"I can just imagine," Adrian said bitterly, "what she must have said. That I'm only interested in you because of the money you might inherit from your grandfather. That was probably the least of it."

"No, that was about it," she said, her voice low.

"And you didn't know me well enough to realize that I'm not like that!" Adrian said. "At first, I was angry with you, for falling for something as obvious as that." He grinned. "But when I thought about it, I couldn't really blame you. This whole situation was so bizarre, you were right not to trust someone you barely knew."

"Thank you," Maggie said, relieved. "I was more than a bit confused, and I just didn't know what to think." She stared down at her hands. "Then, when I finally figured out the truth about Claudine, I didn't know how to say to you that I was sorry for thinking what I'd been thinking."

Adrian stepped closer, took her hands in his. "Look at me."

Calmly as she could, she looked into his eyes.

"Yes, I did go out with Claudine a few times. But that was before I came to work here. By the time I got the job here, I already knew that I wasn't interested in any kind of long-term relationship with her. I was willing to be her friend, but that was all. I tried, many times, to make that clear to her, but she was very possessive. Most of the time, I ignored that. But when you came, she started up again the minute she realized we were attracted to each other."

Maggie smiled. "I see that now."

Adrian held tightly to her hands. "The question is, where are we now? You're about to go back to Houston, and I still have a job here, as long as I want it, that is."

"There are telephones, and there are airplanes," she observed.

"I know," Adrian sighed. "But I don't know how I feel about a long-distance relationship. I mean, there are bound to be all sorts of guys in Houston who are hanging around you. I remember what those grad school Lotharios are like. What if you like one of them more than you like me?"

Maggie grinned. "You know, sometimes you talk entirely too much." She kissed him.